SON OF SUN

Girl of Glass, Book Four

MEGAN O'RUSSELL

Ink Worlds Press

DEDICATION

To those who dare to step beyond the glass

SON OF SUN

CHAPTER ONE

S hadows pressed in around her, snapping the thin thread of her courage. The scent of old blood and rancid rot hung heavy in the air.

Jeremy's silhouette moved in front of her, broken bits of concrete crunching under his feet.

Nola followed his gaze as he squinted into the darkest corners of what had been the club at 5th and Nightland. Not so very long ago, the room would have been packed with vampires dancing as though the world weren't ending.

How many of them are dead?

Jeremy reached into his pocket and pulled out a flashlight, holding the beam level with the barrel of his Guard gun.

Nola pulled her weapon free from her belt, holding her breath as Jeremy shone his light into every crevice. Portions of the walls had caved in, whether from the fire that had destroyed the city above or from the domes' raid on Nightland, Nola didn't know.

Jeremy froze as his light fell on a human form on the floor. A woman with long blue hair, half-buried under a giant chunk of fallen ceiling. A length of rebar stuck out of the woman's head. The rodents of the city had feasted on her flesh.

Nola bit her lips together, blinking back the tears that burned in her eyes.

No life should end like that.

"Which way?" Jeremy whispered.

Nola stepped around him, heading toward the door that led to the main tunnel of Nightland.

Jeremy held out a hand, blocking Nola's path. "Let me stay in front."

"It's that way."

She stayed close behind Jeremy's shoulder as they wound through the debris toward the broken archway. The steel door that had once been heavily guarded lay on the floor to one side. Rubble had been dragged away from the passage as well, leaving a clear path to the corridor beyond.

"Somebody put a lot of effort into clearing this," Nola whispered.

"Let's just hope it's someone we want to see," Jeremy said.

Nola touched his arm with her free hand. "We'll find her, Jeremy. We'll find Gentry."

"Keep close." Jeremy stepped through the archway, sweeping his light across the hall.

Shattered remnants of light bulbs hung uselessly from the ceiling. A section of wall had crumbled, spilling dirt into the hall. Dozens of footprints leading in both directions marked the ground.

"Keep going forward," Nola said. "I only know one path to Emanuel's old house."

They crept down the hall, Jeremy setting a slow and deliberate pace, stopping every few feet to listen and sweep his light over the corridor behind them.

The plan had seemed so simple aboveground. Kieran, Raina, and Julian would hide from the sun in the ruins near Nightland. Nola and Jeremy would check the tunnels to be sure the domes' guards weren't patrolling. The Outer Guard would kill a vampire on sight, but two people who had, until a few short weeks ago, lived in the domes might give them pause.

Now, moving silently through the tunnel, the idea that Nola could face an Outer Guard and hope to survive became unforgivably naïve. The thought that Jeremy could fight against Gentry, his own sister, lost all reason.

He'd do it for me. He'd fight her to protect me.

What if I can't protect him?

A hollow ache gnawed at Nola's chest.

Ahead, another section of the tunnel had collapsed. A chest-high pile of rocks blocked their path.

"Stay back," Jeremy whispered.

"No."

Nola stepped up next to him, aiming her Guard gun at the debris.

Jeremy shook his head but didn't fight Nola staying at his side as they approached the barricade.

Her heart thudded in her ears. There could be nothing behind the mound. Or a rat. Or an Outer Guard waiting to kill them.

Jeremy picked up a fist-sized rock and backed toward the remnants of the wall, keeping Nola pressed behind him. He tossed the rock over the mound and into the shadows beyond, where it landed with a *clatter*.

Nola's nerves zinged as she waited for vampires to spring over the barrier, werewolves to howl their rage, or guards to fire their weapons. But nothing came, not even the scurrying of frightened rats.

Keeping his flashlight and weapon pointed toward the hall beyond, Jeremy moved closer to the barricade, sidestepping to block Nola from walking next to him.

Nola barely caught the quick movement as Jeremy bent his knees and dove over the fallen rocks, landing on the far side with barely a sound. His flashlight's beam darted around the tunnel before he beckoned Nola across. She bent her knees, trying to judge the height and distance of the obstacle in front of her and the amount of space she had between the barrier and the low ceiling.

A few short weeks ago, such a leap would have been completely impossible. But she wasn't human anymore. Graylock had changed her, granting her the ability to survive the contamination outside the glass and giving her body unnatural strength.

"Are you all right?" Jeremy barely voiced the words, yet she could hear him perfectly.

Nola bent her knees and dove over the pile of rubble. As she cleared the mound of dirt and rock, the floor on the far side became horribly real. She pulled her legs forward, trying to get her feet under her. The ground came too quickly, and she stumbled, landing on her knees.

"Are you okay?" Jeremy glanced at her, his eyes quickly flicking back to the dark corridor ahead.

"I've never tried that kind of jump before." Nola stood, shaking the pain from her legs.

"You did great." A hint of a smile touched the corners of Jeremy's eyes before vanishing. "Let's keep moving."

The stillness of the corridor devoured the muffled noise of their footfalls as they moved farther down the hall. Away from light and fresh air. Away from escape.

A door came into view, hanging off its bottom hinges.

"There," Nola said. "Through that door."

She had run through it before. Fled from her own people and locked the door behind her. But the door couldn't be locked now. There would be no hope of blocking danger with something as simple as a door.

Shadows from a different life drifted across the doorjamb. Faint shapes moving as though Nightland had found a way to survive the dome-made massacre in the city.

"Turn off the flashlight," Nola said.

Jeremy flicked it off without question.

Shadows moved across the doorway, cast by a light source Nola couldn't see.

She stilled her heart, listening to the sounds around her. Whispers filtered through the doorway.

Jeremy leaned close to Nola's ear. "Stay here."

"No." Nola met Jeremy's gaze, willing him to understand that she would no more let him walk through that door alone than he would let her.

Jeremy's neck tensed with unsaid words, but he nodded and didn't try to block Nola as she followed him toward the door.

The light from the tunnel beyond flickered, like someone had lit torches or lanterns. The whispered voices grew stronger, as though the speakers waited just out of sight.

"I don't want to be a meal," a male voice said. "I didn't spend this long fighting for survival to become a meal for a Vamper or wolf."

"I don't know what else you want me to do," a female spoke. "We're out of the weather. We've got some water and a bit of food."

"No enough to last," a second female said. "We're going to need help. There has to be someone in this nightmare who has food to spare."

"And what kind of angel would swoop in to save us?" the man said. "There is no help. No one is coming to save us. You've got to understand that."

A sniffle of stifled tears tugged on Nola's heart.

Nightland's home in the mountain had food, water, and solid walls.

The rats will sink the ship. Raina's words echoed through her mind.

"We need weapons," the man said. "If we can fight, we might be able to take what we need."

"I never thought stealing would sound like a good idea," the first female said.

Jeremy crept closer to the door. The nearer they got to the entry, the clearer the shadows became. One of the people sat in front of the light source, while the other two stood near the wall.

Two against three isn't bad.

Jeremy leaned against the wall right next to the door, keeping his eyes focused on the shadows.

"Stay out of sight," Jeremy mouthed.

Nola shook her head.

"I don't want to play our whole hand." Jeremy pressed her against the wall.

She wanted to refuse. To insist on walking through the door by his side. Danger for him should mean danger for them both. But Jeremy had been training as an Outer Guard when he abandoned the domes, had been raised by the head of the Outer Guard.

I was trained in growing food, not fighting.

Nola nodded, hoping she was right to trust Jeremy's instincts.

Squaring his shoulders, he stepped in front of the door, leveling his weapon at the corridor beyond. He took a step forward, moving through the door and out of sight.

Her heart rocketed into her throat. She strained her ears, trying to hear the sound of his footsteps.

"I don't want to be sitting ducks when the Vampers come for a meal," the first woman said.

"What the—"

A terrible *shriek* of metal against stone cut through Jeremy's words.

"Jeremy!" Nola leapt forward as a sheet of steel crashed down, blocking the doorway.

CHAPTER TWO

"Nola, run!" The metal barrier muffled Jeremy's shout.

"Jeremy." Nola stumbled in the pitch black of the hall, falling into the steel door that separated them. "Jeremy!" She pounded on the metal.

"Get out, Nola!"

She ran her fingers along the steel, searching for a handle or lock. Dents and scratches marked the barrier, as though it had slid into place many times before.

"I can't find a way to move the door." Nola's hands trembled as she reached up to the corners of the doorjamb.

"It's a trap. The voices came through a speaker," Jeremy said. "Nola, get out. Go back to the others."

"I'm not leaving you." Nola kicked the door.

"Nola you have—"

"I said I'm not leaving you!" Nola kicked the door again.

"I think there's gas in here," Jeremy coughed.

"Make the other people help you look for a way out." Nola knelt, digging her fingers into the dirt under the metal door.

"There are no other people," Jeremy said. "They're dead. They're all dead."

Her fingertips found the edge of the metal. Gritting her teeth, she lifted with all her might. A scream of rage and fear escaped her.

"Nola," Jeremy's voice rasped.

"Cover your face," Nola said. "I'm going to get you out."

"I love you."

Panic and outrage sliced into Nola's chest, stealing the strength from her limbs. "You're going to be okay." She pushed herself to her feet. "You promised you wouldn't leave me. Don't you dare break your promise, Jeremy Ridgeway."

She needed a light and a crowbar. Or explosives to blast away the door. A hundred impossible ideas raced through her mind.

She tore her fingers through her curls.

Jeremy trapped with dead people. Jeremy dying.

"Stop panicking, Nola Kent. You can't help him if you're panicking."

The people who built the door wanted her to panic, wanted Jeremy to die. What kind of monster would be evil enough to build such a trap?

The domes.

"Jeremy, the other people, are they just dead on the floor?" Nola leaned against the metal.

"No, staged like they're alive." Jeremy's words slurred. "Ropes. Puppets."

"Then they had to open the door." Nola pushed away from the metal, fumbling toward the wall beside it. Starting at the base of the wall, she ran her hands across the packed dirt and stone. "Please," Nola begged the darkness. "Please, please. I will not lose him."

She moved to the other side of the steel, feeling the outline of the broken door that hung off its hinges, her heart racing faster with every second that passed. The tips of her fingers caught on a ridge in the wall, a metal square packed with loose dirt.

"I found something," Nola shouted through the door. "Jeremy?

Jeremy!"

"I'm here." His voice barely carried through the door.

"Hang on." She dug into the loose dirt. Her fingers found something hard and metallic. A lever packed in with the dirt. She tried to push the handle up, but it wouldn't budge. "Come on." She shoved the metal down, but again the lever stayed firmly in place. "Open, dammit." She planted both feet on the wall and pulled backward with every ounce of strength Graylock had granted her. The handle moved a fraction of an inch.

A slit of light appeared at the bottom of the door.

"Move!" Nola yanked harder, ignoring the pain in her hand as a bone cracked under the strain.

The door slid up farther. Fingers appeared, reaching through the gap.

Nola screamed as another bone snapped. The door raised a foot.

Jeremy dragged himself through the gap and lay gasping on the tunnel floor.

Nola let go of the handle and ran to his side. The door snapped shut, leaving them in darkness.

"Jeremy." Nola fumbled blindly for him, not caring about the pain in her hands as she felt his chest rise and fall.

"I'm okay." Jeremy's voice came out as a rasp. "I can heal, I'll be okay."

"The shot of Graylock, you need it." Nola reached for his belt, for the case that held the one dose of the medicine they carried.

"No." Jeremy rolled over, moving the case out of her reach. "I just need a minute, I'll be okay."

Nola felt his face. Sweat slicked his clammy skin. She leaned down, pressing her lips to his. His breath tasted of chemicals.

"What was the gas?" Nola said.

"I don't know." Jeremy clicked on his flashlight.

Deep purple patches mottled the skin on his face and hands. Bright red veins marked the whites of his eyes.

Nola swallowed her tears. "Are you sure you're going to be okay?"

"I can breathe better already." He pressed Nola's palm to his lips.

"Why would the domes build something like that?" Nola asked.

A part of her expected Jeremy to argue. To say the domes would never build something so terrible. But they'd seen the city burn, run into the flames that killed thousands. People who were willing to slaughter an entire city could build a trap to kill underground.

"Trying to round up vampires, I expect." Jeremy pushed himself to sit up.

Nola wrapped an arm around him, steadying him as he swayed.

"Lure blood drinkers in with the promise of a good meal then trap them." Jeremy's voice came out stronger than it had moments before. "There was solid metal on the other side, too."

"And the people?" Nola asked.

Jeremy shuddered. "Too far dead to be a meal for anyone."

Nola swallowed the bile that shot to her throat. "That's sick. Absolutely disgusting."

"We should get away from here." Jeremy knelt. Nola took his elbow, helping him to his feet. "The domes might have a way to track when the trap is tripped."

"Should we search for another way to Emanuel's?" Nola asked. "I don't want to have to try coming down here again."

"It's not worth it." Jeremy kept his arm over Nola's shoulder as they started back the way they'd come. "If they put a trap here, they put in others. There isn't a way to hide in the Nightland tunnels. Not anymore."

"Raina is going to be so pissed," Nola said.

"Yeah."

The steady pace of Jeremy's steps eased Nola's worry.

Graylock saved him again.

Chemicals blended as medicine to save them from the chemicals contaminating the world that had killed so many humans. The domes had hated the vampires and werewolves for turning to drugs like Vamp and Lycan to survive. Then the domes made Graylock, their own version of altering the body, exchanging human DNA for survival.

Nola had despised them for betraying the mission of the domes: to preserve human life in the dying world. A person who could heal from being stabbed in the stomach with no more than a little rest couldn't really be called human anymore. But Graylock had saved Jeremy. And her.

She leaned in closer to him, listening to his rattling breaths.

They reached the barricade of debris.

"Let me go first." Jeremy lifted his arm from Nola's shoulder.

"I don't think you'd make it." In one swift move, Nola leapt up, landing in a low crouch on top of the pile. Nothing waited in the shadows beyond to attack her.

"You can't blame me for trying." Jeremy reached for her hand.

Nola grabbed his wrist and hoisted him up to sit on the pile. Even though he was tall and had the broad build of one born for fighting, his weight didn't strain her muscles.

"My hands." Nola let go of Jeremy and jumped down on the other side of the rocks.

"What about them?" Jeremy jumped after her, tipping forward as he landed.

Nola caught his arm and held him on his feet.

"I broke my hands opening the door, but they don't hurt anymore," Nola said.

"Probably a hairline fracture," Jeremy said. "Those don't take very long to heal."

"Wow." Nola opened and closed her fists. "I could get used to this superhero thing."

"Good." Jeremy smiled. His eyes scrunched up at the corners. The red in them had already begun to fade.

Before Nola could reach out to touch the creases, his smile faltered.

"We'll find her, Jeremy." Nola raised her weapon and started down the tunnel. "It might not be as easy as we'd hoped, but we're going to find Gentry."

"We have to." Jeremy stepped in front of Nola, his gait even as they moved toward 5ᵗʰ and Nightland. "If she really did stand against the domes to try and help the people in the city, she can't go back. Not to our domes or any place under Incorporation control. If she's stuck out here, she should be with me."

"I know."

They walked in silence for a long while. The end of the tunnel came into view.

Jeremy slowed and moved Nola right behind him as they approached the open doorway.

Nola strained her ears, listening for the *thump* of heavy boots or the tiny *pop* of silver darts being fired.

The wall on this side of the door hadn't suffered as much damage as the inside of the club. The stone remained intact with only a few cracks taunting the tunnel's ability to crumble and trap them.

The urge to dart around Jeremy and run for the open air tensed Nola's muscles. She tipped her gaze higher, to where light and open space waited just above them.

Words painted above the door caught her eye.

There is no life left in Nightland.
Death is all that awaits us.

The warning had been painted in black, the letters crooked as though the one writing had hurried to their own escape.

"Look above the door," Nola said.

Jeremy froze, aiming his weapon at the words.

"What do you think it means?" Nola asked.

"That someone smart was here." Jeremy stepped up to the door, pressing Nola to the side as he peered through the entry to the club.

A chill tickled the back of Nola's neck.

There is no life left in Nightland.

Did an Outer Guard write the words, or a vampire who had tried to return to the refuge Emanuel built?

Nola stayed close on Jeremy's heels as he stepped through the doorway. There was no *whine* of deadly doors as they passed into the club. Bits of stone clacked under Nola's feet as she skirted around the body of the blue-haired woman. Perhaps she had met a kind end after all. Better a quick blow than a slow death by poison.

A bright shaft of sunlight streamed down from the hole that led to the street. Nola's shoulders relaxed as they neared the path to freedom.

"I'll go up first," Jeremy whispered. "I'll call when you can follow."

"We should go together," Nola said. "You're sick. You almost died."

"If I get attacked, I'll scream extra loud." He put his flashlight in his pocket and jumped to the street above.

"Be okay," Nola whispered. "You have to be okay. You have to be okay."

"It's clear."

Relief flooded Nola's chest as she bent her knees and pushed off as hard as she could. The wind raced past her as she leapt out of the ground, cleared five feet of open air, and landed on what remained of the cracked sidewalk.

She took deep, gulping breaths of the wonderful oxygen that had seemed too polluted to be safe for human lungs when she'd lived trapped in the domes but now granted her blissful freedom.

Jeremy coughed a laugh. "Nice jump." The purple patches on his face had turned a pale pink.

"Thanks." Nola touched his cheek, savoring the roughness of his stubble. "I've had a pretty great teacher."

Jeremy laughed again, his lungs wheezing from the effort.

"Let's get to the others." Nola took his elbow, leading him across the street.

There were no signs of life around them. No humans, vampires, werewolves, zombies, or Outer Guard moving through the burned out skeleton of the city.

They reached a house where some of the bricks had managed to stay upright in the inferno. Jeremy didn't insist on climbing the cracked steps first.

"Raina," Nola said, "it's us."

Nola hesitated on the threshold, counting to ten before stepping through the gap that should have been a door. Most of three walls of the building remained, surrounding piles of ash and scorched rubble that took up the center of the space.

"Raina," Nola said. "Where are you?"

Thin shadows shaded the corners of the walls, but nothing dark enough to protect a vampire.

"There." Jeremy pointed to a gap in the rubble.

The floor had fallen away, leaving a hole where the steps to a lower level should have been.

Nola tightened her grip on her weapon as Jeremy stalked toward the opening and pulled his flashlight from his pocket.

"Raina," Jeremy said. "Julian?"

"They've got to be down there," Nola said. "They wouldn't leave without us."

Jeremy glanced to her, one eyebrow raised. He turned back to the gap, shining his light on the ground twelve feet below.

"What if the domes rigged another trap?" Nola asked.

"We'd still need to go down and see if the others are alive." Jeremy picked up a blackened brick and tossed it into the basement. The brick fell to the ground with a *thud*. "Good enough, I guess."

Jeremy jumped down into the darkness.

Nola bit her lips together as he landed and swept his light around the space below. He beckoned for her to follow.

Checking her grip on her weapon, she jumped down into the hole. The feeling of being swallowed by the earth pressed against her ribs.

Not far down. Not too far down.

She stood in the sunlight, her Graylock-given vision allowing her to see even in the deep shadows.

One side of the basement had collapsed. The charred remains of shelves and tools littered the dirt-packed floor.

A sheet of scorched plaster had fallen from the other side, revealing a wall that had been cracked and singed but otherwise left untouched by the blaze that had claimed the house.

A heavy metal hatch had been built into the wall, and scratches marked the dirt where the door had recently been dragged open.

Nola filed in behind Jeremy as he moved toward the door. A narrow corridor waited beyond, leading toward what should have been the basement of the building next door.

Faint voices carried down the passage.

"It may not be what we set out to find, but that doesn't mean it isn't valuable." Julian's voice came from the far end of the tunnel.

"I'm not carrying any of this," Raina said. "And if someone kills you because you decided to weigh yourself down, I will only feel moderately guilty."

Nola dodged in front of Jeremy and darted down the tunnel. The dim glow of flashlights filled the space beyond, barely lighting the corners of the room where shelves were lined with beakers and bottles.

Three people stood in the middle of the room. Julian holding a rack of vials, Raina playing with her knife, and Kieran clutching a microscope to his chest.

CHAPTER THREE

"The lovebirds are back so soon?" Raina said, her scathing look bordering on comical in her baggy, tan sun suit.

"Booby traps." Jeremy leaned against the wall just inside the door. "There's no one living in the tunnels. The domes made sure of that."

"Those evil bastards." Raina threw her knife at the wall. The blade sank into the dirt between two stones.

"Are you sure?" Kieran asked.

"Positive," Nola said. "Jeremy nearly died before we even got into the housing tunnels."

"Damn." Julian set his rack of vials on the floor. "I didn't hold much hope of discovering allies below, but I thought we might be lucky enough to find sanctuary."

"Fuck." Raina scrubbed her hands over her face.

"What about the little tunnel?" Nola's chest tightened at the thought of crawling through the darkness. "The one you brought me through before."

"No one we want to see would be able to find that way in," Raina said.

"We need to move," Jeremy said. "If they have a way of

knowing when the trap is tripped, this whole area could flood with guards."

"Who will be really mad when they find out Jeremy escaped," Nola said.

"I didn't escape." Jeremy took Nola's hand. "You saved me."

She leaned her cheek against his chest, hating the stench of poison that clung to his clothes.

"So we head up to the streets and then what?" Kieran said. "We came here to get information for Emanuel. We need to know why there were Domer zombies on the mountain."

"Well, our only way under the river to the domes has just been cut off." Raina yanked her knife out of the wall. "We haven't seen anyone in the city. So unless you have a boat you've been hiding or know a great place we can find some secret information, looks like we're shit out of luck."

"It's not as though the trip has been entirely wasted," Julian said. "The things we've found here are incredibly useful."

"You didn't know this was down here?" Nola asked.

"I knew there was a basement," Raina said. "I'd gone to ground here a couple of times when I got home too late and the door to the club had already been barred for the day. The former owner never showed off the giant hidden door or their side business."

"Side business?" Nola stood up straight, examining the shelves. "Doing what?"

"This is a Vamp lab," Kieran said. "And from the looks of it, not the kind that made the pure stuff."

"I'd be willing to wager more than one person who sought salvation from the Vamp made in this lab ended up a zombie," Julian said.

"And here I thought they were just nice people who were willing to save a vampire from the sun," Raina said. "Did they really think having me on their side would save their lives if Emanuel found out they were poisoning people?"

"Some of the equipment can be salvaged," Kieran said. "My father could use these things to make ReVamp."

"So we close the door behind us and come back when there aren't guards wondering how lover boy escaped from their trap." Raina waved them all toward the door. "Maybe we'll get lucky and capture a guard, ask them some very friendly questions." She winked at Nola.

Nola waited for her stomach to squirm at the thought of taking a Domer prisoner.

They're the enemy.

"Fine." Kieran set the microscope carefully in the corner. "But I'm coming back. Dad and I could both use these things for our work."

"You can't work if you're dead," Jeremy said.

Kieran looked up, meeting Jeremy's gaze.

Raina took Nola's shoulders, pulling her out from between the two boys.

"A microscope isn't as useful as your brain," Jeremy said. "So let's get out of here while we can."

Kieran gave a jerky nod. "There are some things I won't risk leaving."

"The doctor and his son. Trying to save everyone as the world burns," Raina said. "If it weren't so poetic, I would laugh."

"Being able to make medicine isn't a laughing matter." Kieran lifted two small jars filled with white powder, one jar of clear liquid, and a metallic tin off the shelf.

"Stash them in your suit and let's move," Raina said. "We have another stop to make before we can head back."

"Where?" Jeremy asked.

"Not the domes if you were hoping for a little trip home." Raina strode past Jeremy and into the narrow corridor, pulling on her sun hat and lowering the veil that protected her face.

"My home is in the mountain," Jeremy said. "My home is with

Nightland, but we still need to..." His voice trailed away as Raina raised a warning hand.

Nola gripped Jeremy's arm, unwilling to risk being separated from him.

Raina wiggled her finger, beckoning them forward.

Nola pulled her weapon free as she followed Jeremy into the corridor.

The distant thumping of boots carried through the shadows as they neared the first basement.

Raina stayed close to the walls, out of sight should anyone look down from above.

There were no voices to go with the heavy footfalls as the people moved away, toward the entrance to 5th and Nightland.

Nola pressed herself into the shadows, still clinging tightly to Jeremy's arm.

Julian and Kieran stepped out of the tunnel.

The footsteps stopped.

Raina folded her arms and shot Kieran a glare before striding back down the tunnel.

Nola looked to Jeremy and mouthed, "Do we go back in?"

Jeremy shook his head.

Nola watched the sunlight filter in through the hole in the ceiling above them. Where there had once been a staircase, now only charred bits of wood remained. But someone had lived in this house. Someone had gone up and down the stairs to the basement without ever thinking the whole building could burn.

Someone who had made poison.

Images of people with red and black sores on their faces swam unbidden into Nola's mind. People who had tried to take Vamp or Lycan, searching for a cure as the outside world slowly murdered them. The poorly made drugs changed them into prisoners in their own dying bodies, with no thought left but to attack those who somehow still survived.

Low voices rumbled through the silence. Nola tried to listen but couldn't make out anything beyond the vague sound.

A soft scraping came from the lab where Raina had disappeared.

Minutes ticked by. The voices outside didn't disappear, nor did the footsteps move.

Nola wanted to close her eyes, to curl up and pretend life hadn't led her to a world of tunnels and fear.

Then I'd be in the domes. I'd still be one of them. I'd be a murderer.

There was no way to deny what her former home had become. A glass castle filled with killers.

Raina stepped out of the hallway, two large glass bottles in her hand. She looked to Kieran with a glint a mischief in her eyes, held up both bottles, and winked.

"What?" Nola whispered.

Kieran looked to Jeremy.

Jeremy stared at the bottles in Raina's hands for a long moment.

"What?" Nola stepped between Raina and Jeremy.

Jeremy kept his gaze over Nola's head and nodded.

"Jeremy?" A sense of dread squeezed Nola's throat.

"Stay back." Jeremy stepped around Nola, blocking her from the gap in the ceiling.

Raina handed one of the bottles to Kieran.

He pulled down the veil on his sun hat as she counted down from three on her fingers. Together, the two of them jumped up through the ceiling and out of sight.

The dull creaking of the floor above gave the only sign of the two landing at street level.

Nola waited for shouts or the sound of weapons.

A second ticked past. Then another.

Bang!

The sound itself pummeled Nola's body as the walls around them shook.

"And up we go." Julian ran under the gap and sprang out of sight.

Jeremy grabbed Nola's hand, dragging her forward. Her feet couldn't move. Her mind didn't know how to reason past the *bang*.

Jeremy wrapped an arm around her waist, lifting her as he jumped through the hole and into the open air. Smoke shrouded the other side of the street where the entrance to 5th and Night-land had been. But the chasm had grown, swallowing the sidewalk and half the street.

Raina waited on the steps of the burned out building, a knife in each hand, though Nola couldn't see anyone for Raina to stab.

The others started to run, following Raina away from the smoldering ruins of the club.

Jeremy kept his arm around Nola's waist, carrying her as he sprinted down the stairs and up the street. He ran at an incredible pace, leaving the world to whip by in a blur of destruction.

"I can run," Nola said as sense battered its way through shock. "I can run fast, too."

Jeremy didn't set her down. He kept her pinned to his side as he tore past an open square where a park might have been a long time ago. Past a wide building with a metal fence melted around its ruin.

"I can do it," Nola said.

Jeremy let her feet touch the ground but kept a hand on her hip as they ran.

The speed didn't bring any stress to Nola's limbs. The steady movement soothed her nerves.

I am not helpless.

She ran faster, catching up to Julian.

They turned down a narrow alley between buildings. The reek of rotting flesh stung Nola's nose. They sprinted onto a larger road before Nola could spot the unfortunate cause of the stench.

Raina cut right, onto a road lined with melted lampposts. The fire packs the domes had dropped on the city hadn't spared any of the houses on this street. The wide stone stoops had cracked. The front façade of one home had toppled, leaving debris strewn all the way to the other side of the road.

"Bellevue," Nola said, the word coming out easily despite how far they'd run. "Raina, your sister's house is gone. I'm so sorry."

Raina slowed her pace as she neared the crumbled stoop. "It wasn't Nettie's house. It was mine."

"There's nothing left here," Julian said.

"Of course there is." Raina kicked a chunk of cement the size of a backpack out of the way. "You people, all of you grew up in the privileged society of the domes."

"But..." Nola's voice trailed away. She'd forgotten Julian had once lived in a different, far away set of domes.

"You grow up convinced you'll always have food and a safe place to sleep, and it changes the way your brain works." Raina lifted a burnt slab of something and tossed it aside. "You don't think. You don't plan for what you're going to do if the whole world goes to shit and no one wants to feed you anymore."

She cleared the top of the stoop and stomped hard on the ground. "Not me. Being a kid in the brutal outside world, you learn that nothing is guaranteed. Not love. Not family. Not living to see the damned sunrise." The thumping of the stoop under her foot changed, the sound becoming thinner. "So you learn to plan. To have a backup plan for your backup plan."

Raina kicked down on the steps, pummeling the ground again and again.

"Raina." Kieran ran up the crumbled stairs. "Raina, you're going to hurt yourself."

The stone beneath her cracked.

"Don't worry, kid." Raina tore away a hunk of stone. "I know what I'm capable of."

Jeremy's touch brushed the back of Nola's hand. She laced her fingers through his, fighting the urge to help as Raina dug deeper into the stone.

"The domes have taken too much from all of us," Nola said. "How can they just keep going? Do they not see how evil they are?"

"Evil is in the eye of the beholder," Raina said. "The exterminator doesn't think he's evil for killing the rats. The domes have never seen any of us on the outside as anything better than vermin. There you are, beautiful." She bent low, yanking something free from the hole she'd created.

Raina held a black metal box up to the light. The size of a shoebox with only a latch to hold it closed, the case didn't seem worthy of holding anything that might help them.

"Now we can head for home and find a new plan." Raina jumped off the steps.

"What's in the box?" Kieran asked.

"Wouldn't you like to know?" Raina said.

"Do we just go back the way we came?" Nola squared her shoulders, trying not to look daunted by the thirteen mile run.

"Do you have a better idea?" Raina said. "Or better yet, a hidden boat?"

"No," Nola said.

"We didn't find the information we wanted." Kieran climbed down to the street. "But at least we know the whole city isn't swarming with Outer Guard."

"Which could leave them across the river organizing to attack us." Jeremy rubbed his hands over his face. The purple splotches had disappeared entirely, leaving him looking tired but healthy.

"So let's take a pass by the river on our journey home," Julian said. "It shouldn't be hard to see if the domes falling caused the creation of the Domer zombies who stumbled up our mountain. There's also a good chance of us spotting a giant helicopter parked out front."

"I hate running errands." Raina sauntered down the street, carrying the black box. "It always seems like such a waste of time.

Ah well, best view of the river is right this way, ladies and gentlemen." She didn't pick up her pace as the others followed.

Nola kept her fingers laced through Jeremy's as they walked. The feel of his palm pressed next to hers sent warmth tingling up her arm. Even as she searched the corners of burned out buildings for hidden guards and listened for the sounds of impending attack, the delightful warmth didn't fade away.

Jeremy raised their hands, pressing his lips to her wrist.

"What was that for?" Nola asked.

"Saving my life." He kissed the back of her hand. "You never cease to amaze me, Nola Kent."

"Good." A smile curved Nola's lips.

They rounded the corner, and her smile vanished.

The rancid river flowed in front of them, the stink of its water slamming into Nola's nose more fiercely than even the forgotten corpses. And on the far bank, the domes glittered in the sunlight.

CHAPTER FOUR

The domes were perfect, just as they had been designed to be. A series of glass structures centered around one tall concrete tower. No cracks marked the giant door of the Atrium. No smoke or frantic movement signaled distress. The wreckage of the bridge reaching toward the city gave the only sign the domes had ever been attacked.

"Well, that answers that," Raina said.

Nola squinted toward the distant domes. Amber Dome where her mother would be hard at work putting in new plants to feed the Domers. Bright Dome where Nola had lived her whole life.

"Just because the glass isn't shattered doesn't mean there's nothing wrong," Jeremy said.

"If you'd like to swim over and peek in to see if everyone looks like happy little mass murderers, feel free," Raina said. "I, however, am going to report what we do know to Emanuel."

"We can't get across the river," Nola said. "There's nothing more for us to learn."

Jeremy's neck tensed, displaying the thick cords of his muscles. "You're right."

"After me, then?" Julian turned away from the river without waiting for a response.

Jeremy tugged on Nola's hand, guiding her away from the domes. She kept staring at the glass until they turned onto another street and a tower of burned bricks blocked the river and her former home from view.

"Did you ever go back, Julian?" Nola asked. "To see your home domes?"

"I never had the opportunity." Julian led them down a different path toward a part of the city Nola had never entered. "When they cleared out the population of our city, they gave the citizens three days to evacuate the area. By *area,* they meant a thirty-mile radius. Anyone left within that circle without authorization after the three days was to be considered a hostile threat. As I fled the city with those being evicted, I no longer held any authorization."

"That's terrible," Nola said.

"I made it thirty-eight miles before the time passed," Julian said. "I was lucky enough to be healthy from living in the domes. Many of the city dwellers didn't even make it five miles."

"How could they?" Nola said. "How could they even consider..."

"Genocide," Kieran said. "That's the word you're looking for Nola, genocide."

"The domes shift from indifference to slaughter so quickly," Julian said. "Their complacency allows them to feel nothing while they watch others suffer. Their righteousness allows them to kill when murder fits within the domes' cause."

The group fell silent as they passed a row of burned bones laid out on the street. The bones weren't in the shape of the bodies they'd once belonged to, nor were they randomly strewn about as though dragged by animals.

Seven charred and cracked skulls sat in one line above eight femurs and a grid of small bones.

"Domers didn't do this," Jeremy said.

"Too good for organization but not murder?" Raina leaned over the bones.

Nola gripped Jeremy's hand tighter, trying not to lose the hope that came with his touch.

"No," Nola said. "It's not about *too good*. It's just...wrong. There's no reason for it. When have the domes ever put effort into anything that didn't directly benefit them?"

"Sampling the dead for some reason?" Julian asked.

"They'd have to bring the samples back to the lab," Kieran said. "There's no way they'd let anyone as valuable as a doctor or scientist come near the city."

"It feels wrong," Jeremy said. "I know the Outer Guard. I know the domes. This isn't them."

"So who then?" Nola glanced around the buildings, searching for people collecting bones.

"It could be any crazy," Raina said. "Someone who lost their family in the fire. A vampire so far gone with bloodlust they forgot you can't drink blood from burnt bones."

"Please don't." Nola pressed the back of her hand to her mouth. Dirt from the tunnels coated her lips.

"I don't fancy the idea of lingering here," Julian said. "These remains were either laid out by someone with a specific mission in mind, in which case I have no interest in standing in their way, or this is the work of one whose mind is lost—"

"In which case I'd rather not be here when they come back," Kieran said.

"Exactly," Julian said.

"Let's go," Nola said. "Please."

Julian nodded and jogged down the street. He kept to a human pace, like he was simply a rich person, who owned a sun-blocking suit, out for a bit of exercise.

Down one street and onto another. The pavement had been

cleared of debris, like someone had hoped to drive a car down the pothole-ridden road.

"Damn." Julian stopped before the others rounded the corner.

Nola opened her mouth to ask what had happened, but before her lips could form the words, her thoughts shattered, leaving nothing but numb horror behind.

A pile of skulls three feet high blocked the middle of the street. Long bones stuck out of the pile like spikes. Small bones littered the ground around the pile, as though daring anyone who wanted to approach to tread on the dead.

Jeremy wrapped an arm around Nola's waist, holding her close to his side.

"Definitely not the domes." Raina pointed to the front of the building nearest the pile. The four walls remained relatively intact even though the center of the building had collapsed.

Words in red paint had been scrawled across the black brick.

It is not the living the killers need fear.
It's the dead who will haunt their every step.
The dead who stand in judgment.
The dead who will form a mountain of bones the living can no longer
ignore.

Nola shivered, the feeling of being watched by thousands of eyes setting goose bumps on her flesh.

"This took time," Raina said, "and a hell of a lot of work."

"By whom?" Julian walked as close to the pile of skulls as he could without stepping on the scattered bones.

"Is it bad if I really don't want to know?" Nola said.

"No," Jeremy said.

"Change of plans, kids." Raina pulled her knife from her belt. "We aren't going to pack it up and go home just yet. This city just got a lot more interesting."

Kieran turned away from the painted words. "How are we going to find them?"

"We're not," Jeremy said. "We're not going to go looking for a crazy person. There would be no use in it."

"I do not believe this is the work of one disturbed individual," Julian said.

"Exactly," Raina said, "and a whole band of crazies, that's something I can work with."

"How do you expect to find a bunch of lunatics when we can't find Gentry?" Jeremy's voice echoed off the brick walls.

"We're not going looking for the crazies." Raina laughed. "We're going to make them come to us."

"But—" Jeremy began.

"Feel free to run back to the mountain on your own, if you like," Raina said. "Of course, you would be disobeying your commander since Emanuel placed me in charge. I speak with his voice. And I say we're staying."

Jeremy tightened his grip on Nola. "Yes, ma'am."

"Perfect." Raina clapped. "Now, let's set fire to this pile of bones and see who comes running because we ruined their art project."

"What?" Nola said.

"I liked the *yes, ma'am* better," Raina said. "Kieran, give me your burny bottle."

Kieran placed his hands over his pockets. "I need it. I can use it—"

"I can use it to make a fire," Raina said. "A big fire."

Kieran stared at Raina for a long moment.

Nola wished she could see behind the thick veil that protected his face from the sun.

"Fine." Kieran pulled a bottle from his pocket. "And if this doesn't burn bright enough, or whoever built this doesn't come but the Outer Guard do?"

"Then we get to kill a few Outer Guard," Raina said.

Jeremy stiffened.

"Sorry," Raina said. "We get to kill a few mass murderers to go with the set we blew up by the tunnels. You didn't seem too mad about spilling Domer blood then."

"We weren't looking for a fight then," Jeremy said. "We were trying to get out of a hole in the ground without being penned in and slaughtered."

"We're always penned in." Kieran threw the glass bottle at the base of the skull pile.

Nola covered her eyes as the glass smashed, but no explosion came. A scent of chemicals strong enough to strip flesh from bone wafted over her. She peered between her fingers.

"No big bang this time. Give me your knife." Raina held her hand out to Nola.

"Why?" Nola gripped the hilt of her blade.

"Because I like my knives and know how to use them," Raina said.

Julian walked to the front of the building, yanking a chunk of mortar and brick free.

"Knife." Raina snapped her fingers. "Now."

"I'll keep you safe." Jeremy placed his hand on Nola's back.

She pulled her blade from its sheath, feeling naked as Raina lifted the knife from her palm.

"This should do." Julian passed the chunk of debris to Raina.

"You know me so well." Raina took the hunk and threw it at the base of the pile where the bottle had landed. She flipped Nola's knife over in her hand a few times as though testing the balance, then threw the blade at the stone.

A hint of a spark flashed before a cloud of flames soared five feet into the air, enveloping the skulls.

"And now we hide." Raina skirted around the side of the building where the words had been painted.

"What was that?" Nola covered her nose with her shirt as she ran after Raina.

"One of the base chemicals in Vamp," Julian said. "I suppose it's not a wonder that when poorly used, the results are disastrous."

"The explosion at 5th and Nightland," Nola asked, "how did she do it?"

"Mixed two chemicals together that hate each other," Kieran said.

"Is that kind of stuff in Graylock?" Nola asked.

Raina leapt over a seven-foot high portion of wall and out of sight. Kieran jumped out of view behind her.

"I wish I knew." Jeremy stopped before the wall, waiting for Nola to jump up and in.

Nola bent her knees, judging the height of the wall as she leapt. The freedom of flying sent a thrill through her as she reached the apex of her jump and looked to the ground below.

Raina and Kieran stood together, facing twelve people with arrows nocked in their bows.

Nola couldn't change the trajectory of her jump. Couldn't do anything but land boxed in with the enemy. Stumbling as her feet hit the ground, Nola opened her mouth to scream, but an arrow three feet away pointed at her face kept her silent.

The *thump* of Jeremy landing came an instant later. Nola didn't see his arm move as he grabbed her, shoving her behind his back.

Another *thump* came as Julian landed.

Nola tried to move enough to see the enemy they faced, but Jeremy kept both arms behind him, holding her still.

"Now that our numbers are better balanced," Raina said, "let's have a chat."

CHAPTER FIVE

The heat of Jeremy's back pressed on Nola's face, making it difficult to breathe.

"You don't have anything to say?" Raina said.

The shuffle of moving feet came from the other side of the room.

"You just want to stand there and point arrows at me and my friends?" Danger dripped from Raina's words.

"Perhaps we started off on the wrong foot," Julian said. "We aren't here to hurt anyone. In fact, we had assumed this building to be empty. Our mistake, of course. We're more than happy to be on our way."

"You lit a fire," a female voice said. "You desecrated the dead."

"I think the person who jumbled a bunch of bones together is really the one who started the desecration game," Raina said.

Nola pushed against Jeremy's arm, inching far enough to the side to peer around his shoulder.

The twelve still faced them, pointing their arrows at Jeremy, Kieran, Raina, and Julian. The bows were the only sign the twelve belonged together. Their clothes were a tattered mix of leather like the vampires wore, the scraps homeless city dwellers survived in, and clothes that looked like factory uniforms. The woman in the center of the group wore a black, dome-issued jacket, and stood with the air of a leader.

"We came here to honor the dead," the leader said. "We came to this city to be sure the world would never forget the atrocities committed here. Now murderers have ruined our monument."

"We aren't murderers," Nola said.

"Monsters," a man dressed in leather hissed.

"That is a more accurate description," Raina said.

"You've done enough damage," the leader said, "and you'll never stop." She pulled back her bowstring.

"We haven't done any damage." Kieran stepped to the side, blocking Nola's view. "We set the fire outside, but it was only because we wanted to find whoever built the monument."

"Maybe not my best idea," Raina said.

"Crazies," a man said. "You called us crazies."

"An evidence-based term," Raina said.

"Raina, play nice," Kieran said. "We didn't understand why you'd put the bones together, but it makes sense now. A few hundred years in the future, when people have forgotten about this city and the terrible things the domes did, someone will find that pile of bones, and they won't be able to deny something horrific happened here. Maybe they won't understand the details, but they'll know. Humans lived in this city. They had children and homes. And they all died."

"Because of you," the leader said. "A whole garden of people wiped out by your hand."

"Nope," Raina said. "That's where you're just plain wrong. I can see where the confusion comes from, what with our fancy sun suits and those two looking so healthy and strong."

"Dome blood," a voice whispered.

"Look at my eyes," Raina said. A *rustle* of fabric came from her direction. "I'm straight out of Nightland. So are my other fashion-ably-dressed friends."

"Vampires? Here?"

"We came to see if the Outer Guard were still in the city," Julian said. "We wanted to know if they were still hurting people."

"That's why we wanted to talk to you," Jeremy said.

"You're not a vampire," a man said.

"No." Nola wiggled out from behind Jeremy, pushing against his arm until he set her free. "We did live in the domes. After they blew up the bridge, we knew we couldn't stay anymore. We escaped and found our way to Nightland."

"You have strong dome blood," the leader said. "Like the ones who slaughter."

"We're not like them," Jeremy said. "They're murderers. That's why we left."

Nola took Jeremy's hand, offering the only comfort she could.

"We'd very much like to talk to you," Julian said. "Perhaps if you could lower your bows—"

"Vampires who are afraid of bows?" a boy said.

"I was shot by one of your people only last night," Julian said. "I honestly don't care to repeat the experience."

"We didn't shoot you," the leader said.

"He was shot with an arrow." Kieran turned, showing the bow he had across his back. "We were attacked in the dark without warning."

"Not us," a man with a white beard said. "We don't do that sort of thing. Them, not us."

"Them?" Nola asked.

"Very descriptive," Raina said.

"We don't hurt people," the leader said. "We only defend, never attack."

"It's a miracle you're still alive." Raina laughed, her shoulders easing.

"It's not about living," the boy said. "It's about what will come after."

"What do you mean?" Nola stepped closer to him.

The ground crunched beneath Jeremy's boots as he moved up right behind her.

"After we're gone," the leader said. "When we're nothing more than bones."

"Ah," Julian said. "I can see why you're so upset with our disturbing your work. You have my deepest apologies." He gave a bow, which the leader acknowledged with a nod of her head.

"I'm sorry," Nola said, "I still don't understand."

The leader lowered her bow, though the other eleven stayed alert.

"Our lives can be nothing but pain," the leader said. "The death that will claim us is the peace of oblivion. When those who come after find this place, they will know our stories. Our work will live on. Our blood and pain will teach those who come after not to commit the same terrible mistakes that led us here."

"You're teachers," Kieran said.

The leader spread her hands toward the sky. "Of students who will live long after we're gone."

"We should leave you to your work," Julian said. "Our task is very different from yours, but we must attend to it nonetheless."

"We will not harm those who do not harm us," the leader said. "We will not have murder be the lesson we leave behind."

"Thank you," Julian said.

"Can we ask you something?" Jeremy stepped in front of Nola.

The leader stared at him for a long moment. "There is no danger in questions, only in answers."

"There's a girl," Jeremy said. "She'd be in a guard uniform but not working with the Outer Guard. She was helping in the city when the fire packs blew, trying to save people."

"We weren't in the city then," the man with the beard said. "We didn't bring our work here until the city fell."

"There are only guards that slaughter left in the city. The man who looks like a spider made sure of that," the leader said.

"Salinger is still here?" Jeremy clenched his hands into fists.

"Don't know the spider's name," the leader said. "Never got close enough to ask. They prowl the city, looking for anyone they can kill. The city's been declared off limits. People are only allowed on the highway."

"The buildings are too dangerous to go near after the fire." The boy's face twisted in disgust. "Anyone found here is considered an enemy of the domes."

"A hostile threat," Julian said, "to be exterminated by the Outer Guard."

"We've been here for two weeks. There hasn't been anyone but wolves and dying lambs on the streets," the leader said.

"If the girl you ask for really is good, she's either dead or gone," the bearded man said.

"Gone?" Nola placed a hand on Jeremy's arm, stilling his trembling. "What do you mean by gone?"

"To the wilds, the waters, or to them," to leader said.

"You all have spent far too long in isolation," Raina said.

"The wilds." The leader pointed west toward the mountains Nightland had made their home. "The waters." She pointed south. "Them." She pointed north.

Jeremy closed his eyes. "You have no idea where she would have gone?"

"Most go north," the boy said. "But most who go north don't last very long. Too many arrows flying."

"Who are the people in the north?" Raina asked. "Refugees from the city?"

"Been there for a long time," the leader said. "Don't know when it started. Don't know where they hide. But you go there, the arrows fly."

"Thank you for your help." Julian bowed again. "And for the good work you're doing."

"And that's our cue to jump on out of here." Raina turned toward the wall, ignoring the arrows still aimed at her.

"Where did you all live?" Nola asked. "Before you came to the city, I mean?"

"Far from the eyes of the domes," the leader said. "Where we can do our work in peace."

"Right. Thank you." Nola gave a little bow.

"I'll go first," Raina said. "Don't follow until I say so. Not to sound like I don't trust these fine people, but I hate to repeat my mistakes too often." Raina jumped over the wall, disappearing onto the street beyond.

Nola held her breath, waiting for the sounds of an attack.

"Come on out," Raina said. "Nothing here but smoke and bones."

"Kieran," Jeremy said, "you next."

Kieran turned to Jeremy. He froze for a moment before nodding and jumping over the wall.

"Nola, you go," Jeremy said.

She grazed the back of his hand with her fingers as she leapt into the air. The feeling of flying held no joy this time. The street came into view with only Kieran and Raina in sight. Both had their weapons drawn as they scanned the block. Nola landed between them and reached for her knife. Her stomach dropped as her fingers found the empty sheath. She pulled out her Guard gun instead.

Jeremy landed four feet in front of Nola, and Julian arrived a moment after. Jeremy moved to Nola's side, a knife in one hand and a gun in the other.

"You in there," Raina called over the wall. "Either run or find a better place to hide. The Outer Guard are coming."

"What?" Nola asked.

"Listen," Jeremy said.

Nola's pulse thundered in her ears. She listened past the thumping, searching for a different sound. The faster beat of running feet pounded under the rhythm of her racing heart.

"Outer Guard?" Nola asked.

"We need to go," Kieran said.

"What about them?" Nola turned back to the brick wall that blocked the twelve from view.

"We warned them. That's all we can do." Julian took off down the street piled with still-smoking skulls.

"Run, Nola," Jeremy said.

She forced her feet to move. "We started the fire. If the guards are coming toward the smoke, it's our fault—"

"Don't," Kieran said.

Nola faltered as they reached the small bones strewn across the ground. The bones reached too far down the road for her to be able to jump across. She gritted her teeth as the bones cracked beneath her feet.

"We should help them hide," Nola said when her feet found clear pavement.

"They can't run like us," Raina said. "We can't slow to their pace, and there's too many of them for us to carry."

"It's wrong to leave them," Nola said.

"If we stay, we'll have to fight the Outer Guard," Jeremy said.

"Jeremy, I—"

"We can't afford that kind of fight," Jeremy cut across Nola. "We have to get back to Emanuel and tell him what we've learned. We risk all of Nightland if we don't get back to him."

"Right." Nola blinked away the stinging in her eyes. "We have to get back."

"They've survived the city for two weeks," Kieran said. "They've got weapons. The Teachers have as good a chance on their own as they do with us leading them to the base of the mountain and abandoning them."

The rats will sink the ship.

They ran down a long row of tumbledown warehouses and onto the wide highway that surrounded the city. A sprawling mass of tents had sprung up in the middle of the road. Few people moved around the makeshift dwellings.

One man dived back into a red patchwork tent as soon as he spotted them. An older woman sat down on the pavement, as though daring them to force her to move.

"We can't head straight up the road," Kieran said.

Raina took the lead, heading toward the path Nola had always followed to the mountain that had become Nightland's new home.

Nola swallowed her questions as Raina led them past the first set of derelict houses. The fire hadn't spread across the expanse of the highway. These homes had been lost to abandonment long before the Outer Guard decided to extinguish life in the city.

Raina led them off the main road, cutting north through the trees.

Toward them.

They had gone to the city seeking information and were returning with a dozen pieces to a puzzle that made no sense.

Traps set in the ruins of Nightland. Salinger still in the domes. People living to the north. Teachers sneaking past the Guard patrols to leave marks for future generations to find.

If Salinger is still in the domes, what is Captain Ridgeway doing?

Nola glanced to Jeremy who ran by her side, determination burning in his eyes.

She needed to talk to him away from the others.

Soon.

They sprinted past dead and dying trees. The marks of human life littered the forest. A tent someone had abandoned. A wooden cross pounded into the ground. Empty food cans rusting in the dirt. After a few miles, Raina headed west, and the signs of life petered away.

"Why would people head north and not west?" Nola asked.

"Easier terrain to cross," Julian said. "That and fear."

"Fear of what?" Jeremy asked.

"Vampires," Raina said.

The ground sloped up, toward the base of the mountain.

"No one knows where Nightland is," Nola said.

"Of course not," Raina said. "But we had to keep people away while the architects built our home. Having angry vampires prowling the edge of the woods kept people away for long enough that legends spread and everyone started avoiding the area entirely."

"A rather brilliant plan," Julian said.

"Well, I am a genius," Raina said.

They kept to the trees as they climbed the mountain, following an unfamiliar path. Even as the incline increased, Nola's breath still came easily, and the exertion didn't burn her legs.

It's not right.

She missed the burning. The feeling of fighting for each step.

But then I'd be dead.

Familiar mountain peaks came into view. The sun sat high in the sky, giving crisp detail to the trees that still grew near the summit, above the reach of the heavy, acid-filled clouds.

They arrived in a basin nestled in the mountainside. A mossy ledge poked out over the clearing. Raina jumped to the ledge and out of sight without pause. Julian sprang up after her.

Nola didn't bother asking if Jeremy wanted to go next before launching herself at the moss. She planted her palms on the surface, and pushed herself up and over the edge into the entrance of Nightland.

CHAPTER SIX

Three guards stood just out of reach of the sun, each with their weapon raised.

"Knock, knock," Raina said. "Guess who's come home."

"You made it back." Stell, a vampire with bright blond hair let her sword drop back into its sheath. "And here I'd bet you'd be gone for good."

"Don't place bets based on wishes," Raina said. "Now get out of my way."

Stell gave a tightlipped smile but backed against the stone of the corridor wall. The other two guards jumped aside without hesitation.

Raina stepped out of the sun and pulled off her hat, shaking her scarlet and purple streaked hair. "As much as not dying is great, I really hate these suits."

Stell growled.

"Don't bother with jealousy, sweetie. You're not important enough to ever get to wear a sunny," Raina cooed as she sauntered down the hall.

Nola resisted the urge to hide her face as she passed Stell's vicious glare.

"You don't have to antagonize her like that," Kieran said.

"Sure I do." Raina unzipped her suit, letting the upper half fall over her belt, revealing her usual black leather top.

The tunnel wound up through the mountain. Every few minutes, they passed a window cut into the rock wall, looking out over the mountain they'd just climbed.

Nola paused at the last window, leaning out to see the city. The blackness of it all seemed like a sore on the land. A horrible blemish brought on by disease.

"Come on." Jeremy took her hand. "We should get to Emanuel."

"You all go ahead," Raina said. "I'll see Emanuel later."

"Of course," Julian said before Nola could ask why.

The giant metal door to the sparring room stood open. Pairs of vampires sparred in colored squares painted on the ground.

The pair nearest the door spotted Raina and froze, the woman with her knife still raised in the air. Each of the matches stopped as a wave of stillness rippled through the fighters.

Raina raised a hand. "Don't even bother asking."

The fighters cleared a path to the door on the far side of the room.

Despite having chosen Nightland as her home, Nola's skin crawled as she walked the alley between the well-armed vampires.

Raina stopped before the door to the interior tunnel. "Silly me, turn in your toys."

"Really?" Jeremy placed his hands on the weapons at his hips.

"Stell's not fancy enough for a sun suit, and you're not important enough to keep weapons inside Nightland." Raina held her hand out to Jeremy.

He shook his head and unfastened his belt. "Do you really think it's smart to keep people unarmed with Salinger still around?"

"If the domes attack, they'll have to come through the front door," Julian said. "You can claim your weapon on the way to meet them. In the meantime, it's best not to pack a thousand people underground with weapons being carried in the halls. You'll find it greatly increases the mortality rate."

Jeremy handed Raina his belt.

"You too." Raina turned to Nola.

"Just tell them it wasn't me who lost the knife." Nola passed over her belt.

A mousy-looking boy took the weapons from Raina with a bow.

Raina winked at Jeremy and sauntered down the hall with her black metal box, leaving them behind.

"Has she always been like that?" Jeremy said.

"For as long as I've known her," Julian said.

They walked in silence through the stone hallways, passing a woman carrying a crate of mushrooms and a man balancing a stack of clean sheets. Even as they arrived at Emanuel's door, Nola stared longingly down the hall toward the bed that awaited her.

Julian opened the door to Emanuel's library without knocking.

A sense of delight broke through Nola's growing fatigue at the sight of the chandeliers hanging from the ceiling, art adorning the walls, and stuffed bookshelves surrounding the room. In the center of the library sat Emanuel in his red wingback chair, with Eden curled up in his lap as he read her a story.

Emanuel looked up from the book as Julian entered the library.

Nola froze on the threshold, uncertain of disturbing such a rare moment of serenity.

"Go to Bea." Emanuel set Eden down.

The little girl shook her head, sending her black curls flying. "You didn't finish."

"Later, Eden," Emanuel said.

Eden crossed her arms, tucked her chin, and headed for the door at the back of the room.

"Where's Raina?" Emanuel asked as soon as the door shut behind his daughter.

"She'll be here to see you later." Julian climbed out of his sun suit. "This one will need a bit of repair, I'm afraid. I was shot by an arrow."

"An arrow?" Emanuel stood.

"Things didn't go exactly as we'd hoped," Julian said.

"Salinger is still patrolling the city," Jeremy said. "He hasn't gone back to his home domes."

"You saw him?" Wrinkles creased Emanuel's brow.

"No," Nola said. "But we met people who had."

They took turns explaining everything that had happened. Starting with finding people holed up in a house on the way to the city and Julian being shot. Then Nola and Jeremy finding the trap in Nightland. Catching a glimpse of the unharmed domes across the river. Then meeting the Teachers.

"I didn't think the fanatics would come back to the city," Emanuel said. "I was sure they'd died out and we had seen the last of their kind a very long time ago."

"You've heard of the Teachers?" Kieran paused halfway through folding his sun suit.

"Not under that name, but yes." Emanuel tented his fingers under his chin. "I'd heard rumors about people heading north as well."

"Why have I never heard about it?" Kieran asked.

"There are many rumors and legends. I don't choose to waste my time on things that cannot be proven as fact." Emanuel sat in his red chair. "There was talk of tunnels under the city for years before we began construction on Nightland's home underground. If I had listened to them, our people would never have had a sanctuary where we could grow strong enough to come to our true home."

"The people in the north," Nola said, "are they really violent? I mean, if they were killing people, wouldn't the domes have noticed?"

Emanuel looked to Jeremy.

Jeremy ran his hands over his face before speaking. "I never heard anything about settlements beyond the city limits. The domes decreed that people could only live in this area if they stayed between the highway and the river a long time ago. I don't know if they chose to ignore the people lurking in the wild or if they were just so damn cocky and sure everyone would follow their laws they never bothered to look."

"What do we do about them, though?" Nola took Jeremy's arm. "If the people in the north like to attack, what happens if they find us?"

"We need to worry about Salinger first," Jeremy said. "We can defend ourselves against bows and arrows. We can't fight fire packs."

"I need to think," Emanuel said. "You've all done very well. Thank you for risking your lives to protect Nightland."

"Of course." Julian nodded and headed toward the door through which Eden had disappeared.

"I want to get these supplies to my dad." Kieran followed Julian.

"We should find T and Beauford," Nola said.

"You need rest first." Jeremy brushed a stray curl from Nola's forehead. They turned to go back out into the hall.

"Jeremy," Emanuel said, "I'm sorry you didn't find your sister."

Jeremy said nothing as he closed the door.

"Be careful," Nola said in a voice too soft for even Emanuel to hear.

"Of what?" Jeremy said.

"Emanuel isn't a person you want as an enemy." Nola held Jeremy's hand as they walked toward the long corridor of sleeping quarters.

"Why did he need to mention my sister?" Jeremy said. "It's not like he cares about her."

"You're right, he doesn't," Nola said. "He'll never think of a rogue Domer as someone he should worry about." She pressed her fingers to Jeremy's lips before he could speak. "But he cares about us because we help him. Letting us make Nightland our home is in the best interest of Emanuel's people. As one person trying to survive on the outside, Gentry means nothing to Nightland. But *when* we find her, we need Emanuel to see how valuable she is so she can come live here with us. It'll be a lot easier to convince Emanuel that having a second Ridgeway under his protection will be best for Nightland if he likes you."

Jeremy wrapped his arms around Nola and kissed the top of her head. "Isn't it good enough that he likes you?"

"He likes me because I stole medicine from the domes to save his daughter." Nola tipped her chin up, brushing her lips against his. "You've risked your life to find information for Nightland twice now. You've done enough for him to consider you a part of his family. Just try to be civil."

Jeremy kissed Nola.

She stood up on her toes, leaning into their embrace.

"I'll play nice with the vampires," Jeremy said.

"Good."

They stopped in front of the door to Jeremy's room. He lived only a few doors down from the entrance to Emanuel's library, where the leader of Nightland could keep a close watch on the Outer Guard who had betrayed the domes.

Nola leaned in to kiss Jeremy one more time.

"Stay," Jeremy whispered. "Please stay."

A rush of heat flooded Nola's face.

"We both need to sleep." Jeremy caressed Nola's cheek. "Let me wake up knowing you're safe."

A little bubble of contentment grew amidst the worry and

confusion shouting in Nola's mind. "It would be really great to sleep."

Jeremy opened his door, letting Nola enter first.

The small stone room barely fit the bed, dresser, and chair Jeremy had been provided. One light hung from the ceiling, next to a hole that led up to the surface, allowing fresh air to filter in through the mass of the mountain.

Weight pressed on Nola's eyelids at the sight of the bed. "I shouldn't be this tired. I slept a couple of days ago."

"Your brain has processed too much information since the last time you slept." Jeremy tugged on his bootlaces. "Even super-heroes need sleep."

The journey into the city, the time they'd spent there before they'd run back, all of it had taken less than a day. But the running, fear, and pain all blurred together in a swirl that moved too quickly for her mind to focus on one moment at a time.

Nola sat on the chair to untie her shoes, blinking to bat away the excess noise surrounding the failure that hurt most. "We're not going to stop looking for Gentry. You know that, right?"

Jeremy sank down on the edge of the bed. "How can we possibly find her? If she's still alive, which is a big *if*."

Nola sat next to Jeremy, wrapping her arm around his waist. "Gentry is strong and brave. She's had training. She's out there somewhere."

"Where?" Grief filled Jeremy's eyes. "If she left right after the city burned, she could be hundreds of miles away by now."

"I..." There was no argument she could make. With how fast Gentry could move...

We might never find her.

"We'll keep trying," Nola said. "We're not going to give up on her."

"I can't drag you around the wild searching for her." Jeremy dug his knuckles into his temples. "If you had gotten into that room first, if I hadn't been able to figure out how to open the door...I can't risk your life, Nola."

She knelt in front of him, pulling his hands from his face to make him look into her eyes.

"We're in this together, Jeremy," Nola said. "You and me. I love you."

"We can't get to the domes," Jeremy said. "There's no way for us to get more Graylock."

"We can heal without more doses. It'll be slow, but—"

"But what if that doesn't work? Graylock isn't even as old as ReVamp. Our ability to heal could lessen with time. We don't know." He kissed the palm of her hand. "I have to protect you. From Salinger, and whatever drove people from the domes to turn into zombies, and the people in the north, and the vampires here."

Nola sat on his lap. Jeremy laid his head on her chest.

"You can't worry about all of that," Nola said. "It's too much for one person."

"I have to worry about all of it," Jeremy said. "I love you. I have to find a way to keep all of this awfulness from hurting you."

Nola lifted his chin and kissed him, savoring the taste of his lips. She let her mouth linger on his for a long moment.

"You can't protect me," Nola said. "It's not possible. But we can face whatever is coming together. And if that means searching the wild for Gentry, then building a boat to cross the river to the domes, and breaking through the glass to find out how to make more Graylock, we'll do it."

He kissed her again, exploring her lips.

Nola's heart flipped in her chest, shattering the weight the dying world had thrust upon her. She pulled herself closer, wanting to feel the beat of his heart pulse through her.

He lifted her from his lap and laid her down on the bed. Her body throbbed from her toes to the tips of her fingers as she reached for him.

"You should sleep," he said.

"Jeremy."

"We have to sleep." He crawled into bed next to her, staring at the stone ceiling above them.

She lifted his arm, finding the spot on his shoulder that seemed to have been designed as a place for her to lay her head.

"We're going to be okay," she said. "Both of us. We're going to be okay."

He kissed the top of her head but didn't say anything.

Say something. Do something.

She couldn't think of a way to help either of them. Fatigue took her before a plan could form.

CHAPTER SEVEN

"It's really all gone?" T leaned across the table as far as her ever-growing belly would allow, pushing yet another portion of mushroom soup toward Nola.

The scent of the thick soup filled the room Nola shared with Beauford and T.

"There's nothing left in the city," Nola said. "The fire packs got everything between the highway and the water."

Beauford gave a low whistle. "When the domes want a mass slaughter, they do it right."

"I can't even picture it, the whole city just gone. All those people." T brushed a tear off her freckled nose.

"It's awful." Nola fought the urge to lie and spare her friend. "And the people on the highway are in tents."

"They'll be dead soon enough." Beauford pushed away his half-full soup bowl. "One bad sickness, and it'll get almost everyone. Acid rain comes back, and they won't have anywhere to hide."

"There are the houses," T said. "The falling down ones on the little road west of the highway."

"Not enough for everyone," Beauford said. "Unless an illness cuts down their numbers first."

T cradled her belly as she stood and paced the small space between the table and the four beds. "Is there a way we could convince Emanuel to take more people in?"

Nola picked up her spoon and took two bites of soup. Eating didn't make the answer any easier. "We don't have the resources." Self-loathing curdled the food on its way to Nola's stomach. "There are only a few empty rooms left in the tunnels. Those could hold forty people if we packed them in. But then we'd have to feed them."

"Couldn't we make it work?" T said. "Cut down just a bit on how much the humans eat?"

"I—maybe," Nola said, "if we knew when we'd be able to use the garden again. But we can't count on the weather. We don't know how long it'll be before the freezes stop. Forty people could mean the difference of a few more weeks before starvation if it takes too long for spring to come."

"Is it wrong of us not to try?" T said. "There are kids out there. People's children who are hungry and cold. We could at least take in the little ones."

Beauford stood and hugged T. Her shoulders shook with silent sobs.

"I should go," Nola said. "I have work to do."

Neither T nor Beauford said anything to stop her as Nola ducked out into the hall. She closed the door behind her and leaned against the wall.

"I sound like them," Nola whispered.

Which them?

She'd hated the domes for ignoring the suffering in the city. Hated Nightland for causing pain by attacking the domes to steal supplies.

I'm just as much a monster as the rest of them.

Nola walked down the corridor, passing a flock of chattering children surrounding a woman who looked like she hadn't slept in a week. The children had full heads of hair and skin free from sores. They bombarded the woman with questions in voices so loud, the sound could only have been made by lungs undamaged by polluted air.

The children stuck on the outside will never have a chance to bounce around with so much energy.

Nola clenched her fists, letting her nails dig into her palms. She didn't know where her feet were carrying her until she stopped in front of the door to Kieran's lab. She knocked before allowing herself to think.

"Come in," Kieran's voice came through the door.

Nola's hand froze above the doorknob. She worked in the lab, had spent dozens of hours inside.

Don't be an idiot.

She opened the door, stepped into the lab, and snapped the door shut behind her.

"Nola." Kieran looked up from his microscope. "I didn't think you were working on samples today."

"I'm not." Nola's curls bounced around her as she shook her head. "I just needed…"

"Needed what?" Kieran's dark eyebrows pinched together.

"Convince me we're better than them." The words tumbled out. "Tell me why us leaving the people in the tent city is better than the domes leaving the city to rot. Tell me I was right to choose Nightland over the domes. Over my mother. Tell me I'm not a horrible murderer for sitting safely in these tunnels while other people are suffering. That there's a way out that doesn't end with the domes penning us in here and slaughtering the few people Emanuel has managed to save." Nola took a gasping breath. Tears streamed down her face. "A thousand people hidden here in the mountain. And that's it. We're supposed to say this is good enough? The rest of them are just dead whether or not they've stopped breathing?" Sobs overtook her words.

Kieran stood, hesitating before walking over to Nola. "Can I hold you?"

Nola nodded, stepping into the embrace. His body didn't envelope her as Jeremy's broad shoulders did, but a familiar safety came with the feel of his arms around her. She leaned her forehead on his shoulder, letting her tears fall onto his shirt.

"It's not enough." Kieran pressed his cheek to her hair. "The people we've managed to protect in Nightland aren't enough. But we can't take them all in. We can't even get them here without the domes finding us."

"How do we live with that?"

"I don't know. Try to find ways to not feel so helpless. Work to make Nightland sustainable for T's baby so that her child will never understand what we feel like right now."

"I don't want to be like the Domers." Nola wrapped her arms around Kieran. "I couldn't survive being a monster in a glass castle. I don't think I can live as a monster in a stone fortress either. I can't hide and wait for them all to die out."

"I don't think we're going to be doing much hiding."

Nola looked up. Her face was only a few inches from his. Not so very long ago she would have leaned in, finding comfort in the feel of his lips against hers.

"Why won't we be hiding?" Nola asked.

Kieran shook his head and took a step back to the edge of the table.

"Kieran?" She shivered at the hollow feeling growing in her gut.

"Emanuel doesn't like the idea of waiting either. There are too many hostile groups, too many scenarios that end with Nightland being attacked."

"So what does he want to do?" Nola reached for her hip, to where her knife would have rested.

"No idea," Kieran said. "He's planning something. We'll just have to wait for him to tell us what that something is."

"Are you okay with that?" Nola asked. "With waiting for other people to make decisions for us?"

Kieran smiled, and, for a moment, Nola caught a glimpse of the boy she'd once loved.

"I'd rather be in on the meetings." Kieran shrugged and moved back to his microscope. "But then I remember I'm seventeen. Emanuel and Raina have been working to build this place for more than twice my lifetime. Julian's been helping Nightland since before I was born. I want to be a part of the solution, but I have to let them make the decisions."

"And what if you don't agree with the choices they make?"

"We worry about that if the time comes," Kieran said. "In the meantime, we trust them. And we keep working."

"Right." Nola wiped the tears off her cheeks. "Right. I should go get some samples from the field."

"You don't have to," Kieran said.

"I do." Nola moved to her tiny corner of the lab, taking her bag, a case of empty vials, and a stack of clean cloths.

"Is he okay?" Kieran asked.

"Jeremy?"

"Yeah." Kieran pressed his eye to his microscope.

Nola dug her fingers through her curls. "No, he really isn't. My mom is still in the domes, but I know she's not hurting anyone. His dad is still in the domes, but he could have given the order to drop the fire packs. We need to find Gentry, but I have no idea how. He wants to protect me and keep me safe, but I can't protect him."

Kieran laid both his hands out flat on his worktable. "Loving you got him out of the domes. He's here because of you. He's out of reach of the Incorporation because of you. None of us are strong enough to protect the people we love from the nightmares of this world. But he loves you, and you love him. That's a lot."

"Kieran—"

"You should get down to the field." Kieran placed a new slide under his microscope.

"I'll bring some samples back in a bit." The weight of a broken heart pulled against her as she left the lab.

The vials clinked against each other as her bag bounced on her hip. She didn't want to go farther underground. She wanted to be in the fresh air. To stand on top of the mountain under the stars and pretend the human race had never touched the valley below. There would be no city of ash and bones waiting to be found by future generations. No illness, no pollution, no want. Just a rock drifting through space with sparkling stars as its traveling companions.

Nola reached the entrance to the low cave. The door blocking the path had been carved to fit the natural curvature of the stone, leaving gentle waves around the edges.

Just work. The best thing you can do is work.

The door creaked as she opened it, almost as though protesting the existence of the person who had dared to close it.

Nola took one last deep breath and stepped into the narrow tunnel.

The architects who had built the caves had spent years carving out the corridors and rooms that made up the bulk of Nightland. No one seemed to know if the architects had gone looking for the caves toward the base of the mountain, or if they had just stumbled on the path that cut deep into the earth by chance.

Most of the passage had been left in its original state, the floor uneven as the walls bent and twisted to the mountain's will. In places where the tunnel had gotten too tight for a person to pass, the architects had left their mark on the stone, carving out smooth sections to guide the traveler in the right direction, ever downward to the root of the mountain itself.

Nola kept her pace steady, fighting the urge to sprint through the passage and dive into the wide space below.

"I've faced worse than stone. I'm not afraid of you." Even as she said the words, the thumping in her chest beat its disagreement.

At last, the tunnel opened up into a wide cave. Only a few lights had been hung in odd corners, but Graylock gave her the ability to see in the dim shadows. The scent of stone and water filled Nola's lungs, breaking through the hum of her fear. The massive lake at the back of the cavern kept the air moist, allowing Kieran's crops to flourish.

He had carefully placed different types of mushrooms throughout the cave. Some grew by the water constantly dripping down the face of the rock. Others peeped out of crevices where the stone had cracked long ago. But the long mushroom beds built of tarred wood were the real prize for Nightland, even if a few of the residents weren't overjoyed by the thought of anyone feeding them more fungus.

Nola walked the edge of the wide cavern, letting her fingers trail along the cold stone wall. The stalagmites hid troves of mushrooms behind them, but they also provided places for a person to lurk unseen.

Since when am I afraid of people?

She shook her head, trying to fling aside the question.

But the nagging thought remained. If she lined up the evil against the innocent, she didn't know which tally would be higher.

"Maybe the world is right to try and kill us all." Her voice carried around the cavern, but there was no one in the shadows to answer her.

She stopped at the edge of the lake, kneeling down and dipping her hands into the chill water.

Goose bumps crawled up her arms, but the temperature didn't hurt her fingers. Graylock protected her from the cold, as Vamp protected the vampires.

They'd all had to change to fight the disease and contamination that had taken over the outside world.

The domes had locked their people behind glass, relying on technology to filter the air and water and block the worst of the sun's rays.

Nightland had dug deep, relying on the weight of the earth for protection.

"It doesn't make sense." Nola took off her bag and kicked her shoes aside. She stepped out into the water, letting the cold seep through the legs of her pants. She sloshed farther out into the lake. She didn't shiver as the water reached her knees. Her nerves didn't set fire to her skin, warning her to get out of the cold. "It's not right."

She took another step. The ground beneath her disappeared. She plummeted down, falling deeper into the water than she had imagined the lake could reach. The dim light overhead faded, leaving her surrounded by crushing darkness.

Even as her lungs screamed for air, her body cared nothing for the cold.

Graylock protects me.

She kicked up toward the surface, fighting to find the open air above. She kicked again as the horrible thought that she had somehow swum the wrong way pinched her lungs.

A hand reached out, seizing her wrist. Arms she would recognize even after a thousand years wrapped around her, dragging her up. Her head broke through the surface, and she gasped, sucking in wonderful air.

"Nola." Jeremy dragged her onto the edge of the rocks. "Are you okay?" He pushed her mop of sopping curls away from her face.

"I'm fine," Nola coughed. "What are you doing down here?"

"What the hell were you thinking? You can barely swim."

"Of course I can't. We're from the domes. We're lucky they teach kids to tread water in a tank." Nola tried to stand, but Jeremy gripped her shoulders, keeping her sitting in the waist-high water.

"You could've drowned."

"I didn't know there was a ledge." Nola took Jeremy's face in her hands.

"What the hell were you doing in the water?" He pressed his forehead to Nola's. "If Kieran hadn't told me to come down here—"

"Kieran gave you permission?"

"I could've lost you," Jeremy said.

"I needed to see if I would get cold." Nola pressed her lips to Jeremy's cheek.

Even as they sat dripping in the cold water, his skin held onto its warmth. She pressed her lips to his, breathing in his heat.

"Nola," he whispered.

She pulled herself closer, reveling in the faint thumping of the blood pounding through his veins. She wrapped her legs around him, keeping herself pressed to him as her fingers found the bottom his shirt.

He started to speak, but she silenced him, deepening their kiss, only stopping to drag his shirt over his head. His lips found her neck, trailing kisses out to her shoulder as he unfastened the buttons of her shirt.

Flesh met flesh, and the world disappeared.

CHAPTER EIGHT

"We've been thinking about it all wrong." Nola sat at the table in Emanuel's kitchen, Jeremy by her side. "All of us. Nightland, the domes, everyone."

Emanuel leaned back in his chair, but did nothing to silence her.

"In the domes"—Nola looked to Kieran, Julian, and Dr. Wynne—"we always assumed the only way people would be able to survive long term was to lock themselves away from danger."

"It has been a very effective, if morally unsound, solution," Dr. Wynne said.

"The vampires turned to drugs." Nola looked to Raina. "You found a way to change your bodies to survive."

"And it's been grand." Raina raised her tumbler of blood. "Cheers to surviving."

"You copied the domes, Emanuel," Nola pressed on. "You saw them build a home and hide away, and you created your own version here in the mountain. And the domes saw how strong Vamp made you, and they made Graylock to mimic you."

"And now we have two strong opponents pitted against each

other," Emanuel said. "The survival of the domes puts us in danger."

"But see what you just did?" Nola said. "You left out the people to the north."

"I'm not too worried about the people with sticks," Raina said.

"I agree they're not the largest of our concerns, but I must say being shot was wholly unpleasant," Julian said.

"I'm not talking about them attacking." Nola gripped the edge of the table. "I'm talking about them surviving. Emanuel, you made the same mistake as the domes."

"I prefer to think of myself as different from those monsters," Emanuel said.

Nola took a deep breath. "But you're both cocky. I'm sorry, but you are."

Jeremy laid his hand on her thigh.

"You were all so busy thinking you'd found the one path to surviving, you didn't think about there being another way," Nola said. "The way the people up north have been surviving on the outside."

"It's an interesting point," Dr. Wynne said. "In mirroring our enemy, we've been neglecting to look away from our own reflection."

"But you're assuming the people up north are actually living a reasonable life and not starving in a ditch," Raina said.

"If they have enough people to let *arrows rain down*, there's got to be a good number of them," Jeremy said. "If it were only a few archers, it would be easy for people fleeing north to slip past them."

"The person I fought after Julian was shot was human," Kieran said. "No extra strength, nothing like that."

"Which is why you killed him," Raina said. "He's dead, you're alive, so I feel pretty good about our odds of beating the Northerners."

"You don't get it." Nola made herself let go of the edge of the table. She folded her hands in front of her. *Just like Mom.* "I'm not talking about who might come up the mountain to attack us. I'm talking about pure humans surviving on the outside."

"Careful, little girl," Raina said. "Every person in this room would be dead if they had been left as *pure human*. Don't make me think you regret surviving."

"No, no." Dr. Wynne tapped the tip of his nose. "I see what Nola means."

"I'm not sure I do," Emanuel said.

"They've found a way to build some kind of community," Nola said.

"That's got nothing to do with us unless they want to attack," Raina said.

"It has everything to do with us if we don't want to be like the domes." Nola's words echoed around the kitchen. "We can't bring all the people who survived the fire in the city here, I understand that. All our humans would starve if we tried to feed hundreds of extra people. But if we could find out how the people in the north are surviving, we might be able to help the people from the city find a way to provide for themselves."

Kieran pushed away from the wall to pace behind Emanuel.

"I have a thousand people here," Emanuel said. "One thousand lives are depending on my ability to keep them safe."

"I thought Nightland was bigger than that," Nola said. "Do you remember the first time I came to Nightland?"

Kieran froze behind Emanuel.

"You said the domes want to preserve human DNA," Nola said, "but you wanted to protect what it means to be human. Being human means learning and helping. If we ignore the fact that a group of people might be doing what we'd assumed impossible, if we don't take the opportunity to find out if there's a chance to save hundreds of innocent lives, we're no better than the domes."

"The people living on the highway are already as good as dead," Raina said.

"If we accept that, then we're no better than the Teachers," Kieran said. "Giving up on the present and assuming there's nothing left but death."

Nola let a small smile curve her lips. "The second we decide there's nothing we can do to change things, we're nothing more than dust and bones for future generations to find."

"What exactly do you propose we do?" Emanuel asked.

"I want to go north," Nola said.

Jeremy gripped her leg.

"I want to try and talk to the people there." She placed her hand on top of Jeremy's. "See how they've been able to live and see if they'll take in anyone from the highway. They might know something more about the domes, too."

"And when arrows start flying?" Raina asked.

"I'll protect her," Jeremy said.

"How romantic." Raina rolled her eyes.

"What about the Teachers?" Dr. Wynne said. "From what Kieran described, they all appeared to be in relatively good health, and they seem to have been around for a good long while."

"The only direction the Teachers could have come from is south. We can try going south after we're done in the north," Jeremy said.

More chances to find Gentry.

"And how long would that take?" Emanuel asked. "I can't have you away from Nightland that long."

"I…" Nola looked around the room.

Trust them. I have to trust them.

"What if the domes go north and kill the people there before we can learn from them?" Kieran said. "You thought it wasn't possible to have a garden in the city before I built one. We won't know what we could learn unless we try."

Emanuel sat still as a stone for a long moment, his gaze locked on Nola's face.

She held her breath, waiting for his judgment.

"I don't want what my daughter learns from my bones to be that I ignored those who suffered, or dismissed the opportunity to learn when it came," Emanuel said. "One group goes north and one south. You have three nights to gather information and come back."

Three nights.

It was longer than Nola had dared hope for.

"Nola, Jeremy, and Julian go north," Emanuel said. "Raina choose one and go south."

"I'll go," Kieran said.

"No," Emanuel said. "I was foolish to let you go to the city before. I've spent so long building and fighting, I forget it's not only the doctor who does the most good by staying in his lab."

Kieran turned to Nola. She could read the look in his eyes, the words balanced on his tongue. *Then Nola should be left in the lab, too.*

Nola gave a tiny shake of her head.

Kieran hesitated, then nodded. "I'll stay and keep working on the plants. We need to be ready for when the weather warms."

I could help him. I'm better trained in botany. But the tiny voice in the back of her mind, the voice that questioned why she didn't get cold, needed to go north.

"How many sun suits do you have?" Jeremy asked.

"Not enough to spare any more to this venture." Emanuel stood. "Take what supplies you need."

"What if it takes us longer than three nights?" Nola asked.

"You have three nights." Emanuel strode out into the hall, leaving the kitchen in silence.

Dr. Wynne nodded to himself for a moment before wandering out after Emanuel.

"I suppose I should eat a bigger snack before I leave." Raina downed the rest of her blood. "I'm guessing the Teachers won't be very generous hosts. If I even find them while stomping around through the wild." She shot one last glare at Nola before sauntering into the hall.

"We should leave as soon as possible." Julian sat in Emanuel's chair. "Nightfall is in a few short hours. We could cover a good bit of distance tonight, then search for them during the daylight."

"It depends on if we want the element of surprise or don't want to spook them," Jeremy said. "I honestly don't know which would be best."

"We'll have plenty of time to debate the benefits of either course on our journey," Julian said. "I should find nourishment before we leave, and I suggest the two of you see Bea for food to pack. Changed or not, you're going to need to eat a significant amount to run at the pace we'll have to maintain."

"Right." Nola stood, keeping Jeremy's hand in hers. "Let's hope Bea is in a good mood."

Julian laughed as Nola and Jeremy went into the hall. Rooms lined the corridor behind them, but in front, one door blocked the path. Jeremy opened the door with his free hand, ushering Nola into Emanuel's library.

"Why didn't—" Jeremy stopped at the thumping of footsteps behind them.

Kieran stepped into the library and closed the door before speaking. "I can go instead of you."

Both Jeremy and Kieran looked to Nola.

"I'm going." Nola squared her shoulders. "This was my idea, and I'm going."

"You know more about plants than I do," Kieran said. "You run the lab, and I'll go north."

"Emanuel can't spare the sun suit," Nola said.

"Then Julian can stay and just Jeremy and I will go," Kieran said.

"No," Nola said. "Absolutely not."

"We can play nice, Nola," Jeremy said. "It's a good idea."

"I can help him look for Gentry as well as you can," Kieran said.

Jeremy's head snapped up, his eyes narrowing at Kieran.

"I know that's part of why you both want to go," Kieran said. "It's not that hard to see. I like Gentry. She was always decent to me when I lived in the domes."

Nola let go of Jeremy's hand and hugged Kieran. "I know what you're trying to do. But I need to see what's there for myself."

Kieran held her close. "Be careful, Nola. We can't lose you."

"I'm just going for a long walk," Nola said. "Don't let the lab get too messy while I'm gone."

Kieran laughed, but the sound came out forced and wrong. "I won't touch your corner."

"I'll keep her safe," Jeremy said.

"Good." Kieran stepped back. "Nightland needs both of you."

"Keep the path open," Jeremy said.

"See you soon." A lump pressed on Nola's throat. "We should go to Bea."

"I'll let you do the talking." Jeremy held open the door to the hall.

Nola gave Kieran one last smile before going out into the corridor. She reached for Jeremy before she heard the door close behind them. He took her hand, kissing her palm before lacing his fingers through hers.

"You should have warned me," Jeremy said. "Before we went in there to talk to them, you should have told me you wanted to go north."

"I didn't want you to convince me not to talk to Emanuel," Nola said.

"Talking to Emanuel about wanting to learn from the people in the north is one thing. Going north is another. This is too dangerous."

"For me, or for anyone?" Nola asked.

"That's not fair."

"It's completely fair." Nola stepped in front of Jeremy, blocking his path. "I can walk in the sun without protection, so can you. That gives us a unique skill that's valuable to Nightland. Add that to the fact that we need to find Gentry and we can't do it from here, and the two of us going makes the most sense."

Jeremy wrapped his arms around her, enveloping her in a safety she would not allow the horrors of the world to steal. Nola sank into his warmth, a buzz of happiness starting from her stomach and trickling out to her fingers. She rose up on her toes and kissed his neck. "I love you. And it's time for me to help you."

"I know you want to help, and it's one of the reasons I love you so much, but—"

"Don't walk you into a room full of vampires and drop something like this on you again?" She kissed just below his ear. "Okay. I'll make sure I warn you about any crazy plans in the future."

"It's a good plan," Jeremy said. "I just wish you weren't a part of it."

Nola stepped out of his arms, sighing as his wonderful warmth faded from her skin.

"You're just going to have to get used to the fact that your girlfriend is a superhero, too," Nola said.

He took her hand as they headed toward Bea's domain.

"Girlfriend sounds weird, doesn't it?" Jeremy said.

"Do superheroes not date?" Nola raised an eyebrow.

"I think we're making up the rules on that." Jeremy nudged her with his elbow.

"And girlfriend doesn't fit the rules?" Nola nudged back.

"It's just with—"

Nola swallowed her laugh as pink crept into Jeremy's cheeks.

"—it just doesn't sound like enough. I mean, back in the domes, we would have gone to the board, you know."

"We're not of age to have our DNA tested and request to be paired by the marriage board," Nola said.

"There isn't a board here," Jeremy said. "There aren't any rules we have to follow."

"Clearly."

Jeremy's face turned bright red. "What I mean is, we can make up our own rules. You could stay with me in my room all the time. We could decide we want to be a pair without asking anyone's permission."

Nola froze.

Jeremy took another step before realizing she had stopped. He turned to look at her, his face changing from bright red to pale white in an instant. "I'm sorry. I'm sorry, there's too much happening and I always try and go too fast."

"You really want me?" Heat crept into Nola's face. "Just me and that's it forever?'

He gazed down at Nola's hand locked together with his. "With Graylock we might live for hundreds of years. I want to make sure I spend all of them with you."

"I love you. And I want you by my side, no matter what. For as long as we have." She touched his cheek, her heart thrumming as he blushed again. "I pick you as my pair. Whatever the world brings."

"Whatever the world brings."

CHAPTER NINE

T's stomping rang around the pantry. "Again?" She pulled a stack of clean cloths from the shelf filled with jars of preserved fruit. "You're going out there again?"

Nola glanced to Jeremy who shrugged and kept his lips pressed together.

Bea stared at the crates of vegetables along one wall as though she hadn't heard anything.

"We need to know more about the people in the north," Nola said.

"I don't like you leaving like this." T wrapped a loaf of hard seed bread in a cloth and shoved the bundle into Nola's pack. "You should be staying inside where it's safe."

"I'll be fine," Nola said. "I'll be with Jeremy."

My pair.

Her heart flipped and swirled in her chest.

Jeremy smiled at her from across the table where he stored the rations Bea had laid out for him in his own pack.

"We made it through the city to get here, and now you just keep leaving." T shoved apples in after the bread.

Bea banged a wrinkled hand down on the long, wooden table.

"Sorry." T shrank under Bea's glare and placed the dried meat carefully into the bag.

Bea gave a crisp nod that wobbled her sagging cheeks and moved to the barrels in the corner of the pantry.

"I can't just stay here," Nola said. "Not when there could be a way for me to help people."

T *tsked* as she pulled the top of the bag shut with shaking hands.

Nola lifted the pack from T's grip and pulled her into a hug, slouching to reach over the belly between them. "You're not due for another two months. I'll be back in a few days. Beauford will be here with you."

T stepped away from Nola, moving on to the food to be sorted for the humans' evening meal. "If you're going to leave tonight, you should finish getting ready. You wouldn't want to waste any precious hours of darkness staying safe."

"T," Nola said, "please don't be mad. I'm trying to make things better. Make this a better world for your baby."

"I've heard that before." T hid behind the sheet of her hair.

"I'm coming back," Nola said.

T didn't look away from her work.

"I'm sorry." Nola pulled on her pack and headed to the hall, feeling Bea's watchful gaze on her back until Jeremy closed the pantry door behind them.

"I don't want you to think less of me," Jeremy said, "but Bea is terrifying."

"Why do you think Emanuel put her in charge of distributing the food?" Nola gave a laugh that grated against her throat. "No one would dare cross her to steal anything."

"She'll be okay." Jeremy wrapped his arm around Nola, keeping her close to his side as they climbed the hall back to the sleeping quarters. "T, I mean."

"I don't worry about T being safe." Nola leaned her head

against Jeremy. "She's pregnant. The vampires here will fight with everything they have to protect her and her baby."

"But?" Jeremy asked.

"Charles, the baby's father, he went to fight in the domes when Nightland attacked."

Jeremy tensed but kept his arm around Nola.

"Charles was injured at the domes and killed by wolves during Nightland's retreat," Nola said. "He left her behind and promised to come back. Now I keep leaving. I can't blame her for being upset."

"She's got Beauford," Jeremy said. "He'll be here."

"Right. You're right."

Nola stopped at the room she'd been sharing with T and Beauford. She knocked before entering. Four beds sat along the walls, with dressers tucked between them. A table and chairs took up the center of the space. Nola went straight to the dresser that held the few articles of clothing she'd brought with her from the domes. Most of them had already needed mending from the few weeks she'd spent living outside the glass.

"What are we going to do when we go through all the factory-made clothes we have?" Nola tucked her clothes in around the food T had packed for her.

"No idea," Jeremy said. "Maybe all of us will just run around naked."

"No," Nola laughed, the sound coming freely this time. "I don't want to spend my life running around a cave of naked people."

"Then I guess we'll have to figure out how to make new clothes. I'm sure Emanuel's made plans for building spinning wheels."

They stopped in Jeremy's room. His drawers held little more than Nola's. Only the few sets of clothes Nightland had provided and his Outer Guard uniform.

"I don't even want to touch it." Jeremy stared down at the

folded black fabric.

"Do you need it?" Nola said.

"I have no idea." He rolled the uniform and tucked it into the very bottom of his bag.

"It seems like we should be taking more."

"We're going to get weapons." Jeremy slid his empty drawer closed.

"I know," Nola said. "It just seems like a long time to be gone."

He shrugged on his backpack then took Nola's shoulders. "You can change your mind. You don't have to go."

"Yes, I do." She pressed her lips to Jeremy's cheek. "I just wish I felt a little more prepared."

"Me too." He kissed the top of her head.

Nola waited for something to feel different as they walked out of his room and shut the door behind them. Some sort of finality to the *click* of the lock, since the door wouldn't open for days.

It's not that long. Barely any time at all really.

But how much has already changed in a month?

The fighting in the sparring room didn't stop as they entered. Julian waited by the weapons cage at the side of the space, a sword already strapped to his hip. His pack was larger than Jeremy's or Nola's, and a sun hat had been tied to the back. He waved them over, not bothering to try and speak over the chaos in the cavern.

"It took a bit of work to convince them to trust Nola with another knife." Julian handed Nola a belt with two knives and one Guard gun. "Do be careful with them."

"I'm not actually the one who lost the last knife they gave me." Nola fastened the now familiar weight around her waist.

"Anyone coming to see us off?" Jeremy took his belt from Julian.

"I don't believe so," Julian said. "I don't think Emanuel is to too keen on advertising our mission."

"In case we don't come back?" Dread trickled down Nola's

spine.

"In case we find something he'd rather not have people asking questions about." Julian locked the weapons cage. "The peace in Nightland is tentative at the best of times, especially with the threat of Salinger hanging over our heads. The more we can do to keep people calm and grateful for the safety of the caves, the better off we'll all be."

Nola rested her hands on the hilts of her knives as the three of them cut through the sparring pairs toward the exit. No one stopped to bow as they had with Raina. The door at the far side sat open. Chill air swept over Nola's face.

"The temperature's dropped." Nola took a deep breath, feeling the cold rush all the way down to her lungs.

"Hopefully the people in the north will have some fires burning," Jeremy said. "Though, if they've gone this long without being found by us or the domes, I doubt it."

"I hope the people on the highway have a way to keep warm," Nola said.

None of them spoke as they made their way down the tunnel. They passed the first window, and a true gust of cold air blasted against Nola's skin.

She waited for the shivering to start, for her fingers to go numb and her muscles to protest working in the freezing temperatures. But her long sleeve shirt was plenty to protect her from the cold.

Julian stopped by a window halfway between the sparring room and the door to the outside. He pulled a paper from his pocket and laid it on the windowsill under the pale moonlight.

"I don't know how much store we can set by this"—Julian unfolded the paper, revealing a worn and marked map—"but I managed to convince Emanuel to part with a piece of his old collection."

A wide circle on the east side of the river marked the location of the domes. The main streets of the city had been printed on the paper as well. To the far west of the map, the mountains took over the page, though no one had noted the entrance to Nightland.

Gray lines formed the highway that bowed around the city and met up with the edge of the river to the north and south. At the bottom of the map, a set of blue shapes showed the lakes the Teachers had spoken of. By the top, a wide band of green marked a forest Nola had never heard of.

"It's not a very detailed map," Jeremy said.

"The domes took most maps a long time ago," Julian said. "Spread propaganda about the dangers of moving outside city limits. Convinced the citizens to turn in all their maps to protect the youth. The next month they made it illegal to move beyond the highway."

"I can't believe people went along with the domes for so long." Nola traced the circle of the domes with her finger.

"The domes needed supplies from the city," Julian said. "The factories had a reason to run and needed workers. There was nowhere else for anyone who wanted food and money to go."

"Except north," Jeremy said.

"If we are separated for some reason," Julian said, "head east toward the highway. You'll be able to find your way back from there. No matter what happens, we don't risk anyone finding the path to Nightland. Agreed?"

"Agreed," Jeremy and Nola said together.

"Then we begin." Julian folded the map and put it back into his pocket.

Nola's mind wandered as they walked. She'd seen maps before, but never one made of paper. Her father had had a digital map of the city. She had watched him studying the layout of the streets before he went on patrol as an Outer Guard.

I never thought of what lay beyond the city. I was as bad as the rest of the Domers.

They passed the last window. A dull glow glittered in the

distance where the domes waited for the world to end.

I was what they made me.

She reached out, twining her fingers through Jeremy's. He squeezed her hand.

We are what we make ourselves now. We make the rules.

The end of the corridor came into view. Three guards blocked the path to the outside. Two twins with shaved heads and Desmond. Even in the dim light, Nola caught shadows of the scars that marked Desmond's dark skin.

"Heading into the world?" Desmond's fangs peeked out from beneath his lip as he spoke in his deep, rumbling voice.

"Only for a little while," Julian said.

Desmond nodded and stepped aside. The twins followed his movement without argument.

"Thanks," Nola muttered as she hurried past the twins.

Julian didn't slow his pace as he reached the end of the tunnel. He stepped off the ledge and out into the open air as though unaware of the drop.

Nola stopped at the edge, looking to the ground beneath before jumping. For the split second while she fell through the air, her heart seized, warning her of the pain that waited when she landed. But her feet touched the ground without shocking the rest of her body. She took two quick steps forward to balance herself and straightened as Jeremy landed behind her.

"If you please." Julian ran up the mountain.

Tightening the straps on her pack, Nola followed, keeping her ears pricked up for the sounds of Jeremy's footsteps keeping pace behind her.

Julian didn't tear through the darkness as Raina did when she led. He kept to a pace that allowed Nola to see the world as she raced by. They ran through the clearing in the basin that surrounded the entrance to Nightland, then up to the ridge that climbed toward the peak of the mountain where Kieran's garden hid. The steep angle to the ridge would have forced humans to use their arms to haul themselves up. But the speed at which they ran made launching herself up step by step easy, almost fun.

Nola reached the top of the ridge and swayed. The ground dropped away on either side of the thin path, leaving nothing but open air and a fall that could hurt even a vampire.

"You okay?" Jeremy asked.

"Fine." Nola kept running, her eyes darting between the path Julian navigated with ease and the view on either side. The dizzying height couldn't mar the beauty of the moonlight on the mountain.

With only the thin sheen of silver, the terrain became a maze of thick shadows, which seemed to swallow chunks of the world, and delicately textured patches of light. Stands of trees that still clung to life despite the torment the weather and toxic rains had let loose. Mounds of rocks where bits of the mountain had crumbled, leaving swatches of sanctuary where shrubs had found a way to survive.

Before they reached the summit, Julian turned north, cutting down the spine of a smaller, neighboring peak. Here, grass and weeds had managed to grow, sheltered from the worst of the sun by their higher neighbor.

Dense bushes clung to the mountainside, their branches bare, whether from the cold or death, Nola didn't know.

They ran down the spine of the mountain, the pounding of their feet the only sound in the night. A wide span of struggling trees covered the slope below.

Nola looked west beyond the mountain she now called home. The range continued below them, turning into rolling foothills in the far distance. No glimmer of light or barren patches gave a hint of human life ever having existed beyond Nightland's sanctuary. To the east, scars of civilization dug deep into the earth. The ruined highway, a gash through the landscape. The burned city, a terrible wound. Nola kept her eyes on the shimmer of the domes until the trees swallowed the view.

CHAPTER TEN

Sense floated in and out of being. They had been running for a long time, that much Nola knew. Down the side of the mountain, through trees denser than any she had seen before. Past a long stretch of fields thick with high grass as though nature had reclaimed the land once cleared by farmers.

Still, her legs didn't tire, and her lungs didn't burn.

Not needing to rest warped the meaning of effort and the ticking of time.

I could run for days.

A sudden longing pulled at her chest. To run faster and farther. To keep racing forward and see just how far she could make it before she dropped.

"Just a moment." Julian slowed in front of her.

Nola skipped a step, teetering forward then righting herself as Jeremy stopped by her side.

"We'll have to move a bit more slowly, I'm afraid," Julian said.

Nola peered around his shoulder. A patchy swamp of frothy water blocked the way forward.

"Too bad this wasn't on the map," Jeremy said.

"Can we cut through?" Nola pressed her sleeve to her nose, blocking out the putrid stench that filled the air.

"I wouldn't recommend it." Julian stepped closer to the edge of the swamp. The ground squelched beneath his feet. "Pity a true freeze hasn't come."

"What do you mean?" Nola asked.

Julian tapped his toe on the surface of the water. The froth swirled in protest. "I forget how little children know," Julian said. "Or rather how old I am." He cut west, skirting along the edge of the water.

"How old are you?" Nola stayed close behind Julian, mimicking his every footfall.

"Old enough to remember snow," Julian said. "And deep freezes. Proper seasons we could predict."

"It used to snow here," Jeremy said. The sound of the ground squishing under his feet stayed right behind Nola's shoulder. "My dad told me about it. How it used to snow in the winter."

"I loved winter," Julian said. "Snow piled up along the bottom of the domes. The whole world washed in pure white. My partner and I would sit right next to the glass to feel the cold against our skin. We don't have that anymore. There's the hot season and the cold season. But the snow doesn't come. The world has given up on a true healing freeze.

"The temperature creeps low enough to kill poor humans left to sleep in the open and frost over the crops we struggle to grow, then wavers so much from day to day it's difficult to know what time of year it truly is. I miss real seasons, the markers that prove time is passing."

"Does it get easier?" Nola asked.

"No." Julian leapt over a fallen tree. "I do forget sometimes what being human felt like. Letting go of that life makes being a vampire less jarring, but I always miss having time mean something."

"Stop." Jeremy grabbed Nola's arm, yanking her behind him.

"What?" She found what he had seen before the word had fully left her lips.

In the starlight, shapes shifted in the shadows to the north.

Nola held her breath, waiting for arrows to fly as the dark figures moved between trees across the swamp.

Julian rested his hand on the hilt of his sword.

Nola's fingers trembled as she reached for the Guard gun at her hip.

The shadows moved again, crackling through the underbrush.

"Come along." Julian waved them onward.

"What?" Jeremy stayed steady, his weapon aimed at the things moving across the swamp.

"Those beasts won't hurt us." Julian clapped his hands. The sound echoed through the darkness.

The shadows froze for a moment, then disappeared into the trees.

"Why did they run?" Nola whispered.

"Not they," Julian said, "at least not people. Deer, I expect."

He leapt a wide patch of sunken grass and continued west.

"How do you know?" Jeremy kept his weapon out as he and Nola followed Julian.

"A person would have the sense to either be quiet or call out," Julian said. "The poor beasts were only searching for a meal and didn't know what to make of us."

Nola tucked her weapon back into its holster. "Animals and people living on the outside, I just..."

"Just?" Julian said.

"Want to tear through the glass of the domes, find every teacher I ever had, and shake them," Nola said. "There are so many things they never bothered to teach us. I was just supposed to learn how to grow plants and get married and have kids. But when my generation had to teach our children, none of us would have known about deer that still eat in the woods."

"That was the point," Julian said. "I was old enough to understand the choice I was making in entering the domes. I believed in the need to protect the ability of humans to bear healthy children, and I knew what sacrifices were expected of me. Those born in the glass never had the chance to decide if safety and a lofty goal for the greater good were worth spending their entire lives trapped in a place the size of a small village. They were never able to choose between a brief, painful, and chaotic life on the outside or a small, regulated life lacking all compassion within the glass."

The domes had never felt small to Nola, had never seemed like a cold and compassionless place. Not until she'd been to Nightland.

"The vast majority of the world's population has died," Julian said, "just as the Incorporation predicted when they built the domes. Most of those who still live in the open have turned to Vamp or Lycan to survive. Despite those horrors, there are some on the outside who would never choose a life behind glass if the opportunity were ever granted them. And there are those who live in the domes who would choose the open air if they knew such an option existed."

"It's wrong for them not to tell us," Nola said.

"I agree," Julian said.

A row of toppled down trees marked the edge of the swamp. Julian stopped, staring at the path ahead for a moment before shaking his head and walking north.

"I can sort of understand it," Jeremy said. "People on the outside get sick and die too easily. Too many babies are born with birth defects they can't survive. Lying to the domes children is wrong, burning cities is wrong, but making sure there will actually be another generation to take our place? I get that."

Nola reached back, taking his hand, trying to think of something comforting to say.

I don't even know if T's baby will be healthy.

"The fate of the last person alive would be a terrible one," Julian said.

"That's not going to happen," Nola said. "We've got a safe place in Nightland. We're going looking for people we didn't think could survive. The human race isn't done yet."

Julian stopped at the north end of the swamp. "Months ago, when Kieran told me of the wonderful girl in the domes he truly believed had the heart to care for those left to die outside the glass, I thought he was a lovesick fool. I'm glad to know he was right. That there are some who have never known hunger who still care for those who have never had a proper meal."

"Kieran said that?" Jeremy said.

"More times than I can count," Julian said. "I'm afraid the rest of us had given up hope of there being anyone worthy of survival inside the glass."

"Then I'm glad Kieran ended up with you," Jeremy said.

Julian turned to face them, one sleek eyebrow raised.

"Whatever Kieran might have done, he was right about Nola," Jeremy said.

Nola squeezed his hand. "And Nightland. I'll never forgive Emanuel for attacking the domes—"

"But it can't compare to what the domes have done," Jeremy said.

Julian smiled. "I never had children. As much as the Incorporation pushed, I refused the procreation orders. At times like this, I don't mind that my DNA was never passed on. I'm simply proud to have been a small part of the story that led us here."

Fallen leaves crackled under their feet as Julian led the way into the forest. The acid rain hadn't torn through their thin membranes. The leaves had fallen to the ground whole, ready to decompose and give nutrients back to the trees.

Julian headed east, toward the place the animals had been hiding in the shadows, and stopped next to a tree where swatches of bark had been torn away. Hoof prints dented the water-logged ground.

"It really was deer." Jeremy shook his head. "How have they survived?"

"The trees help clean the smog out of the air that hurts people so badly in the city," Nola said. "If there's a stream or some other kind of water that hasn't been contaminated like this swamp and the river, they'd have something to drink. The trees are managing to grow, so they have food."

"By keeping people in the city as labor, the Incorporation condemned them to live with the toxins the domes were built to avoid," Julian said.

"They've been killing people from the beginning." Deep lines creased Jeremy's brow.

"I suppose," Julian said, "but even if people had been told to flee the city and create a homestead far away from industrialization, some would have refused to leave. And those brave enough to head into the wilds might not have survived very long anyway. They might have found cleaner water and soil pure enough to farm—"

"But the weather still would have killed their crops," Nola said. "And the sun would have hurt them, and their kids would still have gotten sick."

A pang cut through the numbness in Nola's chest she hadn't even realized existed. She took a deep breath, letting the stink of the swamp burn her lungs.

"It's okay." Jeremy laced his fingers through hers.

The warmth of his palm traveled up her arm, surrounding the terrible ache. The pain didn't ebb away, but the heat of connection transformed the hurt from a hollow hopelessness to a burning desire to fight.

"If the animals have found a way to survive, then people can, too," Nola said. "This isn't the end of the human race. We're just starting over again as something different. We're evolving to survive."

"Adversity has always required adaptation," Julian said. "The penalty we pay for having done so much damage to the earth is having to adapt so quickly, and not being able to change everyone so they can survive with us. Life will never be what it was before, but perhaps it will endure."

They walked in silence for a long while. The ground firmed beneath their feet as they climbed uphill. They didn't run as they had before. Julian kept them to a steady pace a human would have trouble matching but seemed like nothing more than a brisk walk to Nola.

She listened to the crackling of the brush and fallen leaves under their feet. Even in the darkness, she could see the details of the trees and the individual twigs that had fallen to the ground.

The hill crested in front of them, the rolling line of its edge standing out in the darkness.

Jeremy let go of Nola's hand and reached for his weapon. "Julian, I think you should put that sun suit on."

"The sky isn't even gray yet," Nola said.

Julian stopped in front of them, standing still for a moment, then taking off his pack. "I think you're quite right."

"What's going—"

The breeze shifted, blowing up from beyond the rise. Nola gagged as the horrible stench of decay flooded her mouth.

"We don't want to walk into any surprises with Julian vulnerable to the sun." Jeremy wrinkled his nose, his mouth twisting into a frown.

"What is that?" Nola pressed her sleeve over her face.

"What *was* that is probably the more apt question." Julian pulled the sun suit from his pack, quickly stepping into the over-sized tan fabric and zipping himself in.

"Nola," Jeremy said, "I want you to stay behind me, and trust me."

"I do trust you," Nola said.

Julian put on the wide-brimmed hat, pulling down the heavy veil to cover his face.

"If I tell you not to look," Jeremy said, "I need you not to look."

"Why shouldn't I look?" Nola said.

"Because, sweet Nola," Julian said, "the horrors of the world hurt those with loving hearts worst of all."

A horrible dread weighed heavy in Nola's stomach.

Julian slung his pack onto his back. "After me, I think."

He started toward the rise of the hill, Jeremy close behind.

Nola moved to walk next to Jeremy, but he sidestepped, keeping her behind him.

I've seen terrible things. What could the world have left to torment me with?

She pinched her nose closed as they reached the top of the hill, swallowing the bile that rose in her throat.

"Damn." Julian stopped on the crest of the hill.

Jeremy reached an arm back, trying to keep Nola behind him.

She dodged to the side, taking her place between Jeremy and Julian.

A wide valley opened up below them. Whatever trees had grown in the valley had burned, leaving nothing but charred stumps and ash in their wake. At the bottom of the basin, human figures lay unmoving on the ground.

CHAPTER ELEVEN

"What happened?" Nola took a step forward.

Jeremy grabbed her arm, holding her in place.

Dozens of people lay scattered across the bottom of the small valley, their bodies twisted and broken.

"How did this many people get out here?" Jeremy said.

"I've no idea." Julian started down into the valley, the movement of his hat giving the only sign of his gaze constantly sweeping the burned out trees for danger.

"The Northerners," Nola said. "Julian, be careful. They already shot you once."

"I hope they will have such poor aim should we meet again," Julian said.

A growl rumbled in Jeremy's throat.

"What?" Nola searched his face for signs of pain.

"I should have convinced Emanuel to keep you in Nightland," Jeremy said.

"Why?" Nola freed her weapon from its holster, her ears straining to hear the *buzz* of flying arrows.

"Because I don't want you to see what's down there," Jeremy said. "I don't want you to have to remember this. But I can't leave you alone up here."

"I can take it," Nola said.

"You're strong enough to take on the whole world." Jeremy brushed a curl away from her forehead. "That doesn't stop me from wanting to protect you."

Nola caught his hand, pressing his palm to her cheek. "Thank you."

Jeremy held her gaze for a long moment before turning back to the valley below.

Nola pressed her sleeve to her nose as she followed Jeremy and Julian down the hill. The crackling beneath her feet changed. The leaves had all been burned away by the fire that had torn through the valley but spared the surrounding four hills. Unburnt trees peered up over each of the ridges, as though the flames had known not to move beyond the bounds of the basin.

The bodies weren't burned.

"This shouldn't be possible?" Nola's eyes watered as the stench grew too strong for her to ignore.

Julian reached the base of the valley where the bodies lay. Soot stained the bottom of his sun suit, giving him the look of a strangely tattered warrior as he drew his sword.

They can't be a threat. They're too far gone.

Nola bit her lips together, swallowing her scream as she approached the first of the bodies.

Whoever it was had been dead for days. Animals had already feasted on the remains. There were no gaping wounds from a battle or sores from illness left behind. They had been dumped like compost and left to rot. The taste of blood and bile filled Nola's mouth.

"Are they Northerners?" Jeremy kept his hand to his face as he leaned over one of the corpses.

"No idea," Julian said.

Nola began to ask a question and gagged on the putrid stink

that flooded her mouth. "How did we not smell this from a mile away?"

"The swamp covered the scent until we got close," Jeremy said.

"They weren't killed here." Nola leaned over a tiny corpse. *A child left to decay.*

"Why do you say that?" Julian said.

"People run where they're attacked," Nola said. "It happened in the domes, in the tunnels of Nightland, when the city burned. People ran. These bodies aren't spread out enough to have been running from something, and they aren't packed close enough to have been corralled to be killed."

"She's right," Jeremy said.

"But why go through the trouble of moving so many bodies?" Nola said.

"This valley is useless until the plants grow back," Jeremy said. "You can be seen from all sides, and there's no water source. The smell from the swamp covered the stink—"

"But we still found the bodies," Julian said.

"Because they wanted us to, or because they didn't think we could?" Jeremy's gaze swept the hilltops around them.

"We shouldn't stay here." Nola backed away from the body of a person who had been left naked for the animals to consume. "I don't want to be here anymore."

"We should keep heading north," Julian said.

"If this is what the Northerners do, I don't know how much we'll be able to learn from them before it come down to a fight." Jeremy took Nola's arm, guiding her around the corpses.

A glint of metal caught Nola's eye. Sticking out of the torso of one of the bodies, a thin silver dart that had pierced the doomed person's flesh.

"It wasn't the Northerners," Nola said. "The domes did this."

Jeremy and Julian turned toward her.

She pointed to the dart.

"Damn," Julian said. "I think it best if we run." With barely a nod to either of them, Julian took off, sprinting north.

"Stay in front of me." Jeremy drew his Guard gun, ready to fire little silver darts into anyone who might hurt them.

Nola pulled her weapon from its holster as she tore after Julian.

Footsteps thundered behind her. She wanted to turn and make sure it really was Jeremy following her, but Julian dodged through the burnt out trees with such speed, she couldn't spare a glance behind without risking injury.

"The domes didn't leave them like that," Jeremy said.

Nola's shoulders eased at the sound of his voice.

"It's like the bones, it just doesn't fit," Jeremy said.

"The Outer Guard being this far from the city doesn't make sense at all," Nola said.

"It does if they're searching for Nightland." Julian crested the hill. He paused for a split second before veering slightly left as he continued to run.

"The water bottles," Nola said, "the ones they gave people after they burned the city. We found trackers in them."

"It could have been the bottles," Jeremy said. "Or the Outer Guard could have followed those people here."

"Or those could be the Northerners we've been looking for." Julian led them down a rocky curve in the hillside where water would have run after a heavy rain.

"Sending guards out this far is dangerous," Jeremy said. "They'd have to stay on foot, going through the woods."

"The Outer Guard have always relied on their ability to quickly retreat to safety," Julian said. "Attack a nest of vampires, bundle into their trucks, and be whisked away to the protection of the domes."

A rock shot out from beneath Nola's foot. Jeremy caught her under the arm before she could try and right herself.

"That was before Graylock." Jeremy kept right behind Nola's

shoulder. "They don't need trucks for speed—"

"But they've never been out of the city," Julian said. "The forest and mountains are an entirely different world. It took Nightland a long time to learn that lesson."

"That's why my dad never ran patrols past the highway," Jeremy said. "Even if he took a hundred Outer Guard into the wild, there's too much ground to cover, too many unknowns."

"Does Salinger care?" Nola asked. "Would a monster like him really care that he's putting his guards in danger?"

"No," Jeremy said. "They'd be collateral damage."

They entered a stand of trees with withered and twisted branches. A few thick leaves still clung to life even as the yellow and orange brought on by the cold touched their tips. Fluttering on their perches in the darkness, the waxy coating of the leaves had dulled in patches, marred by the acid rain.

People aren't the only things to adapt.

"Jeremy," Julian said, "I don't mean to be cruel, but I do need you to remember the guards Salinger is sending into the woods, no matter how doomed and helpless they may seem, are still, in fact, our enemies."

"The guards destroyed the city," Jeremy said. "I'm not dumb enough to think any of them are innocent. The only guard I want to find is my sister."

"We're not going to stop looking," Nola said. "We'll find Gentry."

A skeleton lay on the forest floor in front of them. Nola held her breath, waiting to see what horrible thing the forest hid. But the bones belonged to an animal, perhaps a long dead deer. The white of the skeleton shone unnaturally in the first light of the rising sun.

Nola glanced east.

Through the branches of the trees, the sky had barely begun to turn a pale gray.

"We should find a place for you to hide before the sun gets too high," Nola said.

"I have the sun suit." Julian slowed to a walk.

The forest of twisted trees ended, opening up to a wide and barren field. The expanse reached in front of them, leaving a gap as wide as Bright Dome, and stretched in either direction before twisting out of sight.

"I don't like this." Jeremy stood next to Nola, right behind the last of the trees.

There had been trees in the barren strip. Remains of the stumps still stuck out of the ground at odd angles, as though someone had given up on trying to wrench them from the earth. Patches of fire marked the dirt as well, as though an attempt had been made to burn the stumps away.

"It's like they were trying to clear the land for farming." Nola peeked out from behind the tree. "If the soil is good enough for trees to grow, it might be fertile enough for crops. I think someone was trying to make a field." She leaned farther out to the side.

"We should backtrack," Jeremy said. "Head a bit farther into the woods and hunker down for the day."

"I am well protected by the sun suit," Julian said.

"A sword could slice through your sun suit," Jeremy said.

"I've seen pictures of old plows," Nola said. "You could make one from rocks and wood. It might take time to figure it out, but it could be done."

"If there are Northerners or guards watching this strip, I don't want to get into a fight with them when tearing through the suit could get you killed," Jeremy said. "We can wait and try crossing in the dark."

"It could work." Nola pictured it in her mind, a strip of farmland running between the trees. Protected from wind and erosion by the surrounding forest.

We'd have to build shelters from the rain. Kieran could help me.

"How far from the city are we?" Nola asked.

"I'd say about twenty-five miles," Julian said.

"The guards still made it to those bodies," Jeremy said. "We can't take any chances."

"Twenty-five miles from the city should mean the run off from the factories never made it this far. Or if it did, it won't be as bad." Nola stepped out from behind the tree. "There could be a real farm here."

A *whoosh* cut through her thoughts.

"Nola!"

She spun at Jeremy's scream. His eyes were wide with horror as he reached toward her.

Pain shot through her side, buckling her knees.

Jeremy grabbed her before she hit the ground. He dodged to the side as an arrow hit the tree trunk next to his head. He had her under the arms, dragging her sideways, on top of her pack. The movement sent a fresh wave of burning pain shooting through her. Hands pulled her pack away, and she lay flat on the ground.

A scream tore from Nola's throat, but using the air in her lungs only made the pain worse.

"I think we've found the Northerners." Julian had his back pressed against a tree only a few feet from Nola.

"Nola," Jeremy said. "Nola, I need you to look at me."

Nola blinked, trying to think beyond the searing in her side to find Jeremy's brown eyes.

"I have to pull the arrow out." Black blurred the edges of Jeremy's face. "It's going to hurt, but I promise you're going to be okay."

"Jeremy." Nola reached for his hand. Blood coated her fingers. She looked down. An arrow had lodged in her side. Red seeped from the wound, staining her shirt.

"Just hold still," Jeremy said.

But she needed to touch the arrow. To be sure it really was sticking out of her body. She'd been stabbed before, through the chest. The pain felt the same, but her mind hadn't been stolen from her this time.

Her finger recognized the grooves of the hand-carved arrow shaft. The stickiness of her blood made sense.

I am bleeding. I am hurt.

The horrible pain of her wound didn't panic her. She closed her fist around the arrow shaft and pulled.

"Nola, don't." Jeremy reached for her hand, but she kept pulling, dragging the arrowhead back out of her flesh.

Spots of pain danced through her vision as she wrenched the arrow from her body and tossed it aside.

"Well done," Julian said. "But I do recommend you hold still for a bit."

"Don't move." Jeremy pressed his hands over the hole in Nola's side.

"I'll heal." Nola's voice came out rasping, but strong. The pain in her side began to recede, turning from a horrible red to a dull, throbbing gray. "It's already happening, isn't it?"

Jeremy leaned closer to Nola's stomach.

An arrow thudded into the tree behind him.

"Watch out." Nola coughed, and the pain tore itself back open. "Shit."

"Hold still." Jeremy leaned close to her, sheltering behind the same tree that protected her. "Your skin is already knitting back together, but internal organs are a bit more complicated."

"We can't wait, we have to move." Nola tried to sit up, but Jeremy pressed on her shoulders, keeping her pinned to the dirt.

"Waiting a few minutes now will save us a lot of time in the long run," Jeremy said. "They're firing from a distance. We can hide here."

"Why the hell did they shoot me?" Nola said.

"Because this is where the arrows fly," Julian said. "We came looking for survivors of the apocalypse. I never expected to find a polite society."

CHAPTER TWELVE

An arrow shook the tree behind Nola's head as it landed with a heavy *thud*.

"They didn't clear the strip for farming did they?" Nola said.

"It might have started that way," Jeremy said, "but it gives them a clean line of sight for attacks, too."

"No wonder people don't return from the north," Julian said. "I'm not certain even I could make it across the strip alive."

"We can't just turn back," Nola said. The *thud* of another arrow punctuated her words. "Look at what they've done. They have enough people to clear that much land, which means they're managing to feed a real population. We have to talk to them."

"They shot you," Jeremy said.

"Only a little." Nola lifted his hand from her wound. A dull ache throbbed through her side, like a bruise from a bad blow.

"There is no such thing as being only a little shot," Jeremy said.

"We came here for answers," Nola said. "This isn't like the city. The people we're searching for are actually here. We have to talk to them."

Jeremy held Nola's gaze for a long moment.

"I'll go across," Jeremy said.

"Like hell you will." Nola wriggled out from under his grasp to lean against the tree.

"I don't think any of us trying to get across is a good idea," Julian said.

"But—"

"Stop thinking like a guard," Nola cut across. "These aren't wolves on the streets of the city trying to kill you. They aren't mobs attacking the domes. We're invading their home. So let's try and talk to them before anyone else bleeds."

"Okay," Jeremy said, "but you stay behind the trees."

"I think I just learned the value of cover." Nola wiped the blood from her hands onto the cleaner side of her shirt. The red didn't leave her skin. "I don't think I'll forget anytime soon."

"Always good to learn from one's mistakes," Julian said.

Nola shifted to stand, keeping herself behind the tree as she turned to face the strip. Jeremy moved with her, leaving only a few inches between them. The heat from his body radiated toward her. She longed to sink into his warmth and disappear to a place where pain couldn't follow.

An arrow *thudded* into the tree in front of them.

"We didn't come here to hurt you," Nola shouted. She stood frozen, straining to hear any sound beyond her heart thundering in her ears. "I know you don't have any reason to believe that, but it's true. We came here to talk to you. The Teachers told us about you, said you had lived up here for a long time."

She waited again, digging her nails into the bark of the tree.

I will not panic.

She had tried to speak to people who wanted to hurt her once before. That night had ended in blood and fire.

She shifted her weight, letting her back touch Jeremy.

"We found the bodies," Nola called, her voice stronger than before. "Did you move them to the burnt out valley? We know the Outer Guard killed them, but we don't think they moved them. Were they your people, or people from the city?"

"Keep talking," Julian said.

"What the domes did to the city is unforgivable," Nola said. "We have a place where we live away from the city. The domes have tried to come after us. Have they come after you yet? Did they kill your people with little silver darts? If they haven't, if the corpses were just people who fled in the wrong direction, that doesn't mean the domes won't come after you. It only means they haven't found you yet."

"You're one of them," a man's voice shouted across the strip. "I saw the arrow hit. You shouldn't be talking."

Nola closed her eyes, trying to picture the man hiding behind a tree just like her.

Afraid. Desperate.

"I'm not a guard, but I was injected with the same drug that makes them strong. The domes, they'd"—Nola let out a shaking breath—"they'd probably kill me if they knew I'd taken Graylock."

"One of you has a glass suit," the man shouted.

Nola glanced to Julian, whose hat tipped up and down as he nodded.

"He's a vampire," Nola said. "The sun's coming up. He has to wear it to stay alive."

"Prove it," the man shouted.

"Prove that he'll die in the sun?" Nola said. "No. I'm not going to let him leak blood out of his eyes and die a horrible death just to prove a point."

A voice lighter than the man's laughed.

"All we want is to talk to you," Nola said. "We have an enemy that wants to see both of our people dead. There are murderers living on our doorstep. Don't you think having an ally would be a good idea?"

Silence stretched over the gap.

"We need to move," Jeremy whispered. "They haven't had Vamp or Graylock. We can outrun them."

"The entrance to Nightland," the man called. "How do you get in?"

"The tunnels under the city have been rigged to kill," Julian shouted. "There is no entry to Nightland now."

"Not the tunnels," the man called, "the new home of the nightwalkers. How do you get in?"

The subtle sound of Julian's sword clearing its sheath stilled Nola's racing heart.

"You have to jump up," Nola said. "Jumping up is the only way in."

A tree crackled across the strip. A man dressed entirely in brown leapt from the branches, a bow in his hands with an arrow nocked and pointed toward Nola.

"I never thought any of the nightwalkers would come this way." The man squinted in the early morning light, his gaze fixed on the tree sheltering Nola.

"I didn't think we'd be coming here either," Nola said.

"End of the world drives people to all sorts of things," the man said. "I'll let the three of you cross. But there are people in the trees you'll never find. If you show one hint of wanting to hurt us, you will die. Glass drugs in you or not."

"Okay." Nola lifted her pack and moved to step out from behind the tree.

"Me first." Jeremy slipped his Guard gun back into its holster and stepped around Nola. He stood between two trees, facing the man. He raised both hands, displaying his empty palms.

Panic seized Nola's heart. An arrow would fly across the gap and sink into Jeremy's chest.

I won't lose him.

"I was wrong. We shouldn't do this," Nola whispered.

"Just stay behind me." Jeremy stepped out onto the barren dirt.

"I feel it, too, you know?" Nola stepped up next to Jeremy, raising her hands as he had. "The horrible fear when you could be hurt. I hate it."

"You're stronger than I am." Jeremy walked forward. "I've always known that."

Julian stepped up to Nola's other side, his sword sheathed, his gloved hands raised.

"Should things go terribly," Julian said, "find out how they know the entrance to Nightland's new home. More important than how they've managed to survive is how they found us."

"Agreed," Jeremy said.

They were halfway across the strip.

Time stretched as they crossed the barrens. Nola didn't know if it was because she had grown accustomed to moving so quickly, or if dread of the unknown had somehow slowed the seconds.

Nola studied the Northern man. An uneven beard covered his chin, and scars marked the parts of his face not hidden by hair. Not the dots of acid rain burns that marred Desmond's face, or the scratch marks Nola had seen on some of the vampires who attacked humans. These scars were different, varied, as though life had unleashed a hundred unique torments on this man and each of them had left its own individual mark.

His clothes weren't of the make Nola had seen in the city. Baggy and plain, as though someone had made the fabric and fashioned the clothes by hand, their dull brown blended perfectly with the trees, though Nola didn't know if it had been done intentionally or had happened slowly as dirt ground into the fabric.

The man's hands stayed steady, his arrow now pointed at Jeremy's chest, as they reached the far side of the strip

"Thank you for letting us cross," Jeremy said.

"Doesn't mean we won't kill you if you threaten us," the man said.

"I know," Jeremy said, "just like you know we'll defend ourselves."

The man smiled. A gap had taken the place of a tooth in the front of his mouth. "Good to have an understanding."

They all stood silently for a long moment.

"The one who laughed," Nola said, "are they coming out, too?"

"I don't think so," the man said. "It's probably best if we keep our people where they're happiest. *Hidden.*"

"Hard to hide when you've made a wide tract around your land," Jeremy said. "We wouldn't have thought we'd reached you if it weren't for that."

"Blight hit the trees." The man shrugged. "Had to kill the bad ones before the whole forest died."

"That was smart," Nola said.

"I know," the man said.

"What's your name?" Nola asked.

"Doesn't matter." The man slid his arrow back into his quiver and his bow over his shoulder as he walked into the trees, giving a wave for them to follow. "I'm not the one you want to talk to."

Jeremy's fingers twitched as though longing to reach for his weapon. Nola took his hand, tugging him to walk with her. He bit his lips together but didn't argue as they followed the man deeper into the trees.

"Not to be old fashioned," Julian said, keeping pace right behind Nola and Jeremy, "but whether or not you think we're here to speak to you, I still feel incredibly rude not knowing your name."

The man laughed. The sound was more like a cough.

Who did we hear laugh before?

Nola's gaze swept the trees around them, searching for people who could be staring at her, waiting to send another arrow into her flesh. She shivered at the remembered pain.

"You okay?" Jeremy glanced sideways at Nola.

"Fine," Nola said, though her skin prickled with the horrid sensation of being watched.

"My name is Julian, if that helps. I'd take off my gloves to shake properly, but I'm sure you understand why that's not possible."

"I've seen nightwalkers before," the man said. "Some made it this far north. Had to kill them before they bled us."

"I don't blame you," Julian said. "Unfortunately, many of my kind are violent. Letting them into your home might have meant the death of your people."

"But the home in the mountains is different," the man said. "At least that's what everyone is meant to believe."

"Nightland is different," Nola said. "I've been living there. I have human friends who are living there, and no one's ever—"

"Human?" The man turned to them. "Your friends are human, but you aren't?"

"I've been changed." Nola held tight to Jeremy's hand. "I was hurt. I had to be given Graylock to survive."

"And that means you're not human?" The man leaned forward, squinting at Nola's face.

"If vampires aren't human—" Nola began.

"Why shouldn't the nightwalkers be human?" the man said. "They were born, and I know they can die."

"But their DNA—" Jeremy said.

"You were bred in the glass, weren't you?" the man said.

Jeremy glanced to Nola. "I was. I left when I figured out they were murderers."

The man combed his fingers through his ragged beard. "I don't know if that makes you smart or plain stupid. Either way, you're just plain human. You were born human. Whatever they shoved in your veins came after."

"How did you know I've had Graylock?" Jeremy's fingers loosened around Nola's.

The man turned and strode away through the woods. "They let you walk in front, and the girl seems fond of you. She wouldn't have let you do that if you couldn't get shot in the gut with an arrow and walk away same as her."

"Nola," Nola said. "My name is Nola."

The man stopped, grinding his toe into the dirt. "You're the one then?"

"What one?" Nola's mouth went dry. Her fingers twitched, longing for the weight of her knife in her hand.

"The one whose name broke through the noise in the city," the man said. "The one the nightwalkers believed in and the pack folk howled for."

"Yes," Nola said. "I don't know why. There's nothing special about me."

"You're a human and you're alive," the man said. "Isn't that special enough?"

"You're quite right," Julian said. "Being alive is, in itself, a wonderful thing."

"Coming out of your mountain to find us," the man said, "that might be dumber than leaving the glass."

"Not if we can find allies," Nola said. "Then it's worth the risk."

The man gave another coughing laugh. "The whispers are right then. There is one pure idealist left in the world." He looked over his shoulder and gave Nola a wink. "If you're trying to call folks who have strayed from the norm unhuman, you're the least human of us all."

Heat rushed to Nola's cheeks. "I just want people to survive. To have a shot at living in peace."

"She'll like you," the man said.

"Who?" Nola asked.

"Rebecca." He waved for them to keep following.

They went down a hill whose base was hidden in the trees. The same orange and yellow-edged waxy leaves hung from these branches, but the trees grew closer together, as though all crowding in toward the most fertile land. Most of the trees seemed entirely wild, but every now and then the bark would carry a mark of human activity. A hefty stick nailed to the side of a tree to help someone climb up into the branches. A nobble where rope had been tightly tied around a branch while the tree grew.

"How long have you been living here?" Nola asked.

The man cut west, following the edge of a dried stream. The rocks at the bottom of the bed carried no moss or grass, almost as though they had been scrubbed clean.

"I've been here long enough not to remember what the river smells like," the man said. "Others have been here long enough they weren't in the city after the stores shut down. Some have been here for as long as there have been rumors of nightwalkers digging deep to build a home."

"How many years ago was that?" Nola asked.

"I'm not good with years," the man said. "The weather doesn't care about years, why should I?"

The streambed branched off in two directions, one cutting up through the trees and heading farther west, the other cutting north. The man followed the northern fork.

The ground by the stream had been worn down, the fallen sticks driven further into decay by the grinding of many footsteps. The dirt around the bases of the trees had been recently turned and carved into sections.

"Are you going to farm around the trees?" Nola stopped to examine the loose earth. The cold of the night still clung to the shadows. Any new plants would be killed by the frost.

They're planning. Preparing to survive another year.

Nola reached down toward the dirt with her free hand.

"Don't touch it," the man said. "The farmers don't like it if you touch their patches."

"I don't blame them." Nola tucked her hand behind her back.

"Come on."

"It makes sense," Nola said as they followed the man farther up the streambed, then turned west and through a patch of newer, shorter trees.

"What makes sense?" Jeremy ducked under a low branch, snaking sideways to keep his pack from getting caught.

"The trees have developed a way to live through the acid rain," Nola said. "The coating on their leaves, they evolved to survive. If you plant around the base of the trees, the leaves will lend their protection to your crops. It's really brilliant."

"I'm glad you approve," a woman's voice carried through the branches right next to Nola.

CHAPTER THIRTEEN

Nola froze, waiting for the voice to speak again so she could find where the woman hid. There was no movement in the trees. No *crackle* of footsteps coming closer.

"I was training in plant preservation in the domes," Nola said. "I would be very interested to see what other ways you've found to grow crops out here."

The man turned to face Nola, his expression bordering on boredom.

"That's part of why we came here," Nola said. "To learn from you."

"Learn from us?" the woman's voice came from Nola's left.

Nola turned toward the sound but couldn't see a person in the trees.

"You've got medicine to keep you strong, and a mountain to protect you," the woman said.

"And you've managed to survive without any of that," Nola said. "Without ReVamp and a home it took years to build, everyone in Nightland would be dead."

"True." The voice had moved to Nola's right.

"There are people living on the old highway right outside the city," Nola said. "They're going to die, and we can't help them."

"But we should?" the voice moved farther to the right.

The man laughed.

"Not alone," Nola said. "The way we're living, the highway people couldn't replicate it. But they might be able to survive the way you have. If you teach us, maybe we could help them survive together."

"What makes you think I care if the street scum live or die?" the woman said.

Nola's heart stuttered. "Because I have to believe there are decent people in the world. Because even though you've made a home out here, your people must have come from the city. You know what it's like to be cold and sick and hungry. You know what it's like to be afraid."

"You don't," the woman spoke from behind Nola. "The glass blocked the whole world from you."

"But I've learned. I don't want to abandon the people whose city has been destroyed by the domes. I don't want to hide and wait for them all to rot." Nola looked to the man. "If you really believe that all of us are just plain human, then you've got to think it's wrong to hide and do nothing."

"What if the kindest act is to kill them all?" the man said. "Put the street scum out of their misery, save them the pain of a slow death."

"No," Nola said, "the world isn't that far gone. Not yet."

"I like you." A woman stepped out of the trees directly in front of Nola.

Nola blinked, trying to find the trick of the light that had concealed the woman. But the shadows of the rising sun didn't reveal any place the woman might have hidden.

"You're wrong about the people on the pavement," the woman said. "They're too far gone to be saved. Still, I like your heart."

The woman crossed her arms and stared at their group, her

gaze moving from one to the next as though appraising each of them in turn.

She wasn't old, probably not much more than thirty, but there was a weight to her presence that made the examination unsettling. Nola studied her closely-cropped brown hair that matched the color of her sack-like clothing. Her shoes were made of sewn leather, as were the fingerless gloves she wore. The woman had no weapon Nola could see, yet she stood in front of them, not seeming to mind the Guard guns, knives, and sword Nola, Jeremy, and Julian carried.

"I don't like company," the woman said. "Makes the whole place too damn noisy."

"I'm sorry," the man said.

"It's fine," the woman said. "They're as worth it as the last batch. Get back to the gap."

The man gave a nod and slipped between the trees. Before Nola could think whether to say goodbye or thank you, he'd disappeared without even the sound of footsteps trailing behind him.

I didn't notice how silently he walked when we were following him.

"I'm afraid you might be disappointed," the woman said, "coming all this way just to find us."

"Finding healthy people at all is nothing short of miraculous," Julian said.

The woman snorted. "You've been hiding too long. Come on out."

With a faint rustling of leaves, more figures emerged from the trees. Two men dropped into view from high branches. A tiny woman slipped out from under low-hanging leaves. A set of dark-haired twins stepped out to flank their group.

"Best get moving. Daylight is wasting." The woman looked to Julian. "No offense."

"None taken." Julian bowed.

The woman slipped between the trees, heading farther north.

Nola followed, watching the way the woman twisted and bent to avoid brushing against the leaves, always choosing a path that allowed her to continue forward without making a sound.

"Rebecca?" Nola said.

"Yep," Rebecca answered.

"Thank you for agreeing to see us," Nola said.

"Either that or kill you," Rebecca said. "I don't need more death this week."

"The people in the valley," Jeremy said, "the ones the guards—"

"Guards killed them last week," Rebecca said. "They don't count for this tally."

Jeremy reached forward, taking Nola's hand, his pinky draping across her palm.

"Did the guards find you here?" Jeremy said.

"Turned their trail about four miles east." Rebecca skirted around a wide stand of tightly planted trees. "Moved the bodies to the valley to rot."

Nola's stomach churned. "Why did you move them?"

"They died too close to a healthy stream," Rebecca said. "We can't let that kind of decay touch the water, so we moved them to the valley where they can't do any harm. Their bodies will be helping the brush regrow soon enough."

"What burned the valley?" Nola asked.

"Peter," Rebecca laughed.

Nola waited for Rebecca to continue, but instead she stopped next to the densely packed trees.

"Get the other wanderers," Rebecca said to no one in particular before turning to Jeremy. "Don't forget, I've got the right to have you killed if you try to hurt my people." Rebecca ducked between branches and out of sight.

The twins stood next to the place where Rebecca had disappeared.

"Go in," the left twin said.

"Mind your head," the right twin said.

"Thank you." Julian stepped in front of Nola, bowing low to get the brim of his hat beneath the branches.

"What's in there?" Nola asked.

"Rebecca," the left twin said.

"Right." Nola nodded. "Obviously."

Holding onto the straps of her pack, Nola bent over and followed Julian. The tan of his suit had already disappeared into the foliage. The branches tugged at her shirt, finding the place where the arrow had torn the fabric.

I'm following the people who tried to kill me. Going into a dark place. A closed place.

"Jeremy," Nola said.

"I'm right behind you," Jeremy said.

The knot in Nola's chest eased.

"I must say, I'm impressed." Julian's voice came through the leaves in front of Nola.

"Juli..." His name faded from her lips as she stepped into the center of the trees.

A hint of morning light filtered down through the leaves, helping the candles that hung from the branches to light the clearing. Fifty feet in diameter, the space held tables and chairs, as though the Northerners had been expecting to meet for a morning meal. At the far end of the clearing, Rebecca sat at a square table with candles perched on the front corners.

In the golden-green light, Rebecca lost the look of one who only knew the color brown. The glow softened her, giving a sparkle to her keen eyes.

"Welcome to the Woodlands," Rebecca said. "We're not much on visitors, so consider yourselves lucky to have made it this far."

"Thank you." Nola bowed. "How did you build this?"

"We didn't." Rebecca waved a hand toward the canopy of changing leaves. "The forest built this. We only found it and were smart enough not to destroy it."

"It's beautiful," Nola said.

Rebecca scanned the room. "I suppose. We have better places, but those aren't for people like you."

"Hmm." Julian pressed a palm to one of the trees.

"Just because we know your secrets doesn't mean you get to know ours," Rebecca said.

"And how do you know ours?" Jeremy asked.

"You came here to find out how we survive," Rebecca said. "I can believe that. We're a myth, your interest is understandable, but there's more to it than that."

"Really?" Julian said.

"Of course." Rebecca leaned forward, planting her elbows on the table. "Like you said, the same people are trying to slaughter all of us."

"Fair enough." Julian took a chair from one of the tables and set it across from Rebecca. "The real question is what do you intend to do about it?"

"Us?" Rebecca said. "We do what we have to to keep our area clear. We're not like you. My people don't heal after taking an arrow to the side."

"Most of the Domers don't heal either," Jeremy said.

"So we should attack them?" Rebecca said. "Just rush the glass and hope for the best?"

"Of course not," Jeremy said. "The Outer Guard are well trained and better armed than your people could ever hope to be."

"Then you should attack." Rebecca pointed to Jeremy.

"Not possible," Jeremy said. "We can't get across the river, and even if we could find a way to get every fighter in Nightland over the water, it would still be a slaughter. All they would have to do is hold out until sunrise."

"Then we talk to them," Rebecca said, "form a treaty and live in peace."

"I wish I believed that were possible," Julian said. "The territories of our three peoples don't encroach upon each other. There are no resources we are competing for. In a perfect world, we should all be able to live in peace."

"In a perfect world, children wouldn't be born behind glass," Rebecca said, "and I would be able to give you fairy dust to sprinkle on the street scum so they could all survive."

"There has to be something we can do," Nola said. "I refuse to hide and wait for the domes to come for me."

"My thoughts exactly," Rebecca said. "I'd rather see the glass melt than my trees burn. I'm sure you'd rather not see the mountain brought down on the nightwalkers' heads."

Julian nodded.

"Glad to know we see eye to eye." Rebecca pounded a fist on the table and stood. "I wish your leader had come to see us himself, but I suppose Emanuel doesn't often come out of hiding."

"How do you know his name?" Nola planted her hands on her hips to keep her fingers from trembling.

"I know lots of things," Rebecca said. "Just because the night-walkers have ignored everything beyond the tips of their fangs doesn't mean the rest of us have been keeping our heads in the dirt. If we're going to be working together, I'd advise you not to underestimate my people."

"Will we be working together?" Nola took a deep breath, trying to stop the feeling of tumbling through the world too quickly for reason.

"Don't know if I'll have to kill you before the end of the day, but it is nice to know we have similar goals. If you had wanted to take my forest"—Rebecca shrugged—"we could have ended this at the blight field, and I wouldn't have had to waste time on you."

"I'm glad our journey wasn't in vain," Julian said.

"I never said that," Rebecca said.

Too fast. It's all much too fast.

"If you don't have an immediate plan to attack the domes, we'd like to see how you've been surviving," Jeremy said.

"Sure," Rebecca said. "I don't think any of it will help you in the mountain, and it certainly won't help the people dying on the highway."

"Why not?" Nola asked.

"Because what we've got can't be built with steel and glass, or by blasting through stone." Rebecca walked to the side of the space. "You can't remake it. You can't demand it."

"I don't understand," Jeremy said.

"You wouldn't. The glass shattered that part of your soul before you learned to talk." Rebecca slipped between two trees. "Keep up if you don't want the twins to get you."

Nola ran a few steps to slide between the trees before Rebecca could completely disappear.

"Nola, wait," Jeremy said.

Nola reached back, taking Jeremy's hand, but not letting her gaze slip from the heels of Rebecca's leather shoes.

"If they wanted to kill us, they would have tried it already," Nola said.

"Not necessarily true," Rebecca said, "but I'm sure your man was about to warn you of the same thing."

"I was," Jeremy said.

"Ha." Rebecca snaked sideways, twisting around a low bush with nobbles on the branches where berries would grow in spring.

"I've been around plenty of people who wanted me dead," Nola said. "None of them ever turned their back to me when I was armed."

"That makes me foolish, not peaceful." Rebecca stopped at the edge of the trees.

The space in front of them cleared, leaving a patch of bright blue sky above. Weeds fought for life on the forest floor, and moss clung to the trunks of the trees.

"Do you hear that?" Rebecca said.

Nola took a slow breath and listened. The bright scent of the trees and the fresh chill morning air filled her lungs. Below the soft *rustle* of the wind through the leaves, a faint *trickle* of running water carried up from the ground.

"What is that?" Nola asked.

"Humans need air, water, food, and shelter to survive," Rebecca said. "The trees helped us find shelter and purged the worst of the city's filth from our air. Water took a lot longer to sort out."

Rebecca pointed to a pile of rocks across the way.

Scanning the trees for the twins or whoever else might be watching, Nola crossed to the rocks, Jeremy keeping step beside her. As they neared the rocks, the sounds of the water became clearer. Not racing like an underground river, but running calmly, like a steady stream.

The rocks weren't a pile as they had seemed from a distance, but a boundary surrounding an opening that led underground.

"Go on down," Rebecca said. "Took long enough to build it, might as well show it off."

Jeremy stepped in front of Nola, pulling out his flashlight and shining the beam into the darkness.

"Used to be a couple streams running through the woods," Rebecca said. "They'd run clean, then the bad rain would drift northwest from the city and ruin all the water."

A dirt path sloped down into the darkness. Nola stayed close behind Jeremy, testing each step as she went.

"Found a spring down here that runs pretty long." Rebecca followed them into the darkness. "Didn't have much water at the time. We dug out part of a stream to make it cut down to meet up with the spring. Dam that stream up and divert the water out of the woods when the rains get bad. Open it up and get as much water running down here as we can when the raindrops are clean."

A spring ran through the rocks on the tunnel floor, the water bubbling and leaping as it cascaded downstream.

"Wow." Nola knelt by the edge, letting her fingers sink into the chill water.

"We store water for the dry seasons," Rebecca said. "That's the hardest part. Boil it all before we drink it just in case."

"It's beautiful." Nola tipped her hand, watching the water dripping from her palm sparkle in the beam of Jeremy's flashlight.

"You spent too much time behind the glass." Rebecca laughed. "If you think it's pretty, good on you. All I care about is not having lost any of my people to bad water in ten seasons."

"Very impressive," Julian said. "I hadn't imagined such a thing to be possible without filters and electricity."

"That rot is what got all of us into this mess," Rebecca said. "I was born in these woods, and I can promise you, we've never had one hint of electricity."

"Can we see where you live?" Nola trailed her fingers through the water. "Are all your homes made of trees like the place with the candles? How do you farm? Do you store seeds for the cold months?"

"Leave it to Lenora Kent's daughter to worry about the damned seeds," a terribly familiar voice growled from the opening above.

CHAPTER FOURTEEN

Nola felt the impact of hitting the dirt before she registered Jeremy tossing her out of view of the opening to the clearing above. Julian's sword cleared its sheath as she sprang to her feet to see Jeremy pointing his gun at the figure silhouetted by the sunlight.

"Back away," Jeremy said. "You may have the high ground, but do you really think you'll get out of this fight alive?"

"I've made it this far, Ridgeway. If that doesn't prove there's more to survival than contaminating your blood with chemicals, I don't know what does." Captain Stokes limped a step down the dirt path toward the spring.

Nola took a step forward, reaching for her weapon.

"You've even trained the botanist to shoot." Stokes eyed Nola. "I'm surprised you let her move beyond a hot house flower."

"What the hell are you doing here?" Nola asked.

"Surviving," Stokes said.

"Pardon me," Julian said, his sword raised, "but I seem to be at a disadvantage. I have no idea who you are."

Stokes' brow furrowed, joining his eyebrows into one dark line. "Who the hell are you, and how did you get a sun suit?"

"Play nice," Rebecca said. "I don't like this sort of noise."

"He's going to kill you, Rebecca," Jeremy said. "You've got to know that. Stokes will lead the domes here, and they will destroy everything you have."

"A Domer then?" Julian said.

"Arthur Stokes, former Captain of the Dome Guard." Stokes took another step forward, his heavy dome boots sinking into the dirt. The boots were the only bit of dome clothing he still wore. He'd traded his black uniform for the brown clothing of the Northerners.

"Captain of the Dome Guard hiding in the woods?" Julian said.

"Domes be damned," Stokes said. "And I really don't need some hopped up, self-righteous fool's opinion on it."

"Such judgment from someone who's never seen my face," Julian said.

"What are you doing here?" Nola said. "These people haven't hurt the domes. You don't have any right to—"

"I didn't come here to hurt the Woodlands people," Stokes said. "Hell, I didn't know they existed when I left the domes."

"Left the domes?" Nola took a step forward.

"Don't trust him," Jeremy said.

"Even out here the Ridgeways assume superiority." Stokes walked down to the stream, stopping as close to Nola as Jeremy would allow. "I'd love to weave you some story of peace and tolerance, but the truth of the matter is the domes have gone to shit, and there are some kinds of hell no loyalty can bargain for."

"What happened?" Nola asked.

"I don't want to talk about this down here," Rebecca said. "Give the water a hint of how ruined the world is and it might not run so pure."

Stokes glared at Rebecca for a moment, then limped back up toward the clearing. One of the twins reached down, helping him up the last, steepest part of the incline.

"You can't trust him," Jeremy said.

"And I should trust a nightwalker and some runaways from the glass?" Rebecca said. "He's given me a better reason to have faith than the three of you have offered."

What happened in the domes?

Nola wanted to shout the question, but the sound of the stream stopped her.

"We need to get moving." Another vaguely familiar voice came from above. "We've got five miles to cover, and we've got to be at the rendezvous point by noon."

Jeremy stepped out into the clearing first, aiming his weapon, not at Stokes, but at another man. One with short hair and an angry sunburn on his forehead.

"You're from the domes, too," Jeremy said.

"Seems to be a theme," the man said.

Nola narrowed her eyes at the man, trying to place his face away from the golden-green light of the glade. "You're a Dome Guard."

"Was," the man said. "Stokes, we've got to get moving."

Stokes. Not Captain Stokes.

"Let's go." Stokes headed east.

"Where are you going?" Jeremy said. "To lead Salinger here to murder these people?"

"Shove your pious drivel up your ass." Stokes rounded on Jeremy, not seeming to care that Jeremy's weapon was aimed at his heart. "You ran away from the domes like a love sick kid, chasing a girl who helped a bunch of strangers slip through the glass, and in that tiny Graylock-altered mind of yours, you can't even imagine why anyone else would have to leave that tyrannical piece of shit prison after Salinger and his men arrived?"

"What are you doing here?" Jeremy said.

"I don't answer to children." Stokes glared at the bloody tear in Nola's shirt and gave a growl of disgust before stalking off through the trees. He didn't slip silently between the branches like the Northerners, or even try to mimic the gentle way Rebecca walked as Nola had. He stomped through the forest as though every tree were under his command and should leap out of his path or risk their captain's wrath.

"If you want to witness this week's count, you should follow him," Rebecca said.

"What are you talking about?" Nola asked even as she followed Stokes and the other guard.

"You wanted to know what we're doing about the domes creeping through our land," Rebecca said. "We might not have the strength of the nightwalkers or the technology of the domes, but we're far from helpless."

"What are you doing?" Nola asked.

"Making a dent," Rebecca said.

Stokes laughed.

"You can't trust him," Jeremy said.

"Coming from a glass child who lives with the nightwalkers, that means so much," Rebecca said. "Stokes has proven his worth. Same can't be said of you."

Nola bit back her questions as Stokes led them through a glade where huts had been built around the trunks of the trees. A fire pit took up the center of the area. An older woman sat near the cold coals, mending a shirt in the shade of the leaves.

Sounds of life carried from a few of the dwellings. Low voices speaking. The scraping of metal against wood, as though someone carved new arrow shafts hidden behind the thin hut walls.

"Is this where all your people live?" Julian asked.

No more than thirty could fit in these homes.

"All the people in this glen live here," Rebecca said.

"Fair enough," Julian said.

Nola wanted to stop and peek inside one of the huts to see how the Northerners kept warm at night, how they made their beds, and what food they kept on hand, but Stokes stomped past the homes and back into the tangled woods.

"Everyone else dispersed as planned?" Stokes said.

"The unit is carrying out your orders, sir," the guard said.

"Unit?" Jeremy said. "You have a whole unit out here?"

"And the rest?" Stokes ignored Jeremy.

"I personally checked last night. Everything is in place," the guard said.

Stokes gave a sharp nod. "You children might as well put your weapons away. We've got a long walk ahead of us, but since you're all hopped up on Graylock, I doubt you'll care."

Nola kept her weapon in her hand. Each leaf hid a person waiting to attack. Every patch of stone led to an underground tunnel filled with unknown enemies.

"What are you doing out here, Stokes?" Jeremy said when they reached a patch of low-lying bushes that left them a clear view of the sky.

The morning sun beat down on Nola's face. The rays would damage her skin cells, but Graylock would heal her before the sun could move beyond causing simple discomfort.

"Had to get out," Stokes said. "It was either that or lose my soul."

"Soul," Rebecca said.

Nola glanced over her shoulder to see Rebecca walking right behind Julian, carrying a bow and a quiver of arrows over her shoulder, though how she'd gotten the weapons, Nola didn't know.

"Funny how glass people ponder things they don't understand." Rebecca looked up to the sky.

"Why were the domes going to make you lose your soul?" Nola asked.

"This coming from the girl the domes sent out onto a bridge they wanted to blow up," Stokes said.

The other guard laughed.

"They used me to kill those people," Nola said, "not you."

"Things didn't get better when you got out," Stokes said.

They reached a creek that cut through the forest. The trunk of a tree lay across the water.

Stokes grimaced as he climbed onto the makeshift bridge. "When the capture or kill order came down on Magnolia, I thought we'd reached a new low."

Jeremy shuddered.

Nola laid a hand on his shoulder. "I'm okay."

Stokes stopped and turned to watch as Jeremy took her hand, kissing her palm.

"Your father should have known you'd chase her," Stokes said. "Maybe Graylock scrambled his brain."

"That's not how it works," Jeremy said.

"Then I'm sorry you have such a shit for a father." Stokes limped the rest of the way across the creek. "A father worth his salt would have known he was sacrificing his son by giving the kill order on his own child's girlfriend, but Captain Ridgeway sent down the order anyway."

"He was too afraid of the Incorporation to do anything else," the guard said.

"What did the Incorporation have to do with the Outer Guard being ordered to kill me?" Nola jumped up onto the tree and ran across the creek in a few quick steps. She didn't meet Stokes' gaze as she leapt down on the other side.

"When your disappearance was reported, the Incorporation wanted the situation handled," Stokes said. "By any means necessary."

Jeremy jumped down next to Nola. He pressed his arm against hers, as though needing reassurance she was real.

"Sounds like the Incorporation," Julian said.

"You've dealt with them?" Stokes said.

"Once upon a time, I worked in asset management in a set of domes far, far away from here," Julian said.

"Good to know there are people who have made it long term on the outside," the guard said.

"Well," Julian said, "Vamp did greatly increase my lifespan."

The guard flinched.

"Why would the Incorporation care so much about Nola?" Jeremy said.

"One of their own slipped out of their control," Stokes said. "Those sorts of things can't be allowed. They wanted it taken care of *or else*, so Ridgeway sent out the order. Didn't go so well for him."

"What do you mean?" Jeremy said.

"Instead of taking care of the escapee, he lost his own damned kid." Stokes pointed into the trees, gesturing for them all to follow like they were Dome Guard under his command.

"Is my dad okay?" Jeremy asked.

The growth here wasn't as healthy as it had been by the settlement. Brown spots took the place of orange and yellow on the leaves, and rot had eaten away patches of the bark on the trees.

"Last I saw him, he was as fine as an ass-licking buffoon can be," Stokes said.

Rebecca laughed from the back of their group.

"Once the Incorporation heard Ridgeway had lost his own son, they decided the situation had gone on long enough," Stokes said. "They decided to send in Salinger."

"Because of us?" Nola stopped, swaying on the spot. "Salinger came because we left?"

Jeremy wrapped his arms around Nola, pressing his cheek to her hair. "Breathe, Nola."

"Did Salinger order the burning of the city?" Nola said. "Did all those people—"

"Don't," Jeremy said. "You can't think like that."

"Salinger was called in because you ran," Stokes said, "but the fire had already been started. You were just the first sparks to leap high enough to be noticed."

Tears stung Nola's eyes. "But the Incorporation sent Salinger because of us."

"The second the bridge had to be blown, it was done," Stokes said. "The Incorporation was looking for a gap. The orders were coming, all of them."

"All?" Julian said.

Stokes opened his mouth, snapped it shut, and stomped off into the trees.

The guard looked at them for a moment before following his commander.

"What orders?" Nola chased after Stokes. Jeremy's hand slipped into hers as she ducked between trees. "Stokes, what did the Incorporation do besides burn the city?"

Stokes punched a branch that hung in his path, breaking it and sending the stick crashing away.

Rebecca growled.

The scent of Stokes' blood reached Nola's nose.

"When Salinger came, he brought a hundred Incorporation Guard from different domes with him," the guard said. "After two days, he sent a report back to Incorporation Headquarters, all about how our domes had no leadership. How we had failed to maintain control of the outsiders. How our population had been too damaged by casualties from the fighting."

"But that's why they let us use Graylock," Jeremy said. "We'd already told them the Outer Guard were being slaughtered in the city."

"They used that, too." Stokes crashed through the trees, not bothering to shield himself from the sticks that tore at his skin.

"They've used Graylock?" Julian said. "Are there more than a hundred Incorporation Guard with the power of Graylock in their systems just across the river?"

Fear clawed at Nola's stomach.

"No," Stokes said. "The Incorporation and I see eye to eye on Graylock at least. That filth has no place in the domes. If you're going to build glass walls to keep human blood pure, you can't defend the domes by polluting your DNA. It's hypocrisy at an unforgivable level."

"Then how did they use Graylock?" Jeremy said. "You're not making any sense."

"No," Stokes said. "You're not thinking."

The trees opened up in front of them. They'd reached the rocky edge of a cliff that gave them a view of the lowlands beyond. The forest stretched out before them, but whatever evolution had preserved the Northerners' home hadn't touched the woods below.

The few trees that still clung to life had withered leaves hanging from their knotted branches. The trunks didn't grow as wide and steady either. Instead, they listed to the side like zombies stumbling through the wilderness. Even the breeze carried a scent of rot the Woodlands had avoided.

"The Incorporation decided our domes population needed to be increased." Stokes stared out over the decaying forest. "When I read the first part of the message, I thought they meant for some of the guards they'd brought in to stay with us. We had already received some new citizens. It seemed natural they would leave a few more behind. I read that damned message a dozen times before I could admit to myself I'd actually understood."

No one spoke.

Nola watched Stokes, the man she had feared and hated, gaze out over the trees. The sun glinted off the lines in his face.

How did the world manage to hurt such a hardened man?

"It wasn't a relocation order," Stokes said. "It was a breeding order. Dome females between seventeen and twenty-seven had been ordered to breed. The Incorporation sent a list of assigned partners."

CHAPTER FIFTEEN

"What?"

The trees below the cliff swayed, wavering as the world itself seemed to tip.

"Our male Outer Guard had all polluted themselves with Graylock." Stokes' words pounded against Nola's ears. "Too many domes citizens had been killed. The Incorporation had sent the best of the Outer Guard from all the domes into our home. They couldn't waste the opportunity to spread prime DNA."

"They ordered dome women to breed with the guards?" Jeremy said.

Nola clutched Jeremy's arm, holding him close as though he were the safe place in a game of tag.

"They sent a list of pairings," Stokes said. "The optimal matches to create the healthiest children for the domes."

"That's sick." Jeremy held Nola, blocking the swaying trees from view as he wrapped his body around her.

"All for the good of the domes," the guard said. "The domes were built to produce healthy generations of children. How could a loyal citizen argue with the Incorporation's logic?"

"How were they intending to impregnate the women?" Julian asked.

Nola clenched her eyes shut, pressing her cheek to Jeremy's chest, letting his racing heartbeat thunder in her ear.

"Mating." Hatred filled Stokes' voice. The same hatred Nola had heard when he spoke of the vampires, Outer Guard, and Graylock. "Timed mating for the greatest chance of conception. It was deemed a waste of resources to artificially inseminate the women."

"People didn't go along with it," Jeremy said. "It's a sick plan from the twisted Incorporation. There's no way people agreed."

"Some did," the guard said. "After all the hopeless violence, a chance to bring some good into the world, people thought things were finally starting to turn around."

"And those that disagreed?" Julian said.

"Lilly." Tears streamed down Nola's cheeks. "Lilly was seventeen. That's how she ended up on the outside. She said no, didn't she?" Nola twisted just far enough to see Stokes nod.

"There were a few bold enough to outright say no," Stokes said. "Salinger loaded them onto a boat and took them across the river. After that, no one dared argue."

"My sister," Jeremy said.

"Lost the day Salinger dropped fire packs on the city," Stokes said. "She didn't make it long enough to hear the damned order."

"But you did," Julian said. "Slaughtering the city was acceptable, but treating your women as breeding mares was a step too far?"

"I swore an oath to protect the people of the domes," Stokes said. "When the fire packs blew, my place was inside the glass, making sure that monster didn't turn his wrath on his own people. But when word came down that they would be separating husbands and wives—sending seventeen-year-old girls to the beds of strangers —it got pretty damn clear that I only had three options: Roll over and let the devil himself do whatever he damn well pleased, kill the bastard in his sleep and let the domes banish me, or take who I could and get out. Find a way to stop Salinger from the outside."

"So you took some guards and ran?" Jeremy said. "You just left those women—"

"I took the guards I could trust and got them and their families out," Stokes said.

"A lot of good that does for the people you were sworn to protect who are still trapped with Salinger," Jeremy said.

Stokes stepped up to Jeremy. Blood stained his cracked knuckles.

Jeremy shifted, holding Nola with one arm, while planting himself between her and Stokes.

"I took my people into the woods hoping for salvation," Stokes said. "I kept them alive on the slim hope that we might be able to do something for the people we love we had to leave behind. I don't want to hear shit from you about what a brave Ridgeway would have done. Your filthy father is still in the damned domes kissing Salinger's ass. You haven't done anything to help the people still trapped inside. At least I'm trying to do something. At least I'm trying to figure out how to help the women that wouldn't follow me!"

"How old is she?" Nola's throat tightened, pressing down so her words barely came out.

"Twenty-six." Stokes' face crumpled. "The Domes Council had denied her request for another baby. My daughter cried when she heard the order. At first, I thought she was terrified. I was going to tear down the domes pane by pane to save her. Then I realized how happy she was. The Incorporation gift-wrapped torment with the promise of hope. I knew I had to get out and find a way to do something. I've got two granddaughters. I can't let something like this happen to them."

"How can we help?" Julian said.

"Ha." Stokes blinked, brushing away the brightness in his eyes. "I never thought I'd hear a Vamper suggest anything but murder."

"We prefer the proper term vampire, actually." Julian gave a quick nod.

"Can't do anything about what's happening in the domes," Rebecca said. "They've got a giant helicopter and firepower we can't match. So we make a dent."

"A dent?" Jeremy said.

"Throw rocks at the glass until the whole place shatters." Rebecca stared at Stokes, who had looked back out over the cliff to the crooked forest below. "Move, or you'll miss it."

"Right." Stokes nodded. "Let's move."

He limped along the edge of the cliff, following a faint path.

"Don't judge the captain too harshly," the guard said. "I got my wife and little boy out with me, and my brother's wife is five months pregnant. If I'd left somebody vulnerable behind—"

"Are we moving or are we chatting?" Stokes shouted.

Shaking his head, the guard ran after Stokes. Julian followed them, his tan suit not quite hiding the rounding of his shoulders.

Jeremy held Nola tight, pressing his cheek to the top of her head.

"It was inevitable," Jeremy said.

"What was?" Nola wrapped her arms around Jeremy, memorizing the feel of him, blocking out the notion of ever having to know the touch of another person.

"If they'd given that order while we were still in the domes," Jeremy said, "we'd have had to find a way out. Nola, I never would have let them touch you."

"I know," Nola said. "If Gentry had still been there..."

"She'd have killed them all," Jeremy said.

Nola tipped her chin up, kissing Jeremy. "When we find her, we'll go back to the domes and bring hell to the demons."

"I love you."

"Is this what glass teenagers are like?" Rebecca leaned against a tree, watching them.

"Only the ones who have almost been killed a few times, left their home, and keep balancing on the edge of a dying world," Nola said.

"Children should be raised in the woods," Rebecca said. "We don't have this sort of trouble. Move, or we'll lose the others."

Nola took Jeremy's hand and followed the path Stokes had taken.

A bird sailed overhead, cawing her greeting to the bright new morning.

"Do your people have children?" Jeremy said. "Healthy children?"

The bird twisted in the wind, gliding in a wide circle.

"Some," Rebecca said. "Not enough to replace the older ones who die, and not all of them make it to walking age."

The bird dove into the trees, crashing through the branches and out of sight.

"Our numbers getting smaller isn't so bad," Rebecca said. "Less meat to hunt, less food to grow, less water to boil. Our kind spent a long time driving the trees back to where the forests could barely survive. Might be time for the trees to drive us back so they can take over again. I don't see any sadness in it."

A brief *squeak* of pain marked the end of the life of the bird's prey.

"But what if there are no children left at all?" Nola said.

"The last one alive needs to make sure the cook fires are out," Rebecca said. "World's bigger than humans. It'll keep spinning through space without any of us to mark the passing of days."

The path twisted and sloped down, forming switchbacks along the side of the cliff. The path was small, too narrow to have been made by humans. Nola glanced over the edge. It wasn't a far fall. She could jump it if she wanted to. But Julian picked his way along the crumbling rocks close on the heels of Stokes and the guard.

The stench of the trees below worsened as they neared the bottom. The scent of soil crept through the foul odor, but there was something wrong with it, almost as though Nola could smell the fertility being stripped from the earth.

Stokes didn't pause at the bottom of the cliff. He headed southeast, cutting through the tilted trees.

Julian slowed his pace as he reached the forest floor, his hat tipping side to side as he examined the trees.

"What is it?" Nola ran the last switchback to reach him, twisting to keep Jeremy's hand in hers as they moved single file.

"I don't know," Julian said. "Rather, I know what's wrong, but I can't quite pinpoint the root of it."

"What?" Jeremy's gaze swept the trees.

"The dirt here is wrong," Julian said. "The trees here are twisted but growing. Yet the forest right above seems so much healthier."

Nola knelt, digging her fingers into the earth. A yellowish hue marked the dirt. "Something tainted the soil. I don't know what it is from sight, but I could bring some samples back to Kieran."

"Don't know what good samples will do you." Rebecca walked ahead of them, continuing down Stokes' path. "But I can tell you why it's different."

"Why?" Nola wiped her fingers on her bloodstained shirt.

"Floodplain," Rebecca said. "When the streams go over their banks, this whole place goes underwater. Only difference I've seen between here and up on the cliff."

"I wish I could bring Kieran to see this," Nola said. "I might have more training in plant preservation, but I'm not used to seeing contaminated earth."

"If we all make it through whatever storm the domes might bring, perhaps Emanuel will allow you to take Kieran so far from safety," Julian said.

"Maybe." Nola followed Rebecca, her gaze flicking between the invisible path and the forest around them.

She wanted to run, to reach whatever they were heading toward, but Stokes, the guard, and Rebecca wouldn't be able to keep up, let alone lead.

"Did it bother you?" Nola ducked under a tree that had cracked and tipped to pierce the forest floor.

"Did what bother me?" Jeremy asked.

"When I was still normal," Nola said. "When I was slow and weak."

"You were never slow or weak," Jeremy said.

Nola laughed. The sound sent something scampering away through the grayish crumble of the underbrush. "Me before Graylock compared to you after Graylock? You must have thought of me as an eggshell."

"No. I was worried I might be too strong and hurt you, but I didn't think of you as any more fragile. Wanting to protect you never came from you being weak. You're the most precious thing in the world to me. Graylock made me better able to make sure the world didn't take away the person I love most."

A warm glow of heat blossomed from Nola's chest, soaring up to tingle her cheeks. "I love you, too."

"Good."

She could hear the smile in Jeremy's voice.

They walked on, the bubble of happiness in Nola's chest battling against the decay of the forest, which worsened as they walked farther southeast.

Toward the city.

Where the domes had corralled workers, the humans they had deemed unworthy of salvation. Where the factories had poisoned the water. Where smog hung heavy in the air. Where the streets were lined with filth that spread disease.

"Julian," Nola said.

"Yes?"

"When you traveled here, did you pass places where people still lived in healthy cities?" Nola said.

"Not in the way you're hoping," Julian said. "I would love to tell you that all you were ever taught in the domes was pure propaganda and there are places on this planet where human civilization still thrives. But I will not stoop so low as to feed you a comforting lie. The architects have built other safe havens, and there may be more small communities like Rebecca's that have managed to find healthy land where they can survive, but even if they exist, I doubt you could find them."

"Wouldn't have found us at all if it hadn't been for the blight," Rebecca said.

"And shooting me with an arrow," Nola said.

"Ha." Rebecca skirted the bank of a stream.

They followed the water, Nola trying to ignore the yellow froth bubbling against the rocks.

Time dragged on. The sun rose higher in the sky, its rays cutting through the chill of the morning. They reached the edge of the slanting forest and entered what might have been a meadow. All the plants had died, leaving nothing but cracked earth with a yellowish tint behind.

Stokes tromped through the barren dirt without acknowledging its danger or sadness.

The dull pounding of their footsteps became a lament, a dirge for the dying world. Their trek, a dutiful viewing of all that had been destroyed.

Nola hadn't been able to stand being locked in safety while those outside suffered. She had seen ill humans. Had witnessed the violence of desperation. But there was more to the end than the pain people could feel.

We made everything around us hurt, too.

A heavy stone weighed down her lungs.

This isn't the time to grieve.

Stokes slowed his pace as he moved out of the clearing and

into a forest that had rotted much like the trees along the river by the domes.

Shaking her head, Rebecca moved to the front of their pack, slipping silently between the trees.

Stokes drew his weapon. The guard did the same.

As though a silent signal had been given, Jeremy stepped in front of Nola, leaving Julian at the back. The *rasp* of Julian drawing his sword sent Nola's heart racing, anticipating whatever enemy approached them. She drew her weapon, forcing herself to take slow, deep breaths even as the air stung her lungs.

A glint of metal up ahead caught her eye, but Rebecca kept moving forward.

She opened her mouth to shout a warning, but Stokes spoke first.

"Damn fine job you did, boys."

CHAPTER SIXTEEN

Nola's grip on her gun faltered as she tried to decide between aiming at Stokes or the glint of metal in the trees.

"Not too hard," a female voice answered. "We're still waiting on two of the boys though."

"This should be enough." Rebecca stood under the glinting metal. "Sixteen marks all running together. That should scare the spider into coming."

The metal shifted, twisting in the breeze. The thing was tiny, too small to be a weapon.

"What is this?" Jeremy stepped forward, his gaze sweeping the trees.

The *click* of a weapon sounded up ahead.

With enough force to break normal bones, Jeremy knocked Nola to the ground. Something hard slammed into her shoulder.

"Hold your fire!" Stokes shouted.

"What the hell is going on, Captain?" a man asked.

The pain in Nola's shoulder faded as her body raced to heal.

"Found Ridgeway with Rebecca," Stokes said. "He's not an Outer Guard, not anymore."

"You're sure about that?" the female voice asked.

"I left before any of you did." Jeremy stood, lifting Nola with him and keeping her pressed to his back. "I've got more reason to doubt you than you do me."

"Is that Magnolia Kent?" the female voice asked.

Nola peeked around Jeremy. A woman stood between dead trees, her gun pointed at Jeremy's chest.

"I know you," Nola said. "I talked to you in the domes."

"So the Ridgeway boy really did run after you." The woman laughed. "I didn't think Graylock left enough human in a person to love like that."

"It does." Nola stepped out from behind Jeremy. "He gave me a dose, too. Everything I feel is the same as before. My body is just stronger."

"Don't happen to have any extra doses of Graylock around?" A man stepped forward to lean against a tree.

Nola had seen him in the domes too, but his time on the outside had affected him more than it had Stokes. The only color left on his face were the dark circles under his eyes and red patches where the sun had attacked his skin.

"Not enough to change you," Jeremy said, "and we aren't sure how to make more."

"Figures." The man shrugged.

A crashing carried through the trees.

Stokes, the guards, and Rebecca all spun toward the sound, their weapons raised.

Nola followed their gaze, leveling her own weapon. Instinct told her to step away and let the former Dome Guard fight whatever demon they had brought down on themselves.

I'm stronger than they are. They know more, but I'm stronger.

"Get me a string," a voice shouted.

"Neelan." The female guard ran toward the man who puffed into view.

"They're behind me. I tried to meet Cass, but they were already coming," Neelan said. "I caught sight of them a mile back.

I don't know how fast they're heading this way." He opened his palm, displaying a tiny square of metal.

Stokes grabbed the square, passing it to the sickly guard who stuck it to the end of a string hanging down from the branch of a decaying tree.

"That's a tracker," Nola said. "Why do you have a dome tracker?"

"We've got more than one." Rebecca pointed at the tiny bits of metal glittering through the trees.

More than a dozen trackers hung from the branches, twisting in the foul breeze.

"The Outer Guard are coming after the trackers?" Nola said.

"We didn't expect them for another hour," the sickly guard said. "Cass should have had more time."

"Shit we can do about it. Take your posts," Stokes ordered, every bit the captain he had been inside the domes. He hurried to the northern side of the trees as quickly as his bad leg allowed.

"What do we do?" Nola turned to Jeremy.

"Come with me." Rebecca beckoned them farther east.

Nola wove between the trackers, keeping close on Rebecca's heels.

"You found the trackers in the water bottles?" Nola said.

Rebecca ducked under a pile of fallen trees. "You don't think we were smart enough to notice that everywhere a cluster of refugees settled, the spider's men came swooping in to rain down hell?"

Nola stooped under the tree, expecting to continue on but finding herself in an enclosed space instead. The downed trees looked to have collapsed in on themselves as the ground beneath them sagged. But the dip in the earth had been hollowed out, allowing room for Rebecca, Nola, Jeremy, and Julian to all duck into the shadows. Gaps had been made between the rotting branches of the trees, creating sight lines in every direction.

"When we kept finding groups of dead, the only thing they all had in common were the bottles," Rebecca continued in a whisper. "Didn't take long to find the false bottom and the beacons."

"Why did you hang them out there?" Jeremy leaned toward the gap in the northern part of their hiding place, peering in the direction Neelan had appeared.

"To make a dent," Rebecca said. "We can't attack the domes, but we're stronger than they are out here."

"You're leading them toward your home," Jeremy said.

"We're far enough away," Rebecca said. "One skill they never thought to pass on to your glass soldiers: tracking."

The dull *thump* of heavy boots caught Nola's ear.

"They're here." Nola inched toward Jeremy to peer out into the woods.

The thumping of the boots slowed.

Nola scanned the trees, waiting for fire and death to surge toward their hiding place.

The thumping came closer, bringing the Outer Guard into view. Their black uniforms blared against the dull brown of the trees. They approached slowly, their faces hidden in their helmets. The one in front kept looking at something in his hand.

Nola wished she could see their eyes so she could know if they'd spotted the trackers in the trees or the people hiding around them.

Rebecca nudged Nola out of the way, claiming a spot at the gap and nocking an arrow.

Nola stooped, peering over Jeremy's head while the Outer Guard drew closer still.

Have I met you before? Or are you very far from home? Were you paired with Lilly?

The rifles in the Outer Guard's hands kept her from calling out.

Rebecca shook her head, working her lips against each other but not saying anything.

The seven Outer Guard stopped just shy of the cluster of trees where the trackers hung.

They know something's wrong.

Nola gripped Jeremy's shoulder, leaning down to whisper in his ear.

But a *buzz* and a *thwap* cut through the air before she could speak.

The Outer Guard at the front of the formation stumbled back as an arrow hit him square in the chest.

"We're under attack!" a voice shouted from the guards' ranks.

A *pop* sounded from the trees to the right, and one of the Outer Guard fell. Another *pop* brought a third guard down, but the guard that had been hit by the arrow had already pushed himself to his feet. His heavy Guard vest did more than block the weather and sun—the armor within the fabric had shielded him from Rebecca's blow. He leveled his gun, shooting into the trees to his right, while another guard fired toward the left.

Rebecca let another arrow fly, hitting one of the Outer Guard in the shoulder. The man cried out in pain.

Another *pop* from an unseen weapon sounded as Rebecca let loose another arrow. Two of the guards started toward the downed trees where Nola hid.

Rebecca shot another arrow, hitting one in the thigh. The other moved his finger to pull his trigger.

Jeremy knocked Nola backwards. She listened while she fell, waiting for the burst of *pops* that would try to kill them, wondering if the chemicals on the deadly darts would be strong enough to kill her and Jeremy.

But a *swoosh* and a *bang* came before the *pops*. The ground beneath Nola shook, and the dead trees above her sent a cascade of rot onto her face.

Rebecca let another arrow fly as a string of *pops* filled the air.

The stench of burning reached Nola's nose just before a triumphant *whoop* carried from the trees.

"Went smoother than last time." Rebecca looped her bow over her shoulder and ducked back out of their hiding place.

"What just happened?" Nola squirmed out from under Jeremy.

"I'm impressed." Julian followed Rebecca.

"Impressed by what?" Nola crawled after them.

The stench of burning was stronger outside the shelter of the trees.

Stokes and his guards had already crept out from wherever they'd been hiding, all heading toward the downed Outer Guard.

Wisps of smoke drifted up from a crater that had appeared in the earth. On the far side, three of the guards lay still on the ground.

"The *boom* should have been bigger." Rebecca pulled her arrow out of the thigh of one of the guards.

He lay still, not flinching as the arrow left his flesh. The sun caught a tiny piece of silver metal sticking out of his neck.

"Helmets off." Stokes knelt next to the first guard who had fallen and yanked their helmet free.

A face Nola didn't recognize emerged. A tiny hitch of panic tightened in her chest as the woman knelt beside the next Outer Guard.

Nola felt Jeremy next to her and reached for his hand without looking.

The next Outer Guard she recognized. She had seen him in the corridor of the Outer Guard barracks.

Nola ran her thumb along the ridges of Jeremy's palm, needing to feel the texture of his skin against hers.

A woman in her forties was next.

"Hmm." Stokes pushed himself to his feet. "Take what we need and dump them all into the pit."

"Dump them into the pit?" Nola stepped forward to stare down into the ditch.

The pit had been dug before the explosion had gone off. Singe marks from whatever the explosive had been lapped the top foot of the dirt. Four Outer Guard lay at the bottom, their clothes charred and bodies twisted.

"I had hoped my arrows would all make it through." Rebecca frowned at the burned bit of wood sticking out of one of the guard's shoulders.

"We can't just drop them down there," Nola said. "They could wake up."

"None of them are waking up," Stokes said. "I left behind the flaccid Dome Guard tranq darts when I took my men and ran. We only carry ammunition that kills now. Neelan, strip the bodies."

"But what about the one with Graylock?" Nola pointed to the man she recognized.

"We stab him through the heart," Rebecca said. "Want the pleasure, Julian? It might be a nice change for a nightwalker."

"You can't just stab him," Jeremy said. "He could have information. He could just be trying to get back to his family that's trapped in the domes."

"Do you really want me to let an Outer Guard who's had Graylock wake up?" Stokes said. "What kind of fool do you take me for? Neelan, get to work."

"Neelan." The female guard turned toward the trees. "Neelan?"

The sickly guard ran faster than Nola had thought possible toward a subtle rise in the dirt. "Dammit." He hopped down on the far side of the mound. "Neelan's dead, Captain. Two darts to the face."

"Shit." Stokes scrubbed his filthy hands over his chin. "Shit."

The woman let the Outer Guard helmet fall from her hands as she moved toward the mound. "We're carrying him back to camp. He should be burned."

"We can't move anyone until we take care of these demons." Rebecca knelt next to one of the Outer Guard, unfastening his belt and pulling the weapons free.

"We can carry Rivers back to camp, too," Jeremy said.

Rivers. I should have known his name.

"No," Rebecca said.

"I'll carry him myself," Jeremy said.

"You'll carry him and what?" Stokes said. "Do you have chains strong enough to hold him? Are the Woodlands people supposed to dig a prison? If we carry him back to camp and he wakes up, he could hurt people. If he gets free, he could lead Salinger to the forest. Do you want that kind of blood on your hands? I already have to tell Neelan's damned wife her husband is dead. Don't try and make my day worse by getting more innocent people killed."

"We can't just kill a man in cold blood. We're not the—" A crackling cut Jeremy off.

"Report in." The tinny voice carried from the Outer Guard helmet at Stokes' feet. "North team, what's your status?" Captain Ridgeway's voice asked.

CHAPTER SEVENTEEN

Nola placed a hand on Jeremy's chest, stopping him from stepping closer to the helmet.

"North team, report immediately."

"We knew they'd start watching more closely," Rebecca said.

"North team, report." There was no anger in Captain Ridgeway's voice. No panic either.

"How many times have you done this?" Jeremy asked.

"This?" Rebecca said. "None. Dented their numbers? A few."

"North team, report."

"How many Outer Guard have you killed?" Jeremy stepped forward.

Nola pushed against him. He looked down, his gaze finding Nola's hand on his chest.

"Not as many as Salinger killed in the city." Stokes rolled the female guard into the pit.

"North team, status report now." The resignation in Captain Ridgeway's voice pulled at parts of Nola's heart she hadn't known existed anymore.

The guard who had traveled with them from the forest pulled a sack from his pocket, holding it open as Stokes and Rebecca filled it with weapons, boots, and first aid pouches. She opened Rivers' vest, searching his pockets with a practiced motion.

"Wait," Jeremy said as Rebecca pulled a black case free from Rivers' belt. "Can I have that?"

"Can I kill him?" Rebecca said.

"I need the case." Jeremy lifted Nola's hand away from his chest.

"And I need to not haul a traitor home," Rebecca said.

"North team," Captain Ridgeway said. "We are instituting Beta Protocol. Get the hell out."

Each of them froze as Ridgeway's voice crackled through the trees.

"What's Beta Protocol?" Nola said.

"Time to get the hell out." Stokes kicked an Outer Guard into the pit, leaving only Rivers still above the dirt.

"We don't have time to bury them," the female guard said.

"Blame that on the spider," Rebecca said. "Cut the beacons down."

The female guard darted from tree to tree, tearing the trackers from their strings.

"Rivers might know what Beta Protocol is," Nola said.

"So we carry him, ask him, then kill him?" Rebecca said.

"We don't have time to argue," Jeremy said. "I'll carry him, and if it comes to it, I'll kill him."

"We need to move." Rebecca grabbed the sack of weapons and ran, not the way they'd come but farther east, away from the woods.

"I can't let you do that," Stokes said.

Nola didn't see the steel in Stokes' hand until he'd already plunged the blade into Rivers' heart.

"You bastard," Jeremy growled.

"You'll thank me for that someday." Stokes ran after Rebecca. The other guards stayed close behind, two of them carrying Neelan's corpse.

"We should follow," Julian said.

"Follow murderers?" Jeremy shook his head.

"We're all murderers," Julian said. "The world has become too ruthless to leave any of us innocent."

Blood seeped from the wound in Rivers' chest. The same red that had painted the halls of the domes, had been spilt in the tunnels of Nightland, had coated the streets of the city.

"Come on." Nola grabbed Jeremy's hand, dragging him away from the clearing. "Whatever your—whatever Beta Protocol is, we can't be here for it."

Jeremy followed her, though his gaze didn't leave Rivers until the trees blocked his body from view.

Rebecca and the guards wove through the trees ahead of them, slipping in and out of sight.

"He wasn't a great guy," Jeremy said. "I punched him once."

"Why?" Nola kept her eyes on the trees as they ran, catching up to the guards.

"He made a joke about you," Jeremy said.

"What kind of joke?" Nola asked.

"He said I was lucky to have a girl who wasn't dome prim. Something about you learning to sneak into dark corners from the Vampers in Nightland," Jeremy said. "I broke his cheekbone."

"Seems fair," the female guard said.

"He'd already had Graylock. His face healed before I was called to be reprimanded. Dad said..." Jeremy's voice faded away. "He said if Rivers didn't talk so much, maybe he wouldn't end up accidentally banging his face into a wall."

"Ha." Sweat slicked the female guard's brow. "I didn't know Captain Ridgeway had a sense of humor."

"He doesn't," Jeremy said.

"What's your name?" Nola asked.

"Alice," she said. "Jude is the splotchy one."

"Thanks, Al," Jude puffed.

"Preston." Al nodded toward the guard who had come with them from the woods.

No one tried to say who Neelan had been.

They reached a rocky patch where the twisted trees hadn't even attempted to grow. The rocks slipped out from under Stokes' feet as he tried to make his way across.

"We need to move faster," Julian said, only loud enough for Nola and Jeremy's Graylock-enhanced ears to hear. "If Beta Protocol involves fire packs, I don't want to be anywhere near here."

Al and Preston slid on the rocky terrain, trying to keep Neelan's weight balanced between them.

"Let me take him," Jeremy said.

"We can take care of our own." Preston spoke through gritted teeth.

"Leave him or pass him over." Rebecca leapt from rock to rock, quickly overtaking Stokes. "If the Outer Guard catch us in the open, we'll all be dead and there won't be anyone to carry Neelan back to the woods."

"Let me help," Jeremy said.

"Okay." Al stopped, not flinching under Preston's glare.

Jeremy lifted Neelan, draping him carefully over his shoulder.

"We need to run," Julian said.

A cold dread settled in Nola's stomach. She searched the trees and ground for whatever had made Julian's tone so crisp.

"Not all of us are Vampers." Jude gasped for breath as he moved barely faster than a jog.

The rocky patch sloped up, leading to rolling hills covered in scrub brush.

A *hum* shook the air.

Jude glanced up toward the sky. His foot slipped out from under him.

Nola leapt forward, catching him before his face hit the stone, lifting him back up to his feet, and keeping her arm around him as they ran up the slope.

The *hum* in the air had developed texture in the few seconds it had taken to get Jude running again, a thumping that dug into Nola's ear with every beat.

"Damn," Julian said.

Nola glanced back, following Julian's gaze. A black dot appeared in the sky to the south, heading straight for the point where they'd left the guards.

"I suppose Beta Protocol involves Salinger's helicopter," Julian said.

"Get up here." Rebecca stood at the edge of the bushes on the hill, holding back the thick branches for Al and Preston, who dove beneath the dying leaves and crawled out of sight.

Stokes reached the bushes a moment later. He stopped at the edge, looking back toward the rest. Jeremy stayed behind Nola with Julian, and Nola fought with every step to keep Jude from tumbling out of her grasp.

"Get in, you buffalo," Rebecca said.

"Not without my men," Stokes said.

Nola tightened her grip on Jude, dragging him up the hill, not caring if he kept his feet beneath him. She threw him through the gap in the bushes and dove in behind him.

Jude landed with a *thud*, but she didn't bother to ask if she had hurt him. She scrambled over him, grabbed his arms, and dragged him forward far enough to allow Jeremy to duck under the brush.

Al crawled forward, taking Neelan's shoulders and helping guide his body into an open space under the branches.

Julian dived into the shadows a second later with Stokes at his heels. Rebecca slipped between the branches and let them go. The *swish* of the leaves rustling back into place barely carried over the *thump* of the helicopter's approach.

The branches sheltered them from the sun and hid the trees beyond from sight. If Nola had been a very little girl, she would have felt safe beneath their browned leaves. Hidden beyond reach of danger.

"Do you think they saw us?" Nola whispered, sure no one from the helicopter would be able to hear her but unable to convince herself to speak more loudly.

"If they kill us, we'll know they did." Rebecca sank to her knees.

The bushes were five feet high in places, but the uneven growth left some no more than two feet tall. Each of their group nestled beneath the branches as the thumping grew louder.

"We should keep moving." Julian twisted to crawl.

"Do you really think we can outrun them without being seen?" Jude lay on the ground, sweat glistening on his splotchy brow.

"Not even I could outrun a helicopter," Julian said. "But until we know we've been seen and are being followed, I suggest we keep moving as quickly as concealment will allow. There is a radius to every blast, and I would like to be as far from whatever Beta Protocol might be as possible, even if we only make it a hundred yards."

"Agreed." Rebecca's gaze swept the bushes for a moment before she began crawling north.

"What about Neelan," Jeremy said. "Should we...what do you want me—"

A piercing sound cut across Jeremy's words.

Nola crept toward the edge of the bushes, peeking out between branches.

"We have to move," Stokes ordered.

It's too late.

The helicopter flew in a slow circle around where the dead Outer Guard lay. If the people in the helicopter could see their compatriot's corpses, they didn't seem intent on retrieving them. They didn't drop black and silver fire packs on the dead trees either.

No fire. No blasting. Only a shimmer as they sprayed something into the air.

Nola leaned closer to the edge of safety, trying to get a better look at the mist.

"We have to go." Julian grabbed her arm, dragging her backward through the bushes.

"What is it?" Nola twisted around, gaining her own footing.

"We have to go south," Julian called to the others who had been following Rebecca north. "Leave the body, Jeremy."

"Are you—"

"Do not sacrifice the living for the dead." Julian let go of Nola's arm and stood doubled over to run southeast at a pace the humans would have trouble matching.

Nola glanced back, needing to be sure Jeremy was the one crashing through the brush behind her.

"What the hell is going on?" Stokes ran next to Julian, hunched over and red-faced.

"There are demons in the Incorporation's past even you are too young to remember," Julian said.

"Where are you trying to go?" Rebecca stayed on Julian's heels.

"Against the wind."

Rebecca nodded and took the lead, cutting between bushes as though running doubled over with a sack on her back were nothing.

"Jude," Nola said, "we can't leave him."

"I've got him." Al had an arm around Jude's waist. His face had already turned a bright shade of red.

"Let me." Jeremy looped around, half-draping Jude over his back.

"Are you going to leave me under a bush, too?" Jude asked.

"Not as long as you're breathing," Jeremy said.

The weight of another person wouldn't slow Jeremy, but the size of two people together shook the bushes.

"If they fly this way, they'll see us moving," Nola said.

"If we don't keep moving, most of us will die," Julian said.

Nola ducked under a low branch. "Why? Why are we running from mist?"

"It's not mist," Julian said. "They are using one of the Incorporation's worst mistakes to try ridding themselves of enemies. How quickly they forget what the true meaning of evil is. A little more east."

Rebecca shifted their path.

Nola tried to feel it, the breeze that guided Julian away from whatever had scared the vampire so badly. All she could feel on her skin was the brushing of leaves and scratching of branches.

She took a deep breath, trying to scent the wind. A horrible sting filled her nose and burned its way down her throat.

"What is that?" She choked on her question, muddying the words beyond recognition.

They reached the crest of the hill where the bushes were too thin to hide them completely from view. Nola glanced back toward the helicopter.

The mist had become a haze that hung heavy over the trees. For a moment, Nola thought her eyes had failed her in her panic as the trees beneath seemed to melt into the ground.

CHAPTER EIGHTEEN

Nola stared horrified as the trees shrunk, melting beneath the spray from the helicopter.

"We need to move." Al seized Nola's wrist, trying to drag her away from the hilltop. But Al wasn't strong enough to make Nola's feet move.

Neither was Nola.

She couldn't tear her gaze from the trees slumping to the side in their final death throes before dissolving into the barren forest floor.

"How?" Nola shook her head as her whole body trembled. "That's not possible."

"Nola!" Jeremy's shout cut through the storm of confusion battering her mind.

"What are they doing?" Nola chased after Jeremy, glancing over her shoulder to see the helicopter move on to the next patch of trees, wiping away the forest as though it had never existed.

The bushes tore at her skin, but the rough touch seemed to come from far away. From a dream where trees could disappear.

It's not a dream. Not even a nightmare.

"What's in the mist, Julian?" Jeremy kept right in front of Nola, Jude draped over his shoulder, bouncing with every step.

They sprinted down the far side of the hill, Preston supporting Stokes, Rebecca leading with Julian and Al close on her heels.

"I'm not a chemist." The wind shifted, whisking Julian's voice away and surrounding them with the stench of the mist.

The sound of the helicopter came closer, pounding behind the rise of the hill.

"We're not going to make it," Al said.

"Just keep moving." Rebecca veered farther south. "How much of that stuff can they get in the air?"

"The allotment was 4.35 barrels per acre," Julian said. "If they kept the helicopter to its prescribed load, they should have enough Nallot to clear just under eleven acres."

"That's a lot of forest," Al said.

"Not so much we can't outrun them," Jeremy said.

They reached the bottom of the hill, where the bushes grew thicker with branches unwilling to bend as they ran past. Each *crack* as they crashed through the growth echoed in Nola's ears like a rifle shot.

"That's assuming they spread the shit in actual acres." Jude spoke between coughs. "If they spray in a straight line, they could cut a path from here to the domes."

"Can the mist eat concrete?" Rebecca said.

"Not as quickly as it can eat wood," Julian said. "But given enough time, I'm not sure there's much Nallot couldn't destroy."

"Then we'll just have to hope they don't rain death on us." Rebecca raced farther south, toward a wide expanse of rotting trees.

A million questions jumbled in Nola's mind, but one carried over the din.

Why?

With a grunt, Stokes tipped forward, falling into the dirt.

Preston grabbed his arm, yanking him up. Before Stokes had gotten to his feet, Julian wrapped an arm around the captain, lifting him as he kept right behind Rebecca.

"Leave me alone." Stokes pushed against Julian's chest.

"Leave you to die?" Julian said, the sideways tilt of his torso the only indication of carrying Stokes' weight. "Don't tempt me."

The horrible need to laugh bubbled in Nola's throat, but the thumping of the helicopter drawing near killed the urge.

"We need to find cover," Nola said.

"We know," Al panted.

The trees here had no leaves on their branches and didn't grow close enough together for their shadows to offer anywhere to hide.

Nola scanned the dirt, searching for a place they could dig a shelter.

Not fast enough, we couldn't dig fast enough.

The tree line broke in front of them, leaving the terrain even more exposed.

A sound carried beneath the noise of the helicopter—the rushing of water against rocks.

"They're coming over the hill!" Preston darted behind a tree.

But Rebecca didn't hesitate as she ran toward the water.

The stench of the river broke through Nola's panic and the sting of Nallot in her nose.

Rebecca dodged north and disappeared from view.

Nola ran faster, reaching Jeremy's side as Julian, Stokes, and Al vanished.

A mound in the ground where the entrance to a concrete structure had crumbled poked out of the earth.

"Get in," Rebecca shouted.

"Nola, go," Jeremy said.

She didn't argue. There wasn't time. She dived into the darkness, stumbling on a steep ramp. Hands grabbed her, jerking her out of the way as Jeremy rushed into their shelter.

"Preston!" Stokes bellowed. "Get in here you damned—"

The helicopter blades whirred overhead, their rhythm pounding into Nola's chest.

Jeremy laid Jude on the ground and moved to Nola's side. She threaded her fingers through his, feeling the racing of his pulse as his wrist pressed against hers.

Should I shut my eyes against the end?

If Nallot could melt trees, it would burn through bone. There would be no knife through the heart or slice through the neck to end her second life.

Not even the Teachers will find me.

The thumping of the air changed.

Jeremy pressed Nola to the concrete wall behind her, curving his body around her, sheltering her from the end.

It won't help.

She couldn't bear to tell him, wouldn't take away his final act of shielding her.

A scream cut through the pounding of the helicopter's blades. A blood-curdling cry that shook Nola's bones.

"No!" Julian shouted.

The *thud* of a landed punch punctuated Preston's last painful shriek.

Nola buried her face in Jeremy's chest. She took a deep breath, reveling in his scent of fresh earth, with the hint of something else. Something uniquely hers that hadn't existed when they lived in the domes. Their life together had left a mark in his blood.

I love you.

Jeremy held her tighter, as though he had heard the words in her mind.

The thumping of the helicopter's blades changed, whirring as the craft surged forward across the river and away from their hiding place.

No one spoke as the noise faded away. Silence filled the darkness, leaving Jeremy's heartbeat as the only sound Nola could hear.

"We have to see if he's dead." Al spoke first.

"No one survives screaming like that," Rebecca said.

Nola wrapped her arms around Jeremy's waist, holding him as though the helicopter would come back to rip him away.

"We still have to check," Al said.

"Do you think it wise to go out into the open?" Julian said.

"We don't know if they dumped the stuff right over our heads," Jude said. "Do we want to hunker down here and see if we're melted into nothing, or get the hell out?"

"I'll go up," Rebecca said. "Stay down here."

"Preston—" Stokes began.

"I don't think there'll be anything left of him to carry back," Rebecca said. "I won't lie if I'm wrong."

There was no sound of Rebecca leaving the safety of their hiding place.

"Are you okay?" Jeremy whispered in Nola's ear.

"I'm…" She faltered on the easy lie. "I'm alive."

"I don't want to rain on the beauty of youth," Julian said, "but somedays *alive* is the best you can hope for."

Jeremy stepped back, holding Nola tightly but shifting the bulk of his shoulders enough for her to see the space around them.

Stokes slumped against the cracked concrete wall, nursing a fist-sized bruise that blossomed across his cheek.

Jude struggled to sit up. Bright red patches dotted his sweat-slicked skin.

Al stood at the top of the ramp, staring at the open ground around them, clutching the rusted rebar that poked out from the doorframe.

"What is this place?" Nola's voice wavered.

"I'm not sure." Julian moved toward the far end of the space.

Nola turned to peer past Jeremy's other shoulder, unwilling to relinquish the comfort of contact.

The space stretched back thirty feet. Empty shelves leaned against the cracked back wall.

"Looks like storage," Jeremy said. "But storage for what?"

"Dock maintenance," Rebecca said. "Dock crumbled, but this hole is still pretty sturdy."

Jeremy stepped away from Nola, sliding his hand down to find hers.

"We took everything good out of here ages ago." Rebecca stood in the doorway. The light from behind shone so brightly, Nola couldn't make out her face.

"Did they..." Nola's voice faded.

"There's nothing to carry back," Rebecca said. "We need to get moving."

"Moving where?" Stokes growled. "Back across the hills? Hope they don't come sweeping down on us again? Take a nice walk through the land they just demolished like they were melting ice?"

"We can't stay here." Rebecca hoisted the sack of weapons they'd taken from the Outer Guard over her shoulder. "They spotted Preston, but we don't know if they saw us. They could bring back more guards, more Nallot."

"So we run from here and see how fast they find the Woodlands," Stokes said. "Your people have nothing to protect themselves from this hell!"

Jude wobbled to his feet. "Captain—"

"Don't *captain* me," Stokes spat. "I lost two men today. I don't know where Cass is. He might be melted to nothing right now. What am I supposed to tell the people waiting for him in the Woodlands? I dragged ten guards and their families out of the glass, and for what? To watch them die? To watch their kids get sick?"

"To save them," Julian said.

"My men are dying!" Stokes shouted.

"I didn't say you were saving them from death," Julian said. "You didn't leave the domes in search of paradise. You left for a chance at redemption."

"Does redemption happen to cure whatever the hell is wrong with me?" Jude asked.

"No," Julian said, "but better to die than live as a minion of a monster. Believe me, I learned that lesson a long time ago."

"I have people counting on me," Rebecca said. "I can't stay here mourning for lost men when there are still living people in danger in the Woodlands. I'm going. If you want to come, move fast. If you want to stay, don't come back to my home. I can't risk you leading the Outer Guard to my woods."

"We're coming with you," Jeremy said. "We came here to learn from you. This hasn't changed anything."

"I don't know if I can get very far," Jude said. "But I say we make a break for it. I've still got a few breaths left in me. Don't want to waste them in a concrete hole."

"I'll help you," Julian said. "You won't fall behind."

Jude nodded. Julian wrapped an arm around his waist.

"Stokes?" Al said.

"Where the hell are we supposed to run to?" Stokes said.

"I've spent my life in these hills. Don't doubt me." Rebecca stepped out of view, heading north.

"You two should go next," Julian said. "Don't worry. I'll be right on your heels."

Nola led Jeremy to the door, stopping next to Stokes. "You weren't wrong to help your guards escape. The people I let out of the cells, one died in the first couple of hours. But I know she wasn't sorry we got out."

The left side of Stokes' face had begun to swell. Blood stained his top lip.

"Not all of us get to survive," Nola said. "That doesn't mean you don't have to try."

She walked up the concrete ramp and to the outside.

The fumes of the Nallot pressed on her lungs. Jeremy twisted as they walked, blocking the place where Preston had died from view. She didn't try to look around him.

There are still horrors I'm not ready for.

She kept her gaze fixed north. For a moment, she was afraid Rebecca might have run too far for her to track. But Rebecca waited a hundred feet away, standing at the edge of the trees, staring at the strip of barren land next to the bank of the river. Nola blinked at the blackened ground, wondering what awful thing had stained the dirt such an unnatural color.

"It's a road." Nola walked straight for the strip of black, tapping the pavement with her toe. "Is this the road to the city?"

"Yep." Rebecca pointed south, along the current of the brown river.

Barren islands split the river in places, but none of them blocked the view of the oxbow downstream. The edge of the ruined city peered out over the water, and high on the hill, the domes glistened in the sun.

"They still look perfect," Nola said.

"Looks can be deceiving." Jude leaned on Julian's shoulder.

"Hmm." Rebecca turned north, heading into the barren trees.

"Where are we going?" Nola asked.

"Somewhere we can shelter for the night," Rebecca said. "If the Outer Guard don't find us by morning, we'll start the long way back to the Woodlands."

"Long way," Jude said. "Sounds great."

Just keep running.

The thumping of footsteps pounded up from behind.

Jeremy let go of Nola's hand, drawing his weapon.

Nola glanced back as her fingers closed around the hilt of her knife.

Stokes and Al ran side-by-side, racing to catch up to the group.

CHAPTER NINETEEN

Nola didn't want to look at the forest as they trekked through the trees. Didn't want to think of how easily the domes could destroy everything around her.

Think of better things.

Like what?

Jeremy next to her, healthy and whole.

Julian cradled Jude in his arms. Jude hadn't made it past the first few miles on his own feet. Julian had been carrying him for hours as the sun rose in the sky and began its long journey back to the western horizon.

Better things.

T and the baby.

The baby whose father had already died. The unborn child who could be killed by the domes and their horrible weapons.

"Breathe, Nola," Jeremy whispered. "Just breathe."

Nola took a deep breath. They had stopped running hours ago. They walked up hills and past creeks that smelled of rot. Trudged around a pond covered with a cloud of bugs and through woods so far beyond life, no leaves or needles textured the ground.

But walking, walking and trying to find one hopeful untainted thing, was what stole Nola's breath away.

She clutched Jeremy's hand tighter.

"Why did they make Nallot?" Nola asked.

"Murder would be my guess." Rebecca's uneven words were the first sign of fatigue she'd betrayed.

"No," Julian said, "though Salinger does seem to be making a habit of reusing the Incorporation's mistakes as weapons. As foolish as it may sound, Nallot was designed to combat invasive species."

"What?" Nola stumbled over a rock.

"Not all domes are situated in the same fashion as yours," Julian said. "It's a bit complicated, I'm afraid."

"Well, talk." Rebecca set her sack down and leaned against a boulder, which lay nestled next to the rocky side of a low-hanging cliff. She fished in the folds of her pants, pulling out a leather drinking pouch.

"I've got water for us," Jeremy said.

It wasn't until he said the word *water* that Nola noticed the burning in the back of her throat.

Al sank to the ground, wiping the sweat from her forehead with her sleeve and pulling out a water pouch like Rebecca's. Sun and exhaustion had turned her face a bright shade of red.

Nola took the metal bottle Jeremy handed her, taking a slow sip that washed away the grit in her throat.

"I'd offer you some water," Rebecca said, eyeing Julian, "but I suppose you won't drink it."

"No indeed," Julian said. "Don't worry. I'm just fine."

"Good," Rebecca said, "then talk while we drink."

"Of course." Julian laid Jude on the ground.

Nola crouched by Jude. "Can you drink?"

"If you're offering." Jude gave a wavering wink.

"The location of these domes was chosen for its proximity to a city small enough to be controlled yet large enough to manufacture. The mountain range, river, and high number of streams were also considerations, but not all domes were placed for the same values." Julian paced between trees. "The far south domes were placed for their proximity to an excellent seaport."

"Civilization has fallen," Al said. "Who the hell has goods to ship to a port?"

"You're too young," Julian said. "Even though you were raised in the domes, you don't remember the beginning. The city was needed for manufacturing, but the Incorporation didn't plan on the city surviving in the long term. The world was already too far gone for sustainable urban survival before the first pane of glass was put into place. The Incorporation was looking toward the day when the river would have cleansed itself, the mountains would offer a home to the wildlife the domes have fostered, and the land would be ripe for farming. Placement by a port situated that domes' citizens to be able to travel and spread across the coasts when the ocean has stabilized and become a source of safe food once again."

"That still doesn't explain—" Jeremy began.

"Nallot was created for a set of domes in the southern hemisphere," Julian said. "Farther away than even I have traveled."

"What was so special about the location that the Incorporation wanted to build somewhere that would require Nallot?" Rebecca said. "From what I hear, the world is still pretty damn big even if it has gone to shit."

"The soil around those domes was fertile beyond compare," Julian said. "So much so, farmers had brought in non-native crops. Which inadvertently brought in non-native species and pests. The Incorporation decided purging the area of invasive species and allowing the land to naturally reclaim the region over the course of many years would be the best solution for recreating the ecosystem for a time generations from now when citizens would finally leave the domes."

"They destroyed all the land around their home?" Nola dug

her nails into her palms, trying to keep from screaming. "Nallot melted through the trees. The land where they sprayed—"

"Will now be abundantly fertile." Julian tapped his lips through his veil. "On a rudimentary level, Nallot turned those trees into pure fertilizer."

A *crack* shook the air as Stokes punched a tree.

"You said Nallot was a mistake," Jeremy said.

"The Incorporation does seem to forget they are not infallible," Julian said. "They sprayed the area, clearing every plant and animal around the domes."

"And?" Nola shivered.

"The domes were new at the time," Julian said. "The council of those domes became very comfortable in their secluded location. They hadn't been monitoring their systems as closely as they should. The glass in one of the agricultural domes hadn't been properly secured. Fumes were trapped with the workers. Twelve people were killed that day. The Incorporation banned the use of Nallot after the incident."

"Until now," Jeremy said.

"They sprayed the mist miles from the domes," Julian said. "I'm sure the Incorporation set a safe distance for its use."

"The Woodlands are far outside that area," Rebecca said. "They could destroy my entire forest."

"If they have enough Nallot, they could," Julian said. "I don't know how they transferred the Outer Guard here from their home domes. I don't know how much Nallot they brought from the Incorporation's headquarters. I wish I had something comforting to say, but all I can offer is *I don't know*."

Rebecca ran her hand over her head, ruffling her short hair. "Shit we can do about it now." She walked around the side of the boulder and out of sight.

"The barren strip," Nola whispered in Jeremy's ear. "If they saw it from the helicopter—"

"I know." Jeremy nodded. "We could warn them."

"I doubt we could find them on our own," Julian said. "And to travel slowly is to risk being followed."

Stokes glared at Julian, who stared placidly back through the slit in his veil.

Stokes didn't hear me. He can't run to the Woodlands tonight. He's just plain human.

"Nobody wants to rest?" Rebecca called from around the corner.

"I'll get you inside." Julian lifted Jude from the ground.

Jude gave only a faint murmur of thanks as Julian carried him away.

"Captain," Al began.

Nola tugged on Jeremy's hand.

"I'm not going to lie down for a nice rest when Cass could still be out there somewhere," Stokes said.

"I'm not sure I'll be able to sleep." Nola spoke louder than she needed to, trying to drown out Al's reply.

They rounded the boulder. A gaping void in the cliff greeted them on the other side. Tufts of dead grass waited just inside the lip of the cave where the greenery had flourished until the cold snaps had killed it.

"You're not going to find him, sir," Al said. "This isn't the domes. We can't do a floor by floor search."

"You want me to leave your fellow guard for dead?"

"We should try to rest anyway," Jeremy said. "Who knows how long it'll be until we get another chance?"

"I'm asking you to trust his training," Al said. "Or did what you see in the years of us serving under you convince you of our incompetence?"

Nola scampered into the cave.

Rebecca knelt next to a ring of burned logs. "Want to gather some wood?"

"There is nothing I could have taught any of you to prepare you for this!"

Nola flinched at Stokes' shout.

"I'll get the wood then." Rebecca stood and stormed out of the cave. "Shut the hell up, Stokes."

"Back here." Julian beckoned them toward the far end of the cave.

"Unless you've got a way to sniff out where—"

"Nice to have some cover for the night." Jeremy's voice echoed off the back wall.

The hollow in the cliff side reached less than forty feet. Julian knelt in the shadows where the rock ceiling hung too low for him to stand.

"Glad Rebecca's good at lighting fires." Jude's voice crackled.

"How about another sip of water?" Nola sat, carefully lifting Jude's head into her lap.

"Don't know if you should waste it," Jude said.

Nola's eyes flicked to the leather case on Jeremy's belt.

"We need to look in the bag," Jeremy said.

"Which bag?" Julian said.

"Rebecca's." Jeremy started toward the sack by the entrance of the cave.

"Should we wait for her?" Nola asked.

"There isn't a way out of this." Stokes' shout shook the cave.

"I don't think we have time." Jeremy opened the sack, carefully pulling out the rifles, checking each of them before laying them on the ground in a perfect line.

"I'm impressed she carried the weight for so long," Julian said.

"She's been carrying the weight of hundreds of people for a long time." Jude's laugh turned into a cough.

Nola slipped her pack under Jude's head, braving being closer to Stokes to be nearer to Jeremy.

Jeremy pulled the handguns from the bag, checking the darts in each before placing them in a line below the rifles.

"Which kind of darts were they sent with?" Jude asked.

"The killing kind," Jeremy said. "They didn't even give them a non-lethal option. I don't know why I bothered to check."

"You'll keep checking," Julian said. "The spark of hope takes a long time to go out."

"Mine's gone," Jude said. "Guess it figured it wasn't worth sticking around."

"I've often thought mine had disappeared." Julian sat next to Jude. "The brightness of hope would dissipate for years at a time, only to be revived when a hint of goodness breathed in fresh life."

Jeremy pulled the black leather case from the bottom of the sack.

"Nola survived the domes and came to care for those on the outside," Julian said. "Even if I hadn't had the promise of Nightland's new home, Nola would have ignited the spark again."

Jeremy's fingers shook as he opened the case. Nola held her breath, waiting to see the silver syringes filled with the deep black of Graylock.

"Hope is—"

"Damn." Jeremy gripped the case, cracking the sides. "Damn, damn, fucking damn."

"Jeremy." Nola took his hands, pulling the case low enough for her to see inside.

No glittering syringe waited for her. A thin bottle of white pills was all the padded ridges of the case contained.

We need more Graylock.

A guilty weight sank in Nola's chest.

We can wait. Jude can't.

"What's wrong?" Julian pulled his veil back over his face as he moved toward the mouth of the cave.

"There's no Graylock in the triage kit," Jeremy said. "They were sending every Outer Guard out with two doses."

"A couple of Outer Guard were killed in the city," Jude said. "Their doses were taken. Salinger had a fit about the possibility of outsiders dosing themselves. Graylock doesn't move beyond the glass anymore."

"I took four." Jeremy closed the case and unfastened his belt, hooking the box in place. "It might've just been me."

"Or someone else on the outside could have more doses," Nola said.

"This whole world has gone so far to shit, I don't think you'll ever know." Jude's eyes drifted shut. "Guess Salinger doesn't care how many guards die. They'll just breed more."

"We have to do something," Nola whispered.

"We can keep him comfortable." Rebecca returned with an armful of wood. She dropped the load onto the cold coals. "We'll keep him warm and fed."

"If no one's chasing you," Jude said, "try and bring my body back to the Woodlands. I might not have family, but Stokes will give me a proper send off."

"We'll do our best," Rebecca said.

"There is another option," Julian said.

"We don't have enough Graylock," Jeremy said. "Even if we could get him back to Nightland in time, we don't have three full doses. He'd die without the third injection."

"There were ways to save lives before Graylock." Julian moved back into the deep shadows of the cave, pulling off his hat. "It wouldn't be an easy road, and I don't think you could return to the Woodlands, but there is a way for you to survive."

A chill knot of fear settled in Nola's throat.

"I have one dose of ReVamp with me," Julian said. "The injection would be enough to save your life. We'd have to leave immediately for Nightland. Our doctor would be able to administer the other doses."

"You want to stick him with a needle and run for it?" Rebecca said. "Hope the spider and his men don't follow you home?"

"I mean no offense, but I don't think we would be followed," Julian said. "We can move much faster on our own."

"Move faster to where?" Stokes stepped into the mouth of the cave.

"To save your guard's life," Julian said.

"What the hell are you talking about?" Stokes stomped over to Jude. "Get up, Jude."

"I don't think I can, Captain." Jude didn't open his eyes.

"I know your opinion on vampires," Julian said, "and I will freely admit that some of my kind deserve the revulsion you feel. But this man will not live through the night. If he prefers to die, I will not argue with his choice."

Nola gripped Jeremy's hand.

Julian reached into his pack, pulling out a narrow container. "What sort of a monster would I be if I had a way to save a life and didn't offer to help?"

"He'd never be able to walk in the sun again." Al stood in the entrance to the cave, her hands clasped under her chin.

"But he would still be alive," Julian said.

"He wouldn't be Jude," Al said.

"He would," Nola said. "ReVamp is different than Vamp. He'll be healthy and strong. He won't be able to go into the sun, and he'll have to live off blood. But he'll still be the same person."

"You can't know that." Jude's words came out a rasped whisper.

"I do," Nola said. "My best friend was given ReVamp. It saved his life, and it didn't change him."

Jeremy pressed his lips to the top of Nola's head.

"I don't want to die, Captain," Jude said.

Stokes stood over Jude. His dark brow wrinkled in something between loathing and disgust.

"You've been a good guard, Jude," Stokes said.

Nola moved to step forward, ready to plant herself between Stokes and Jude. Jeremy wrapped his arm around her, keeping her pinned to his side.

"Your work isn't done yet, Guard," Stokes said. "So you take that damned shot, and you get ready. Because we've got one hell of a fight in front of us."

———

CHAPTER TWENTY

———

"It's not a pleasant process." Julian knelt beside Jude. "I'm afraid there will be a fair bit of pain."

"Can't be too bad when you lay it out next to dying," Jude said.

Nola wrapped her arms around Jeremy, trying to push away the horrible memory of ice taking hold of her veins.

The ice has already changed me. It can't happen again.

"Once I've administered the injection, we'll have to leave." Julian took the syringe from its case.

The metal of this syringe seemed somehow less frightening than those that held Graylock. Whether it was from the metal gleaming less brightly, or the faint, shimmering liquid held within the glass, Nola didn't know.

"You're just going to take Jude away?" Al knelt next to Jude, holding his hand.

"He'll have to be protected from the sunlight," Julian said. "Though it won't be completely deadly to him right away, it's unwise to risk exposure."

"So stick him with a needle and run. Go back to hiding in your mountain. Wait to see if the Woodlands are destroyed." Rebecca knelt next to the coals, striking two bits of stone together, throwing sparks onto the crumpled bits of brush. "I'd come to think better of you than that."

"I don't think any of us are dumb enough to think we can hide from the domes," Jeremy said. "But Julian's right, we have to get Jude to Nightland."

"Then what?" Al said. "You keep Jude with you forever?"

"The mountain is the safest place for a vampire," Julian said. "But once his transformation is complete, it will be up to Jude to decide where he wishes to live."

"And if the Woodlands have been melted by the spider before Jude's turned into a full nightwalker," Rebecca said, "you'll just have one more for your ranks and one less to be counted among my dead."

"You'll have one more alive and fighting on your side," Julian said. "Nightland will stand with the Woodlands."

"How?" Rebecca blew life into the embers, sparking a blaze that danced against the backdrop of the setting sun.

"We have to talk to Emanuel before we can do anything," Jeremy said. "He's the one who controls Nightland. He needs to know what Nallot can do."

"He'll never let any of you leave the mountain again," Rebecca said.

"He will," Nola said. "Even if it means breaking every pane of glass in the domes, we have to stop Salinger. There's no other way out. Not for us. Not for the people on the highway. We have to fight."

The weight of Jeremy's arms wrapped around her did nothing to stop Nola's hands from shaking.

"I hate to agree with you," Julian said, "but I don't think there is any other choice. The domes have chosen to wage war on all who survive outside the glass. If we hide, we allow them to slaughter more innocent people. They've proven themselves to be horrible monsters. We can't turn our back on that sort of terror and have any hope of retaining our souls."

Jeremy clutched Nola closer to his chest. "We have to find a way across the river, and a place for the vampires to go to ground close enough to the domes to stage an attack."

"If I can do that, you'll fight with us?" Rebecca stood, dusting the soot off her hands.

There is no way across the river. There is no shelter big enough to hide the vampires of Nightland.

"Fight how?" Stokes asked.

"Emanuel will have to give the order," Julian said.

Jude gave a rattling gasp that shook his whole body.

"Jude." Al gripped Jude's sweat-slicked hand. "We're talking about attacking the domes, Jude, so wake the hell up."

"Give him the shot." The words stole the breath from Nola's body. "We can't stand here talking while he dies."

"No." Julian pulled open the top of Jude's shirt. "Though, from experience, it is easier to inject someone who has already lost consciousness." He raised the needle over Jude's chest. "It might not lessen the pain of changing, but having a still target does make my job much easier."

In one swift movement, he plunged the needle into Jude's heart.

Jeremy gasped, tightening his arms around Nola.

"It's okay," Nola whispered.

Jude took a shuddering breath, and screamed. His pale fists clenched. The muscles in his neck bulged.

"What the hell did you do to him?" Al leapt to her feet, aiming her gun at Julian.

"ReVamp is not a kind drug," Julian said, "but it will save his life."

A moan escaped Jude's lips as he began to writhe on the ground.

"Is this what happened to me?" Nola asked. "I remember not being able to move—"

"You didn't." Jeremy shook his head. "You were so still I thought I was too late."

Nola kissed Jeremy's cheek. "You weren't. I'm still here."

With a gasp, Jude went still.

"Is it done?" Stokes asked.

"He won't wake for several hours," Julian said. "Frankly, I don't envy what he's feeling trapped inside his body right now, but all of our ReVamp is made by Dr. Wynne, who the domes so graciously tossed into the outside world. The batch is good. Jude will wake up. I think it best if we are far from here by that time."

"Right." Al laid Jude's hand on his chest. "You're right."

Julian pulled off his sun suit, carefully folding the material and sliding it back into his pack.

"What if you don't make it by sunrise?" Stokes said. "Are you going to leave him out to die?"

"We'll find a place to hide," Jeremy said. "We aren't the domes, Stokes. We don't believe in murder."

Julian lifted Jude, draping the unconscious man over his shoulder.

"One of my people will come to you," Rebecca said. "The one I send to the ledge will speak with my voice. I'll deliver the path to ending the domes."

"We will be waiting for them." Julian gave a nod.

"If they don't come," Stokes said. "If that bastard gets all of us—"

"We'll still break through the glass," Jeremy said. "Salinger isn't staying in there with your granddaughters."

"Then run," Stokes said. "Get Jude to safety before the sun comes back."

"Travel well." Julian skirted around the fire and out into the night.

"Stokes," Jeremy said, "if you find my sister, keep her with you. Don't let her disappear."

Stokes nodded. "That girl was one hell of a fighter. I'll try to get her on our side."

Say something. Say that I'm sorry for the girls who are still trapped behind the glass. That Lilly was right to leave, even if it got her killed. That Stokes was right to take the people he could. To try and save one small part of the domes, even if the rest are doomed under Salinger's rule.

Say I'll fight even if it's against my own mother. That Jude will be strong and able to fight again soon.

Nola met Stokes' gaze. He didn't say anything as Jeremy led her past the fire and out into the night. Neither did she.

The brightness of the flames hid the inside of the cave from view.

"This way." Julian took off, running through the trees.

Nola tore her eyes from the fire, not bothering to ask if Jeremy wanted to be second in their line.

Running felt better than the slow pace they'd been forced to keep before.

When the unchanged humans ran in our line.

The air moved easily in and out of her lungs. The stars provided enough light for her to be able to see the trees she tore past.

She could keep running for a day, maybe more. She and Jeremy could slip so far away Salinger would never find them, not even with his helicopter.

There would be no hope for T. No way to travel that fast with a baby.

We have to fight the domes.

The thought brought with it a terrifying certainty. There was no other way forward. No other path to a future for anyone beyond her and Jeremy. The Northerners wouldn't be able to defend against an attack on their home and wouldn't be fast enough to run away. The vampires of Nightland were defenseless during the day. Salinger could flood the tunnels of Nightland with Nallot, and, as long as the sun was in the sky, the vampires wouldn't be able to flee.

But Jeremy and I could. I could protect him. Lead him far away where Salinger would never be able to hurt him.

She listened to the steady thumping of his boots on the ground behind her.

They could find a place with water and shelter. She could find a way to grow them food. They could figure out how to hunt.

And we would be the last people in this part of the world.

"Nola," Jeremy said, "are you all right?"

"When it's time to fight," Nola said, "we're going together."

"Nola—"

"I wish I could make you hide." Nola leapt across the banks of a frothy stream. "I wish we could live somewhere just the two of us where there's nothing to be afraid of."

"But neither of us could live with that." Jeremy ducked around a tree to run by her side.

"So when it's time to fight the domes, I'm coming with you," Nola said. "I'm fighting with you."

"I..." Jeremy took her hand, his pinky draping over her palm. "I will do everything I can to keep you safe. But I won't take fighting the monsters from you."

"I never thought I'd want to fight," Nola said. "All I ever wanted was to help people. To make all the awfulness we've been stuck with stop."

"We're going to," Jeremy said. "Maybe not the way we'd hoped, but we're going to get Salinger the hell out of here."

"Hear, hear!" Julian said. "I must say, in the years I've known the horror of what Salinger is capable of, I never thought I would be present at his downfall. I don't know how Emanuel will take the news of Nallot or what his plan will be, but I look forward to ending this particular reign of terror."

A reign of terror. And I was bred to be one of the monsters.

Nola tightened her grip on Jeremy's hand.

They stayed behind Julian as he led them farther west. There was no path for them to follow, no sign of the Northerners living in these decaying woods. Twice they were turned back by cliffs too high to jump. But Julian kept running.

Neither Nola nor Jeremy questioned his route. The helicopter and Nallot had ruled out running to the river and following the path back to Nightland from the city. There was nothing to do but run and hope for a clear way to the mountains.

The heat of friction burned Nola's feet, but the pain never progressed.

I should be bleeding. I should be damaged beyond repair.

Julian paused as they reached the top of a hill.

"Is Jude okay?" Nola asked, stopping next to Julian. "Do you need me to carry him?"

"I can carry the weight, Nola." Julian stared east.

Nola followed his gaze.

In the depths of the decaying forest, a wasteland scarred the earth. A wide circle of death where nothing survived.

"If this is what humans insist on doing, I don't blame the earth for trying to rid itself of us," Julian said.

"It's not all humans," Jeremy said. "There are good people, and that's who we're going to fight to protect."

Jude gave a shuddering gasp.

"If you can hear me," Julian said, "I'm sorry for the bumpy ride, but I'm afraid we must keep going. I don't know which will startle Emanuel more, our returning so quickly, or my jumping into the tunnel with a newly minted vampire over my back. We'll find out soon enough, I suppose."

Julian turned south, heading toward the silhouette of the mountains reaching up into the night sky. "We aren't going to reach Nightland before dawn."

"Then we'll find a place to shelter," Jeremy said. "We've made it far enough. I don't think the Outer Guard are going to find us."

"No," Julian said. "I don't think they will. However, Nightland itself could be found. If the Outer Guard are searching so far north, they may be turning their attention west of the domes as well. We would have had to leave Rebecca tonight even if Jude hadn't been in need of another dose of ReVamp. If the Northerners found the path to Nightland, the Outer Guard could as well. If an Outer Guard were to capture a Northerner—"

"They could give up our home," Nola said.

"I'll get you as close to the entrance to Nightland as I can before the sun starts to rise," Julian said. "You'll have to find your own path from there."

"We can do it," Jeremy said.

"Tell Emanuel everything," Julian said. "Make sure he knows to expect a Northern emissary and understands how much of a threat or ally the Northerners can be."

Nola touched the hole in her shirt where the arrow had pierced her flesh. "We will."

"Good." Julian ran south toward the jagged outline of the mountains.

CHAPTER TWENTY-ONE

Nola stood on top of the ridge, looking down at the uneven mound of earth far below.

"You know," Jeremy said, "when we had all those classes in Green Dome on how to properly plant things, I never thought I would be using those digging skills to bury two vampires."

Nola squinted down at the freshly turned earth. From this height, there was no hint of the two men hiding from the sun beneath the layers of dirt.

"I hope we dug deep enough," Nola said.

"Julian said to go. We have to trust him."

Nola looked toward the summit of the mountain. High above, a familiar divot marked the place where two peaks joined, sheltering Kieran's garden. Taking a deep breath, Nola sprinted up the slope.

A faint fatigue pulled on her limbs.

Sleep. I'll have to sleep soon.

The *clatter* of rocks beneath Jeremy's feet followed her up the mountain.

What if Salinger's found Nightland? What if everyone's dead and we're racing back to a tomb?

"Say something nice," Nola said.

"What do you mean?"

Nola could hear the hint of a smile in Jeremy's voice.

"I need to think about something other than the possibility of Julian bleeding from all over his body, or Nightland being flooded with Nallot." Nola's breath hitched in her chest. She pushed herself to run faster, tearing around the bend in the ridge and twisting to follow a new ridge east.

"Okay," Jeremy said. "When all of this is over, you and I are going to run to one of these peaks just for fun. And we'll lay under the stars and watch the heavens move, and we won't be afraid of anything."

"That sounds really nice." Tears burned the corners of Nola's eyes.

"It's going to be amazing," Jeremy said. "Every night I get to hold you in my arms will be amazing. And we're going to have so many wonderful nights, Nola. We just have to keep fighting for a little while longer."

"We can do it." Rocks shifted under Nola's foot. She leapt forward without thought, landing without breaking her stride. "You and me together, we can do it."

"Absolutely we can."

The ruins of the city came into view, nestled next to the banks of the rancid river. Nola's gaze followed the path up from the city, through the woods and the field of brambles, up to a basin between two steep slopes.

"I see the path." Nola veered off the ridgeline and onto the steep mountainside. Her feet barely touched the ground as she leapt down the slope.

Bang!

The sound caught her ears while she was midair. She twisted toward the noise, forgetting to keep her gaze on the ground beneath her.

"Nola!" Jeremy shouted as she hit the rocks below.

Instinct told her to fight for her footing, but the ground slipped away beneath her. A sharp stone cut into her arm as she tumbled down the slope. Her pack banged into her spine, knocking the air from her lungs.

"Nola."

She caught a glimpse of Jeremy chasing her. She reached out and seized a rock, but the force of her fall pulled the stone from the mountainside, sending a cascade of rocks down on her.

Pain burst through the back of her head, stealing her vision. A *crack* sent a fresh wave of hurt through her leg.

The pain of stones pummeling her skin didn't stop, but the ground beneath her held firm.

"Nola, are you okay?"

Hands pulled the weight away from her chest.

Nola gulped in a breath. Shifting her ribs even that small amount sent the agony in her head spinning.

"I'm okay," Nola said. "I'll heal."

"Just hold still. Let me get the rocks off you."

Nola blinked, pulling the gray stones back into focus. A rock the size of her pack pressed on her pelvis, pinning her to the tree that had stopped her fall. She lifted her arm, pushing her hair away from her face. Blood coated her skin, though the cuts had already begun to heal.

"What was that *bang*?" Nola asked.

"I don't know." Jeremy lifted away the stone that had pinned down her right leg. "It came from the east."

"Nightland?"

"Farther away, I think," Jeremy said. "We have to get to Emanuel."

"I think I can walk." Nola sat up, biting back her scream as pain shot through her stomach.

"I can carry you."

"You have to be ready to fight." Nola gasped as she put weight on her right leg. "We don't know what the explosion was."

I shouldn't know what that noise means.

"Dr. Wynne might have to reset your leg." Jeremy wrapped his left arm around Nola's waist, taking most of her weight as they headed down the mountain. His gaze darted between Nola's face, the path down the mountain, and the city far below.

"I don't see any smoke," Nola said.

"I'm not sure if that's a good thing."

The pain ebbed away from her pelvis as they reached the tree line. Signs of life marked the trees, things Nola wouldn't have noticed before. Dirt piled at the base of a trunk where some small creature had dug its home. Bark torn away in patches large enough to feed a man-sized animal.

The basin appeared in the trees below, as welcoming as seeing the door to her home in Bright Dome.

"Do you think they know we're coming?" Nola asked. "Have the guards spotted us?"

"I've never been sent to guard the tunnel. I don't know what the sightlines are like."

Nola shook her head. The movement blurred the edges of her vision. "As safe as Nightland is, it's still not enough. I don't know if it will ever be enough."

"It won't. Not until the domes are no longer a threat."

Neither spoke as they walked into the clearing below the entrance to Nightland.

Nola scanned the trees, searching for any sign of a Northerner hiding in the branches. She took a deep breath, trying to catch the scent of human life.

"It's Jeremy and Nola," Jeremy said, his voice barely loud enough for vampires to hear. "We're coming up."

They stood frozen for a moment, Nola feeling foolish as she listened for a voice welcoming them home.

"Me first?" Nola whispered.

Jeremy bit his lips into a flat line.

"If there were Outer Guard waiting up there, they would have fired on us already," Nola said.

"Can you jump it?" Jeremy asked.

Nola tested her weight on her leg. The pressure sent pain shooting from her ankle to her knee, but she stayed on her feet.

"I'll be okay." Nola bent her knees and jumped, planting her palms on the ledge and leveraging herself up and into the tunnel. Gritting her teeth against the pain of the impact, Nola staggered forward, pulling her weapon from its holster.

Jeremy landed by her side with only the slightest *thump* from his boots.

"Who's up there?" Nola said. "It's Jeremy and Nola. We're back from the scouting mission Emanuel sent us on."

Stell sauntered into the shadows, a frown pursing her lips. "Where's Julian? I was told you two went with him."

"He was delayed," Jeremy said. "He sent us ahead with news for Emanuel."

"Hmm." Stell pulled her knife from its sheath, twisting the point into her finger. "What about Raina?"

"We weren't sent the same way as her," Nola said. "We don't know where she is."

"Pity." A drop of blood fell from Stell's finger. "I was hoping you'd say she'd blown herself up. Ah well, a girl can dream."

"Can we pass?" Nola said. "We need to get to Emanuel."

"Oh sure, sure." Stell stepped aside. "You're on the list of people I'm supposed to let in, and I do take my duty to Nightland seriously. After all, there's a big difference between hoping someone won't come back and keeping them in the sun to burn."

"Right," Nola said.

Jeremy wrapped his arm around Nola's waist, easing the burden on her leg. "Thanks for watching the path."

Nola didn't speak as they passed a group of five heavily armed vampires a hundred feet down the tunnel. She didn't say anything at all until they reached the first window looking out over the mountainside and down toward the city.

"It's people like Stell we're talking about taking to the domes." Nola searched the horizon for smoke from whatever had caused the *bang*. "The last time Emanuel led vampires into the domes, innocent people were killed."

"You don't think we should attack anymore?" Jeremy said.

"I do." Nola limped down the tunnel, leaning against Jeremy. "I wish there were another way, but the domes have fallen too far. They're wiping out outsiders, torturing their own women—"

A growl vibrated Jeremy's chest.

"But we have to protect the ones who are being hurt," Nola said. "There are little kids, and girls like Lilly."

"And to get rid of Salinger, we're going to have to use people like Stell," Jeremy said.

"There has to be a way," Nola said. "Some plan to get rid of Salinger and his guards without letting the kids get hurt."

"I..." Jeremy paused, facing the line of ten guards that blocked the metal door to the sparring room. Desmond stood at the middle of the line, his bow staff resting against his shoulder.

"Back so soon?" Desmond asked in a low, rumbling voice.

"Found what we were looking for a lot faster than we thought we would," Jeremy said.

"Found it how?" One of the bald twins pointed to Nola's stomach. "By letting them cut you to ribbons?"

Nola looked down at her shirt. Dark, dried blood surrounded the place where she'd been struck by the arrow. Smaller, fresher patches of blood marked the rest of her clothes, matted in with the dirt from falling down the mountain.

"If you wanted to bleed, you could have stayed here and let us help," the other twin said.

"I can manage well enough on my own, thanks," Nola said.

"Julian will be coming at nightfall," Jeremy said. "He's going to have a fresh vampire with him. Try and convince Stell to let them in without a fight."

"And if a stranger comes," Nola said, "keep them alive until you've heard from Emanuel. We made some new friends"

Desmond raised an eyebrow but gave a nod and stepped out of their way.

One of the twins dragged open the heavy metal door. "If you want to bleed more, we'll be out here until nightfall."

"Sure thing." The din of sparring vampires swallowed Nola's voice.

The familiar *clang* of metal on metal and shouting and jeering of the fighters banged into Nola's ears. But rather than bring terror, the cacophony soothed Nola's nerves.

Nightland is home. Even the fighting and blood are part of me now.

A few glanced their direction as they made their way past the painted squares, but no one stopped them to ask questions.

We're not Raina or Julian. No one expects us to lead.

"Straight to Emanuel?" Nola said.

"We need to get you to Dr. Wynne," Jeremy said. "The sooner he resets your leg, the better."

"I can wait a few minutes. Emanuel needs to know what's happening."

The corridors were quiet as they made their way to Emanuel's library. There were no children tearing past or workers chatting as they went about their assigned tasks.

"We'll have to leave some of the fighters here," Jeremy said. "To keep Nightland safe."

"Not us though," Nola said.

"No, not us." Jeremy stopped sin front of the carved wooden doors to Emanuel's library.

Nola knocked.

Desmond's standing guard, Raina's in the south, Julian's buried underground. We're already spread too thin.

Nola opened the door and led Jeremy into the library.

The red chair sat vacant in the center of the empty room.

A tingle raced down Nola's spine as her uneven footsteps echoed around the library. She stared at the door to Emanuel's home, waiting for Eden to run through laughing or Dr. Wynne to wander past following some vague and invisible idea. But no one came.

Desmond would have told us if something horrible happened.

She knocked on the door to Emanuel's home, holding her breath until the knob turned.

Bea's weathered face appeared in the crack.

"We're looking for Emanuel," Nola said.

Bea shook her head.

"Julian sent us with important information," Jeremy said. "Nightland is in more danger than we thought."

For a moment, Nola wasn't sure if Bea had heard. After a few seconds, Bea nodded and wandered down the hall in Emanuel's home, leaving the door open behind her.

Jeremy raised an eyebrow at Nola.

She shrugged as much as being half-carried by Jeremy would allow and followed Bea.

Bea waited in the entrance to the kitchen, pointing to the door at the back with one hand while pressing a finger over her lips with the other.

Nola nodded, keeping silent as she and Jeremy maneuvered around the kitchen table.

Dim light and a low voice drifted through the door.

"But the frog didn't want to sleep on the lily pad," Emanuel spoke softly. "'No, no, no,' said the little frog. 'While the glow bugs dance, so will I.'"

Nola peeked through the door.

Emanuel sat at the head of Eden's bed, book in hand, as the little girl's eyes drifted shut.

CHAPTER TWENTY-TWO

The bright lights of Dr. Wynne's lab bored into Nola's eyes.

"It's not that I don't believe what you're telling me is true." Emanuel leaned against the door, his hands tented beneath his chin. "I simply can't understand how such a thing is possible."

"I didn't think I was seeing it right." Nola tried to keep her voice steady as the cold of the table drained her courage. "But the mist from the helicopter melted the trees, and Julian knew what it was right away."

"This isn't going to be the most pleasant task." Dr. Wynne rolled his chair up next to the table. "It will feel better once the bone is properly set, of course."

"Rebecca wants to attack the domes," Jeremy said, "and after seeing what Salinger's weapons can do, I have to agree."

"It's times like this when I miss my equipment in the domes the most." Dr. Wynne pinched and poked at Nola's shin.

"I don't know how far we can trust Rebecca," Emanuel said.

"You trusted me when I came here," Jeremy said. "You knew that after what the domes had tried to take from me, I would never betray you to them. One pass of Nallot from the helicopter and the Woodlands would be destroyed. All of Rebecca's people would be less than ash. Emanuel, I don't know how well they'll do in a battle. I don't know if they have the resources to get us across the river or to shelter your fighters during the daylight. But I do know Rebecca wants to fight. Her people will fight. They've got just as much to lose as we do."

"On the count of three, then," Dr. Wynne said.

"What?" Nola squeaked as he tightened his grip on her leg.

"One, two—"

A *crack* reverberated around the room.

Nola screamed before she knew she was in pain.

"Nola." Jeremy grabbed her hand. "She wasn't ready."

"I sometimes find that's best," Dr. Wynne said.

Nola blinked the spots out of her eyes to find Jeremy glaring at a placid Dr. Wynne.

"Lie still for a moment," Dr. Wynne said. "Don't want to risk the bones slipping out of place and having to do this again."

"Nope," Nola spoke through gritted teeth. "I really don't want that."

"Is there anything else you need from me?" Dr. Wynne rolled his chair back to his desk.

"I don't think so," Emanuel said. "Though we will need to impose until Nola can walk."

"Actually, I wanted to show you something, Dr. Wynne." Jeremy used his free hand to open the dented black case on his hip.

"More Graylock?" Dr. Wynne wheeled back.

"We weren't that lucky," Nola said.

"Any idea what these are for?" Jeremy pulled out the bottle of white pills.

"Hmm." Dr. Wynne opened the bottle, dropping a single pill onto his palm.

With a movement so quick Nola didn't think to stop him, the doctor licked the pill.

"Dr. Wynne!" Emanuel lunged forward, snatching the rest of the pills from Dr. Wynne's hand.

"High grade pain killers," Dr. Wynne said. "It's not the sort of stuff I liked to prescribe even in my dome days." He held his palm up, presenting the licked pill to Emanuel. "Where did you find it?"

"On an Outer Guard who'd been given Graylock. Is there"—Jeremy glanced to Nola—"could there be something wrong with Graylock that would have left him in enough pain to need medicine like this."

Dr. Wynne patted his lips. "My best guess, the pills were given in case of injury. If the guard were to be wounded and not have the time to allow Graylock to heal him, the pills would have kept him from feeling any pain."

"Let him keep fighting while he bled." A horrible twisting seized Nola's gut.

"And these are the men we fight against," Emanuel said.

"We don't have a choice." Nola gritted her teeth as she sat up, expecting pain to shoot from her leg. The mending bone answered with a dull throb.

"How soon do you think the Northerner will arrive?" Emanuel said.

"If Rebecca survived and got back to the Woodlands?" Jeremy said. "Someone could be here in a day or so."

"Ha," Dr. Wynne said, "I sometimes forget how slowly normal people move."

"We need to plan," Emanuel said. "We need to know how we want to attack the domes before the Northerner arrives. We need to be sure those we leave behind are cared for while we're gone."

"And be sure they know what they're to do if you don't make it back," Dr. Wynne said.

Nola held Jeremy's hand tighter.

"I'm not trying to say I doubt any of you." Dr. Wynne fluttered his hands through the air. "But I have worked very hard to keep the children and humans of Nightland alive. I wouldn't be doing my job if I didn't see to their safety."

"You're right, doctor," Emanuel said. "Plans will be made."

"Good." Dr. Wynne turned to the stack of papers on his desk. "She should be fine to walk, best to get moving. Circulation will help you heal."

"Right." Nola rolled down her pant leg and kicked her feet over the side of the metal table.

"Careful." Jeremy took Nola's arms as she stood. "How does it feel?"

Nola bounced on her leg for a moment. "Sore but sturdy."

"When was the last time the two of you slept?" Dr. Wynne didn't look up from his work.

"A couple of days," Nola said. "I think."

"Sleep," Dr. Wynne said. "Both of you."

"We need to plan," Jeremy said.

"Of course you do," Dr. Wynne said. "But the brain doesn't work as well when fatigue has taken over. If you're going to be plotting against the domes, it is my medical opinion that you should do it rested. A few hours now could save lives later."

"Go," Emanuel said. "There is work you can't be a part of. Thank you for finding the Northerners. Now it's my job to prepare Nightland."

"Right." Nola started toward the door.

"Emanuel," Jeremy said, "I know the domes' defenses. I know how the guards work."

Emanuel gave a weary smile. "And I'll need all of that, once I know what my people will be capable of."

"Come on." Nola pulled on Jeremy's hand, drawing him out of Dr. Wynne's lab and into the hall.

Neither of them spoke as they passed the kitchen or walked through the library.

"Does he think we can't do it, or I can't be trusted?" Jeremy asked.

"What do you mean?" Nola's eyes grew heavy as they neared the promise of sleep.

"I'm the best resource Emanuel has," Jeremy said. "I'm good enough to run north, but he doesn't want me to help plan."

"You're not one of his people." Nola stopped in front of the door to Jeremy's room. "Everyone else—Julian, Desmond, Raina—they've all been with him for years."

"Dr. Wynne and Kieran—"

"You're asking him to leave his home and fight," Nola said. "To leave the sanctuary he built for Eden. To him, we're children. He's been working to create Nightland since before we were born. And now we're telling him everything he loves might be taken from him. He's scared and tired. A thousand lives depend on his decisions."

Jeremy wrapped his arms around Nola, pressing his lips to her dirt-dusted hair. "I only have you to worry about, and that's enough to steal my breath when I think about the domes getting anywhere near you."

"He's going to need you," Nola said.

"To tell him how to fight against my father."

"Yeah." She leaned her cheek against Jeremy's chest. "I'm so sorry."

"Don't be." He kissed her head one last time then opened the door to his room. "You aren't the monster, my father is. He gave the order to drop the Nallot."

Nola closed the door behind them. "I wish..."

"Wish what?" Jeremy untied his boots.

"That there was something better for me to say." Nola pulled off her dirt-and-blood covered shirt. "That I could tell you your father wasn't to blame, and the domes weren't evil, and it was all going to be okay, and I wouldn't be lying." The words caught in her throat.

"It's not okay." Jeremy took Nola's hands, kissing both her palms. "None of this is okay. But the only thing I need you to tell me is that you love me. I will fight the whole world, Nola. As long as I'm fighting for you."

"I love you." Nola leaned up on her toes, brushing her lips against his. "More than anything I love you. And whoever we fight, whatever we're fighting for, we do it together."

"Together." Jeremy brushed the tears from her cheeks.

Voices pounded into Nola's ears, but she'd stopped following the thread of the words. They talked in circles over and over again. Emanuel had called them to his library at sunrise. Then the planning had begun. Which direction should they attack from? The likelihood of Salinger being ensconced in the concrete tower that housed the Com Room.

None of it will matter if we can't get across the river. We can't fight if there won't be a place for the vampires to hide during the daylight. We're stuck waiting.

But still they planned.

"If you can't get it done first, there's no point in even trying." Jude's unfamiliar voice shook Nola from her thoughts.

Jude paced in a wide circle around the library. Passing Desmond by the door to the corridor, Kieran by one bookcase and Julian by another, lapping in front of Emanuel who sat silently in his red chair, then Nola and Jeremy who leaned against the far wall.

Nola recognized the need to run burning in Jude's newly strengthened limbs. The way he clenched his hands over and over, the unchanging rhythm of his steps.

He can still feel his second dose running through his veins.

"It can be accomplished." Julian reached his mug out in front of Jude, stopping his circle.

Jude took a deep breath, a look of something between revulsion and bliss taking over his face.

"But if you can't, we're all dead." Jude turned his back on the group to sip from the mug.

"We have enough explosives," Kieran said, "and Raina will know how to do it."

Silence washed over the room.

If she gets back.

She'd missed the deadline Emanuel had given them. She should have come back by sunrise, but she hadn't arrived. Neither had the Northerner.

"And I'm supposed to believe this of someone I've never met?" Jude said.

"Once you meet her, you won't have any doubts," Jeremy said.

"If the Outer Guard don't kill us all before she gets back," Jude said.

"Keep drinking," Julian said. "It will calm you."

"Let me give the unpopular opinion," Desmond said. "We can't assume anyone out there is alive. We can't count on the Northerner arriving or Raina coming back."

"She'll get here," Emanuel said.

"We don't know what caused the explosion yesterday," Desmond said.

"Probably Raina," Kieran said.

"If things are as bad as they seem, we can't afford to keep waiting," Desmond said. "It's only a matter of time before Salinger unleashes some fresh hell."

"What do you propose?" Emanuel leaned forward in his chair.

"We send a scouting party to the river," Desmond said. "See if we can find a way across. Find a shelter on the other side ourselves. Then we take a small team and we fight."

"A small team won't make it back," Emanuel said. "If we go in undermanned, no one will get out."

"Then we don't get out," Desmond said. "There are some things worth dying for, Emanuel."

Nola slipped her hand into Jeremy's.

"I agree with the sentiment," Julian said, "but how would those left behind know if the task had been completed? If we send people out and they don't come back, those left behind will be less protected and still not know if they are, in fact, safe."

"I wish we had coms." Jeremy shook his head. "I never thought about it when I was an Outer Guard. But not being able to check in or give orders in real time, it makes everything harder."

"I can't risk losing you, Desmond," Emanuel said. "Not with Raina gone."

"But we have to do something," Jude said.

And the circle begins again.

Nola shifted her weight to lean against Jeremy's side.

I should be doing something. Helping somehow.

There's nothing to do but wait.

"We have to be sure the humans of Nightland are cared for," Emanuel said. "Their safety has to be our first priority."

Bang, bang, bang.

The pounding on the library door jolted Nola, sending her heart racing.

"Emanuel!" A boy's voice came from the corridor.

Emanuel was up in an instant, wrenching the door open.

Nola reached for the knife on her belt, forgetting she wore no weapons within the halls of Nightland.

A teenaged boy stood in the corridor, his eyes wide as Emanuel stepped toward him.

"Message from the tunnels," the boy said. "There's someone outside looking for you."

"Who?" Emanuel took off down the hall.

"I don't know." The boy chased after him, the rest of the group from the library close on his heels. "I didn't see them. Stell sent word."

"Raina wouldn't wait outside," Jeremy said.

"It's got to be someone from the Woodlands." Jude cut around to run right behind Emanuel. "That means Stokes and Al made it. Rebecca got them back to the woods."

Not everyone gets to survive.

The cacophony in the sparring room stopped as Emanuel burst through the door. The fighters cleared a path, and two men pushed open the door to the outer tunnel before Emanuel made it across the room.

Nola faltered before stepping into the tunnel. It wasn't her place to see if allies or enemies had come.

I went north. I saw Nallot work. I should see this, too.

She tightened her grip on Jeremy's hand as they sprinted down the tunnel.

"Jude, stick to the shadows!" Julian shouted as they neared the first window.

Emanuel turned sideways, skirting the deadly rays of the sun.

Jude slowed, turning to face the interior wall and hunching his shoulders as he sidled by the square of sunlight.

Nola pulled Jeremy through the patch of sun, catching up to Emanuel.

The line of guards came into view up ahead.

"Emanuel," Stell spoke in a hushed tone, "there's someone down there."

"Did you speak to them?" Emanuel asked.

"No, they called up that they wanted to see Emanuel, so we sent for you," Stell said. "They've moved out of view from the shadows. I was told to watch for a stranger, and I'm guessing this is them."

"I'll go see," Jeremy said. "If it's one of Rebecca's people, I might be able to recognize them."

"We don't have weapons," Nola said.

Emanuel looked to Stell, whose pale eyebrows pinched together as she handed her knife to Jeremy.

"I need a knife, too," Nola said.

"You don't—"

Nola silenced Jeremy with a glare.

Stell pulled another knife from her boot and handed it to Nola. "Don't lose my knife."

"I'll do my best." Nola gave a sarcastic smile.

"If it's not who we're expecting, get back in the tunnels," Emanuel said.

Jeremy nodded and stepped out into the sunshine.

The heat of the rays tingled Nola's face. The world seemed to have forgotten how cold it had been only a couple of days before.

Jeremy moved silently out to the edge of the ledge. Nola stepped up by his side to look below.

A woman with a long black braid down her back sat on the ground, staring up at them. Her dark skin had no hint of sores or damage from the sun. She wore Northern brown, and a bow and quiver full of arrows lay by her side.

"Who are you?" Nola asked.

"I'm here to see Emanuel," the woman said.

"That doesn't answer my question," Nola said.

"Rebecca sent me," the woman said. "That should be good enough for you."

"She made it back to the Woodlands?" Jeremy said.

The woman stared at Jeremy.

"What made your people create the gap?" Nola asked.

The woman looked to the struggling trees that surrounded her. "Blight. Took months to get rid of the patch, but we kept it from spreading."

"She's from the north," Jeremy said.

"Bring her up." Emanuel's voice came from the shadows.

Jeremy stepped off the ledge and landed by the woman's feet. If the woman was shocked, she gave no sign as she stood, carefully dusting off her clothes before slinging her bow and quiver over her shoulder.

"If I may." Jeremy reached for the woman's waist. When she didn't protest, he lifted her into the air.

Nola reached down and grabbed the woman's hands. A familiar sense of trepidation tickled Nola's stomach as sense told her pain would come from hoisting the woman's weight. She widened her stance and lifted, feeling nothing but the shift in her balance as she brought the woman up to the edge of the ledge, setting her down on her knees.

"You should build a ladder for guests." The woman stood, peering into the shadows over Nola's shoulder.

"We don't generally allow guests," Emanuel said.

"I suppose I should be grateful you made an exception," the woman said.

"I do not wish for your gratitude," Emanuel said. "Though I do hope you came with information."

"I did," the woman said. "Rebecca wouldn't have sent me otherwise."

"Then please follow us," Emanuel said. "We have food and drink for you."

"I'm not going into your mountain." The woman reached into her pocket.

Jeremy jumped up onto the ledge behind her, gripping Stell's knife.

The woman looked over her shoulder, staring blandly at Jeremy as she pulled a leather scroll from her pocket. She passed the scroll, not to Emanuel in the shadows, but to Nola.

"I've been sent with a map," the woman said. "Be at the blue in two night's time. Get there with enough time to cross the water and get to the black before sunrise. You'll shelter there for the day, and we'll attack at nightfall. Rebecca will bring twenty-three of our people. The black can protect thirty of yours."

"Only thirty?" Jude asked.

The woman looked to him. "Huh. You really aren't dead."

"Nightland has more fighters to offer," Emanuel said.

"We don't have more dark," the woman said. "Bring any more than thirty, and their deaths are your responsibility when the sun takes them. Do you have any messages for Rebecca?"

"Only my thanks for her offering shelter to my fighters and a path across the river," Emanuel said.

The woman nodded and turned back to the ledge.

"That's all?" Nola said. "You came all the way here and you're already leaving?"

"I trust Rebecca," the woman said, "but I don't trust night-walkers enough to stroll into a mountain filled with blood drinkers. You have the information I have. Our people will bring arrows and knives and fight to the death. Bring what you will to help stop the spider. My people have chosen their sacrifice. Bring yours to the blue."

The woman stepped around Jeremy to sit on the ledge. Grabbing the rock, she twisted, lowering herself before dropping to the ground so softly unchanged ears wouldn't have noticed the sound.

Trying to ignore the feeling of a hundred eyes watching her, Nola stepped into the shadows, handing the scroll to Emanuel. "I'd like to see the map."

Emanuel untied the thin cord that held the scroll shut.

Jeremy leaned over Nola's shoulder as Emanuel unrolled the map.

Their mountain marked the southwest corner. A red line laid out a path that wound east of the rancid swamp marked in gray paint. The Nallot wasteland had been marked in yellow. The red path led them west of the damage to a blue triangle on the bank of the river.

"What is that?" Nola pointed to a black square on the far side of the river across the hills from the domes.

"I have no idea," Emanuel said. "But I hope it will provide enough shelter."

Nola leaned closer to the map, studying the series of circles that made up the domes.

Home.

CHAPTER TWENTY-THREE

"It's not right," T said.

"What's not right?" Nola peered into the box of apples T had been counting through. The fruit was ripe and undamaged, though none of the produce in Nightland would live up to Lenora Kent's expectation of perfection.

T glanced to Bea's door in the back of the pantry and to Kieran working by the barrels along the wall. "This whole project is pointless," T whispered.

Kieran's neck stiffened.

"We're spending all this time preparing food packages, and for what?" T said.

"Emanuel is being careful," Nola said. "He wants to make sure everyone is protected."

"Protected?" T pulled a bundle of empty sacks from under the table. "He wants to lead an attack on the domes. Fine, I get it. But pretending that, if things go badly, sending the human survivors scattering into the wild with a bag of food will somehow magically keep them alive is nothing more than a fairytale he's feeding the children."

We don't leave for the north until tomorrow night and people are already scared.

"If people have supplies—" Nola began.

"You don't get it," T said. "You've never been hungry. You've never wondered where you were supposed to sleep, or if there would be any water safe enough to drink. We're budgeting out food for people to carry, but if there isn't a way to get more, everyone who takes one of these sacks will die."

"We're giving everyone enough for a week," Kieran said. "That's as much as most will be able to carry. And we're going to put a couple of seeds in each package."

"We'll all be long dead by the time any seeds can grow." T banged her hands on the table. "We don't need pretty promises of safety, or packages of food so it will take us longer to die. This was supposed to be a place where we could survive and it's all just shit!" Hands trembling, T stormed out of the pantry, slamming the door behind her.

Nola stared at the door, her mind warring with her feet's urge to run after T.

There's no truth I can give her that will make this better.

"Well," Kieran said as the sound of T's heavy footsteps faded, "I don't suppose you going after her before she upsets any of the others would help."

"She's scared," Nola said. "Everyone is. T's due soon, and now she's packing food in case she has to deliver her baby on the side of a mountain."

The tang of fear had filled the tunnels of Nightland for the last day, ever since Emanuel had ordered Nightland to begin preparations for battle and evacuation.

"My dad will look after her," Kieran said. "In Nightland or in the wild. He's got his medical bag packed. He'll stick with T and do everything he can to help her."

Nola picked up a sack, shaking it out and starting a neat stack. Hundreds of food sacks had to be packed and distributed.

In case.

We're abandoning them to wait in the dark. Leaving them without any way to know what happened if we don't come back.

"I hate it," Nola said. "I should be staying with T. I'm abandoning her just like Charles did."

Nola shook another sack, sending dust flying into the air.

"Do you want to stay here?" Kieran moved the pile of sacks out of Nola's reach.

"I can't." Nola pinched the bridge of her nose. "I can't send Jeremy without me, without anyone else who can go into the sun unprotected. Emanuel can only bring thirty vampires, adding Jeremy and me makes the number thirty-two. And I don't think I can live with myself if I let Emanuel go after the domes without me."

"Because you'd be ashamed not to fight or because you're afraid of what he'll do?"

Nola looked into Kieran's black eyes. Eyes she'd caught a glimpse of as he fled from the domes, leaving blood and pain behind him.

"I know what the domes did to you and your dad is unforgivable. What they did to me on that bridge is unforgivable. Using fire packs in the city is unforgivable. Spraying Nallot is unforgivable. Making us even consider leaving Nightland to attack them is unforgivable." The table cracked beneath Nola's grasp. She stared down at the ruined wood. "Sorry. I'm sorry."

"You don't have to apologize for being angry, or for being right." Kieran took her hands in his.

"Nikki died, Kieran." Nola blinked the haze of tears from her eyes. "She was shallow and couldn't remember which dome classes were supposed to be held in, but she never hurt anyone. She lived in the domes, but she never understood the harm they were doing."

"None of us did."

"How many more Nikkis are there going to be when Night-land attacks?"

"Emanuel will do everything he can to make sure people who aren't fighting aren't hurt."

"But we get rid of Salinger and then what?" Nola pulled her hands from Kieran's grasp as the need to run seized her lungs. She paced by the table, wishing the pantry were large enough for her to sprint in circles. "We can't just ask him to leave nicely. We're going to have to kill him or force him out. Either way, we'll have to damage the domes."

"You're right." Kieran leaned against the table, his gaze tracking Nola's movement.

"So we shatter the glass and decimate the Outer Guard," Nola said. "Then what?"

"We come back to Nightland."

"But what about the Nikkis we leave behind?" Nola said. "You've heard Julian. The domes are a delicate ecosystem. If we shatter the glass, how will they fix it?"

"We live without glass."

"But what if they can't? Do the pregnant women Salinger will leave behind deserve to die? Because they could. And justified or not, it will be our fault."

"So you think we shouldn't attack?" Kieran leaned on the table, a line creasing his forehead.

Nola recognized that look. The reasoning Kieran. Sorting through a problem that would give their classmates trouble. Sorting through his father's jumbled thoughts to find the spark of genius.

"We have to." Nola leaned against the other side of the table, focusing on Kieran's face.

Get rid of the wrinkle in his brow. Solve that problem first.

"If we don't attack, the domes won't stop until all of us are dead," Nola said.

"But if we destroy the domes, we kill innocent people."

"I don't know if any of us are innocent," Nola said. "But people who have never tried to hurt anyone will die. Even if Emanuel could keep his fighters from killing anyone but the guards, the domes survivors won't be able to keep everything running with the glass shattered."

"Break the glass, and you can't keep the domes functioning," Kieran said. "The entire system relies on technology."

"If the survivors leave the domes, they'll die." Nola dug her knuckles into her eyes. "When the domes kicked you and your father out, your lungs couldn't handle the outside world. You didn't have the immunities you needed. It would be the same for them. And, even if Emanuel would agree to it, we couldn't even take in the domes' children."

"We're doing fine on food, but not well enough to support a few hundred extra food eaters."

"I just can't accept it." Nola dug her fingers into her curls, relishing the pain it brought. "To save people, we have to kill people. I want to survive. I want T and her baby to survive, but I don't want blood on my hands."

"Then we find another way."

"What other way? We can't just hide in these caves and wait to be slaughtered."

The crease disappeared from Kieran's brow as the crinkle of a smile appeared at the corners of his eyes.

"What?" Nola leaned farther across the table. "What?"

"Make it impossible to justify the cost of the fight." Kieran grinned.

"What do you mean?" Nola asked.

"We don't have to win," Kieran said. "We just have to make it impossible for them to."

CHAPTER TWENTY-FOUR

Nola gripped the edge of the bed as her gaze darted from Jeremy to Kieran.

"It makes sense," Jeremy said. "I'm not an expert on how the dome computers work—"

"But the domes have their own experts." Kieran leaned against the door to the hall as though trying to sink through the stone and back out into the corridor. "It's not our responsibility to fix it. We're just trying to leave them with something salvageable."

"Getting in won't be easy." Jeremy ran his hand over the scruff on his face.

"None of this is going to be easy," Nola said. "There is no easy plan, but at least ours might not end with a thousand dead Domers."

"How many dead vampires are we going to have on our hands?" Jeremy met Nola's gaze.

If people die, it will be because of our plan.

"No matter how we attack, not all of us are making it back to Nightland," Kieran said. "Every one of us going knows that."

"You're going?" Nola stood.

"I have to," Kieran said. "I know the domes. None of the others do."

"Emanuel won't allow it," Nola said. "He has to keep you here to grow food."

"He already agreed to let me go. It only took about an hour of me reciting the layout of the domes for him to admit he needs me." Kieran gave a half-hearted smile. "That was before you and I even started on our plan."

"Does he want Nola to stay here?" Jeremy asked.

"I won't." Nola stepped across the tiny room to lay her hand on Jeremy's chest. "If you go, I go. And they'll need both of us to pull this off."

"But he wanted one of you here to make sure the gardens—"

"We've packed up food bags for the survivors to take," Kieran said. "If this doesn't go well, there will be no garden to tend. He needs all three of us at the domes. I spent the time you were gone writing out everything I know about the gardens."

"Kieran." Nola searched his black eyes for a hint of fear.

Kieran shrugged. "Honestly, it didn't take as long as I thought it would. Dad has the papers. He'll keep them safe, and if he has to run, the papers will go with him."

"And he'll be with T," Nola said.

"We can't be everywhere and protect everyone," Kieran said. "All we can do is our best and hope people are strong enough to survive without us."

"He's right." Jeremy wrapped an arm around Nola's waist, letting her lean against his side. "Yours is the best plan we've got."

"Do you still have your uniform?" Kieran asked.

Jeremy kissed the top of Nola's head before letting go of her to open his dresser drawer. His black Outer Guard uniform lay perfectly folded inside.

"It's been torn," Nola said.

"As long as they don't see me in it until after the fighting's started, I don't think any of them will notice," Jeremy said.

"We should go to Emanuel," Nola said.

"See if he'll even agree," Jeremy said.

"Emanuel may be desperate to protect Nightland," Kieran said, "but he's still logical. He'll understand."

"We hope." Jeremy reached for the doorknob.

Kieran placed his hand on the knob first. "Thank you. For listening even though I helped come up with the plan."

"I never said I didn't think you were smart," Jeremy said. "I'll listen to whoever has a plan that will keep Nola safe."

Nola froze, watching Kieran and Jeremy stare at each other.

"It's good to be on the same side." Jeremy offered his hand.

A crack in Nola's chest mended as the two shook hands.

"You get to be the one to talk to Emanuel," Jeremy said. "You know him better than either of us. He's more likely to listen to you."

"Best get to it." Kieran opened the door to the hall. "It's probably good Raina hasn't gotten back yet. She'd fight us on every detail."

"Why?" Raina leaned against the wall in the hall. "What on earth is so important that Kieran and the lovebirds would lock themselves in a room together? Unless the plan *was* to lock yourselves in the room together." Raina winked at Nola.

Heat rushed to Nola's cheeks.

"When did you get back?" Kieran asked. "Were you hurt? What took you so long?"

"Asking too many questions at once bores me," Raina said.

"When did you get back?" Nola asked.

"Not long ago," Raina said. "But I had to talk to Emanuel, tell him all about my southern excursion before I came to find you."

"Do you have any news?" Kieran said.

"Not that has to do with your mushrooms," Raina said. "Though from the looks of it, your interests are branching out."

"Does Emanuel want us in the library?" Nola asked.

"Not as much as I want to know what the three of you are

chatting about that I'll hate so badly," Raina said. "Come on, give me a clue."

"We shouldn't keep Emanuel waiting," Jeremy said.

"Sure." Raina tossed her scarlet and purple streaked hair behind her shoulder. "That could be fun too. It's not like I just spent days stomping all over creation. Let's do what you want to do." She sauntered toward the library.

"What kept you out so long?" Nola said.

"This and that," Raina said.

"Did you blow something up a couple of days ago?" Jeremy asked.

"Wouldn't you like to know?" Raina opened the doors to the library, stepping aside to let Nola and Jeremy pass.

"Jeremy," a female voice spoke from inside the library.

"And boom," Raina said.

A streak of black raced across the room, pummeling into Jeremy.

A head of short, dark blond hair blocked Nola's view of Jeremy's face.

"Gentry?" Nola said.

"You're actually alive." Gentry stepped back, taking her younger brother's face in her hands.

"Like I'd lie." Raina stepped into the library, heading toward three others dressed in filthy and worn Outer Guard uniforms.

"How did you get here?" Tears rolled down Jeremy's cheeks.

"We spotted Raina, and I knew she'd been with Nola when she disappeared," Gentry said.

"That's not really how it happened, but sure," Raina said. "Took me a little longer to get back since even fancy trained Domers are still slow as hell. But it seemed like you might want to see her."

Jeremy stepped away from his sister, reaching Raina in a few quick strides.

Before she could speak, he'd pulled Raina into a hug, his mass covering everything but her brightly colored hair.

"Thank you," Jeremy said.

"Don't get mushy." Raina backed away from Jeremy's embrace. "I'm morally opposed to feelings, and you'll make me regret hauling four lost humans all the way to Nightland."

"Right." Jeremy nodded. "Thanks." He turned to the other three Outer Guard.

Nola recognized the woman from the domes, but she'd never seen the two men before.

"Thanks for sticking with my sister," Jeremy said.

"She's a pretty convincing leader," the woman said.

"And you'll all be an asset to Nightland," Emanuel said.

Nola turned toward his chair for the first time.

Emanuel stood, his gaze drifting from Jeremy to Gentry. "I'm afraid you've arrived at a difficult time. I built Nightland to be a safe haven for vampires and humans, but the domes and Salinger seem determined to destroy everything outside their control."

"Yeah," Gentry said, "that's the gist of it. They wouldn't even let us give an evacuation order before they started dropping fire packs on the city."

"We're going to attack," Jeremy said. "Things have gotten worse since you left. Salinger sent down a mandatory breeding order."

"What?" Gentry said.

"We can't let him stay in control," Jeremy said.

"We have a plan." Nola turned to Emanuel. "One that might end better for everyone."

"Does it involve lots of blood?" Raina grinned.

"Hopefully not," Kieran said, "but it would take some explosives."

"I'm moderately intrigued," Raina said.

"You can't attack the domes." One of the male Outer Guard stepped forward.

"I haul you all the way here, and that's what I get?" Raina said. "A *sorry Salinger is killing people, but don't attack the domes?*"

"It's not that you'd be wrong to do it," the female guard said. "He means it can't be done. Salinger has made them too strong."

"You have no idea who you're dealing with," Raina said. "Spill the plan, Kieran."

"We should go to the kitchen," Emanuel said. "Let our new friends find food and rest. You'll have to forgive us." Emanuel bowed to the guards. "First generation vampires like Raina and myself often forget how immediate the needs of humans can be."

"We can wait," Gentry said.

"I insist," Emanuel said. "Jeremy, Nola, take them down to Bea. She'll feed them and arrange a room for them to share."

"We should stay," Nola said.

"It's okay," Kieran said. "I won't leave out any of the details. Take care of the Domers."

"Thanks," Jeremy said. "Come on, we'll get you fed."

"Sure." Gentry turned to Emanuel. "Thank you for your hospitality."

"In a world where allies are hard to find, we must make the best of those who come our way," Emanuel said.

"This way." Jeremy opened the door to the corridor. "If you've been outside since the city burned, you probably need a good meal."

"Eating would be nice," one of the men said.

Nola watched Emanuel lead Kieran and Raina into his home.

"Does he not trust you or not trust us?" Gentry said.

"You," Jeremy said.

"It's okay," Nola said. "Kieran will convince them."

"Convince them of what?" Gentry said.

Jeremy glanced to Nola. "Nothing that will happen before you eat."

Shaking her head, Gentry followed Jeremy out into the hall. Nola walked at the back of the group.

Am I protecting them, or guarding against them?

"How long have you been here?" Gentry trailed her fingers along the stone wall as they walked toward the pantry.

"We got here two nights after I left," Jeremy said.

"*Left* is a hell of a way to put it," the female guard said.

"That's rich coming from you, Bishop." Jeremy glanced over his shoulder, a grin on his face. "You ended up here, too."

"Shit happens," Bishop said.

"None of us planned on leaving," the older of the two men said. "But when they plant you at the perimeter of a city and start dropping fire packs on it, your day doesn't go according to plan."

"The world isn't split into dome citizens and Vampers," Gentry said. "I swore I would give my life for the domes. I never promised them my soul."

"And how can you let innocent people burn and claim you still have one?" Bishop said.

"We were in the city when it burned," Jeremy said.

"We?" Gentry said.

"Nola and I. We were looking for someone. We found one of the groups you'd tried to save. You left them near Bellevue. The people, they got out."

"Good." Gentry's voice tightened. "We tried to go back for them, but there wasn't a path through the flames."

"The important thing is that you tried," Jeremy said. "The domes decided to slaughter people, and you tried to help. Even if they hadn't made it out, it wouldn't have been your fault. It's the domes."

"It's Salinger," the younger of the male guards said. "I was in the first batch the Incorporation sent. This was going to be my new permanent placement. I thought everything was going to be okay. Then he came in, and I couldn't see anything in my future but blood and death."

"It'll be——" Jeremy cut himself off. "Don't give up. We aren't done yet." He stopped in front of the door to the pantry, knocking loudly before speaking. "Emanuel sent me down with some new people who need food and a bed."

Silence answered.

"Should you knock again?" the young man asked.

"Hungry, Dave?" Bishop raised a singed eyebrow.

"It's best if we wait," Nola said. "No one rushes Bea."

"What sort of food do you have here?" Dave asked.

"I hope you like mushrooms," Jeremy said.

The door to the pantry opened, and Bea peered out into the hall, her already wrinkled forehead furrowing into thick lines.

"Sorry to bother you, Bea." Jeremy gave a polite nod. "This is Gentry, Bishop, Dave, and..."

"Jefferson." The older guard reached out his hand, which Bea stared at without speaking.

"Emanuel wanted us to bring them here to get food and said you could find a place for them to sleep," Nola said.

Bea shuffled away from the door, leaving it open behind her.

"Don't touch anything she doesn't give you," Jeremy said.

"Really?" Gentry mouthed to her brother.

Jeremy nodded and bowed the others into the pantry.

The sacks of packed food waited at the bottom of the shelves.

Only a day before we leave.

I may never know if Bea had to use the sacks.

Nola ended up by Jeremy's side without knowing she had made the decision to move. He wrapped his arms around her, kissing the top of her head as Bea laid out beans, dried beef, and seedy bread.

With a sigh Bea headed for the door at the back of the pantry.

"Eat up," Jeremy said.

"Thanks," Dave said.

Nola twisted, keeping her back pressed to Jeremy.

While the other three guards ate, Gentry stared at Jeremy and Nola.

"You really did leave because of her," Gentry said.

Jeremy tightened his arms around Nola. "They were going to kill her."

"Right." Gentry ruffled her short hair. "Right."

"I didn't ask him to," Nola said. "Everything just sort of spiraled, and we ended up here."

"With everything that's happening in the domes, I'm not sorry we left," Jeremy said. "Gentry, none of us would have been able to stand by and let Salinger burn a city or treat the domes women like animals to be bred."

"I want in," Gentry said.

"What?" Jeremy said.

"However Emanuel is planning on attacking the domes, I want in." Gentry stared at Jeremy, every bit the Outer Guard her father had raised her to be.

"You can't," Jeremy said. "With how fast we're going to be moving, it would take being a vampire or having Graylock for you to keep up."

"So I'm just supposed to sit here?" Gentry said. "After how far we came to get here, I should just relax in a cave? Bond with Nola, since you two are apparently a real thing now."

"I won't be here," Nola said. "I'm going with Emanuel."

"Gonna ride piggy back?" Gentry said.

"Nola's had Graylock," Jeremy said. "When I found her, she was dying, and I had my triage kit."

"What?" Gentry said.

The other guards turned to stare.

"I can run it on my own," Nola said.

"Nola's like me," Jeremy said. "I made her like me."

CHAPTER TWENTY-FIVE

I should sleep.

Nola pinched the bridge of her nose, willing her eyes to find some hint of fatigue. The sun had risen outside the caves hours ago. As soon as the day ended, they would be leaving for the north, running toward the plan Nola and Kieran had built.

If people die, it will be my fault.

Jeremy had taken refuge in the sparring room, fighting away the words Gentry had shouted at them.

Is she mad that he saved me, or that he followed me?

Nola shook her head, trying to break away from the awful thought.

Gentry wanted to take Graylock from the beginning. Now I've had it, and she hasn't. I'm stronger than she is.

T had refused to look her in the eye ever since she stormed out of the pantry. Beauford had taken the same approach, staying close to T's side, as though the evacuation order might come down at any moment.

I'm hurting everyone. All I want to do is help, and I keep hurting everyone.

"I don't want to do this anymore." Her words rang dully

around Jeremy's empty room. "Our room. This is our room, in our home, which I'm trying to save so we can have a life." Nola looked up to the stone ceiling. "And now I'm talking to myself."

She yanked on her shoes, giving one last, longing look to the bed before heading out into the hallway.

A strange scent caught her nose as she moved toward Emanuel's library.

Fresh blood.

Nola shivered but kept moving toward the door. One drop of red stained the handle on the library doors.

"Emanuel?" Nola stepped into the library.

The room was empty. Everyone else in Nightland was either sleeping or preparing.

"And I'm wandering," Nola said. "And still talking to myself."

The scent of blood thickened in the library. Red dots marred the floor, leaving a path to Emanuel's home.

"Eden." Nola sprinted for the door, wrenching it open before knocking. The trail of red didn't lead to the kitchen, but farther down the hall, stopping at the metal door to Dr. Wynne's laboratory.

Nola banged on the door. "Dr. Wynne, are you okay? Dr. Wynne?"

"I'm fine." Dr. Wynne's voice carried through the door. "Quite unharmed. You have no need to worry."

The false brightness of his tone shot fear into Nola's stomach that screaming couldn't have managed.

"I'm coming in." Nola twisted the knob, half-expecting the door to be locked. But the handle turned easily, and Nola stepped into the laboratory. More spots of blood shone on the floor, leading to the metal table where Gentry sat, eyes closed, jaw clenched.

"What happened?" Nola reached for Gentry. "Did one of the vampires attack?"

"No." Dr. Wynne fluttered his hands through the air. "No sort of attack. No harm at all, really. Gentry is extremely healthy."

"But there was blood," Nola said, "down the hall and leading here. Gentry, what happened?"

"Perhaps it's best if we leave her to a nice rest." Dr. Wynne shooed Nola toward the door. "Not long left to get everything ready, and our new, former guard friends have just arrived."

"But—" Nola took a breath to begin arguing with Dr. Wynne, but a scent caught on her tongue. Something more familiar than the fragrance of stone and more frightening than the smell of blood. "What did you do?" Nola rounded on Dr. Wynne.

"It wasn't him." Gentry spoke through gritted teeth. "I did this."

"Did what?" Nola smacked the table where Gentry sat. "Gentry, what did you do?"

Gentry shivered as she looked at Nola. "I will not be left behind while my baby brother fights."

"I didn't think," Dr. Wynne said. "She asked to see the samples. I only turned my back for a second, and then it was too late."

"What do you mean *too late*?" Nola said.

"I've been a guard for two years longer than my brother," Gentry said. "I've fought Vampers and wolves. I've watched my friends die, and I've watched them be changed so wounds can't kill them. I will not sit back and let my brother go up against Salinger."

"We're not—"

"You're going to the domes, and I'm coming with you." Gentry held up a blood-covered palm. The wound on her hand had been completely healed.

"What did you do?" Nola said.

"Asked to see a dose of Graylock and shoved the venom into my veins," Gentry said.

"I really didn't consider she'd do anything of the sort," Dr. Wynne said.

"We don't have enough!" Nola banged the table again. "We don't have three full doses. You're going to die!"

"We all have to go sometime." Gentry stood, her legs shaking beneath her. "You and Jeremy are going to the domes, and I'm coming with you. If I don't get in the glass and find more Graylock, then I die. Do not try to sideline me, Nola Kent. I will do whatever it takes to win."

"It's not worth—"

"Do not tell me what my death is worth." Gentry pushed her shoulders back, showing no fear of the ice that raged through her veins.

"We're leaving soon," Nola said. "We're running north, and you have to have another dose tomorrow."

"I stabbed myself in the heart once. I can do it again." Gentry stepped toward the door.

Nola planted herself in the way, refusing to cower in front of Gentry.

"I need to see Emanuel," Gentry said. "No point in waiting to tell him he's got another fighter running with his pack."

"And if he forbids you from going?" Nola said. "He doesn't know you. He doesn't trust you. He might not want you running right back to your father. Did you even think about that?"

"I am going to fight," Gentry said. "I am going to stop that monster from destroying everything good about my home. If I have to find my own way across the river, so be it. I'm coming."

"And if Emanuel locks you up?" Nola said.

"Then I'm glad I made myself strong enough to fight back."

"If I may?" Dr. Wynne waved timidly. "I have known both of you since you were too young to remember being brought to me for medical treatment. I cared for you during your early years, just as I've cared for Eden. I knew your parents, just as I know Emanuel."

"Thank you for taking care of us," Nola said.

"It's not about thanks," Dr. Wynne said. "I simply want to offer a bit of advice."

"If it involves me not taking Graylock, you're a little late," Gentry said.

"When you speak to Emanuel, don't lie," Dr. Wynne said. "Don't pretend you're going for his good, or for the good of Nightland. Tell him the truth. A monster has taken your home, and you intend to slay the beast."

"With my bare hands if I can."

"Show him that," Dr. Wynne said. "That is a truth he can believe without knowing the teller."

"You think he'll say yes?" Gentry said.

"No," Dr. Wynne said, "but it's the only way I can imagine him not saying no."

"We need to find Jeremy," Nola said. "He should be in the sparring room."

"I'm not asking my baby brother's permission."

"He should know first," Nola said.

He should know the clock is ticking down on your life.

"Where's Emanuel?" Gentry turned to Dr. Wynne.

"I have no idea. Kieran would know, but I'm honestly not sure where he is right now either. He came in a few hours ago to say goodbye." The doctor's voice cracked.

"Not goodbye," Nola said. "Kieran will be back soon. You made him to survive."

Dr. Wynne nodded, puffing his hair into even more of a cloud than usual. "So I did."

"Someone in the sparring room will know where Emanuel is," Nola said.

"Then let's get to it," Gentry said.

"Wait." Dr. Wynne reached into a cabinet, pulling out a syringe filled with deep black Graylock. "Good luck, both of you."

Tears burned Nola's eyes. She nodded to the doctor, not knowing what words to say, and opened the door to the hall.

There were no voices coming from the kitchen or stories being read in Eden's room. The only sign of recent human habitation was the lingering scent of Gentry's blood. Nola breathed through her mouth on the way through the library, trying not to wonder what Gentry had done to her hand to leave such a trail behind.

"I didn't do it to spite you," Gentry said after she'd closed the library door behind them.

"I believe you."

"There has to be a part of this secret plan I can be used for," Gentry said.

Nola stopped in the middle of the hall, closing her eyes and trying to picture actual people carrying out the plan she and Kieran had formed in the pantry.

"You can be," Nola said. "Every vampire in Nightland could be used if there were a way to bring them all."

"Then be grateful for my help," Gentry said. "You've got one more trained and capable person fighting by your side."

"If Emanuel allows it." Nola stopped at the entrance to the sparring room. The thick metal door blocked the path forward. "Why is it closed?"

"I've never walked this direction in this tunnel, so how the hell should I know?"

Gritting her teeth to keep from speaking, Nola raised her hand and knocked on the metal door.

A dull *thunk* carried down the hall.

What if the Outer Guard are here? What if they blocked the passage to save us all?

But the heavy bolts hadn't been slid into the wall.

The door whined as it was pulled open a crack.

"What?" Raina glared out at them.

"We're looking for Emanuel," Gentry said.

"Why?" Jeremy asked from the corridor behind Nola.

Nola spun to face Jeremy. "I thought you were sparring."

"I was." Jeremy's brow furrowed as he glanced between Gentry and Nola. "But we're leaving soon, so everyone who's going is being called to the sparring room. I went to our room to get you."

Heat rose in Nola's cheeks.

"Perfect," Gentry said. "If this is where the squad is rallying to fight, then I've found the right place."

"What are you talking about?" Jeremy said.

Nola backed toward the sparring room door, ducking under Raina's arm and into the giant stone room.

"What the hell were you thinking?"

Nola winced at Jeremy's shout.

The weapon cages were open. Desmond and Julian worked together, pulling out swords, staffs, knives, and guns, making one long line along the far wall. Kieran worked near the outer door, checking the sun suits for damage, preparing them for the vampires who would defend Nightland if their attack on the domes failed.

Emanuel stood in the middle of the room, staring at the door to Nightland.

"I'm going to fight." Gentry's voice rang around the room.

"What's happening?" Emanuel asked.

"Gentry tricked Dr. Wynne and dosed herself with Graylock so she can come with us," Nola said. "She wants to fight."

Emanuel nodded. His face betrayed neither anger, nor amusement. A mask had taken the place of his usual knowing determination.

"Are you okay?" Nola asked.

"I said goodnight to my daughter," Emanuel said. "I won't be here when she wakes up."

"You're coming with us?" Nola said.

"I have yet to meet Rebecca. There are decisions to be made

on Nightland's behalf that I would not lay on anyone else's shoulders," Emanuel said.

"Besides," Raina said, "what kind of king doesn't ride into battle with his people?"

The door from the corridor pushed open. Stell and the twins entered, all of them glancing back at Gentry and Jeremy, who stood close together, speaking in hushed voices while glaring daggers at each other.

"If you want to say goodbye to anyone, now's the time," Raina said.

"I"—Nola tried to swallow, but her mouth had suddenly gone too dry—"I don't have anything to say to anyone that would make leaving any easier."

"For you, or for them?" Emanuel asked.

"Neither," Nola said.

"For what it's worth," Raina said, "T and Beauford made it a long time without you. If you die tomorrow, it'll be just another sad blip on their radar of tragedy."

"Raina, don't," Kieran said.

"I'm not a blip," Nola said. "And neither are you, Raina, even if that's all you want to be."

"I'm not a blip." Raina grinned. "I'm a boom." Tossing her hair over her shoulder, she sauntered toward three large black packs lined up by the far wall.

"Is there anything I can do to help?" Nola turned her tear-brightened eyes away from the door as three large men entered.

"I don't know," Kieran said. "We're traveling so light, there isn't really anything to pack."

"Jeremy and I will need food and water," Nola said, "and maybe Gentry, I guess."

"T made up a pack for you," Kieran said. "She packed enough food for a week. I didn't have the heart to tell her you didn't need that much."

"Then Nola and Jeremy will have enough to share." Gentry

strode up to them, the pink in her cheeks the only hint of her anger.

"We should talk," Emanuel said.

"I have to go with you," Gentry said, her gaze level with Emanuel's black eyes. "Salinger is a demon inside my home."

"And when we have to shatter the glass?" Emanuel asked. "When we have to fight against those whom you very recently called comrades in arms? Will you turn against us, or stay the course? I can't allow you to run by our side if you will turn your weapons on my people the moment Domer blood begins to fall."

"I won't," Gentry said. "Salinger needs to be stopped."

"We won't be fighting one man," Emanuel said.

"Sometimes you have to cut down part of the forest to stop the blight from spreading," Jeremy said. "Gentry understands that."

CHAPTER TWENTY-SIX

The pack weighed heavy on Nola's back.

Faint whispers drifted up from the back of the line. Thirty vampires waited behind Jeremy, Nola, and Gentry, anticipating the setting of the sun.

Jeremy stood closest to the open air, beyond the shadows that protected the vampires, his gaze scanning the forest below. He wore a large black pack and his torn Outer Guard uniform. The sight of him dressed as the enemy sent shivers down Nola's spine.

She looked down at her own clothes. Bishop's shoes had been too large for her to wear, but Nola had pulled on the rest of the former guard's uniform without argument, trying not to let the unfamiliar feel of the oversized clothes swallow her courage.

Jeremy and I are not a part of the domes.

Nola wanted to touch his hand, to feel the warmth of his skin against hers. To say his name and watch a smile twinkle into being at the corners of his eyes.

We don't have time. We're racing the sun itself.

The sky turned from red to gray as the sun dipped behind the mountains.

Gentry inched closer to the opening, standing shoulder to shoulder with her brother.

Nola's heart raced in a way running for hours could no longer achieve.

Jeremy glanced behind to Nola then stepped off the edge of the ledge. Gentry dropped from view a split second later, not even pausing to consider the fall.

Nola stepped off the ledge, her hand instinctively reaching for the knife at her hip.

Jeremy and Gentry had moved to the north side of the basin. Nola darted to Jeremy's side as Julian jumped down from the ledge. He looked up to the sky before clicking his tongue.

Nola sensed rather than heard the vampires surge toward the mouth of the tunnel.

Julian didn't wait for the vampires to assemble before he ran up the ridge. Jeremy nodded to Nola and took his place as second in the long line with Nola staying close on his heels.

Stay right behind him. Stay with Jeremy.

She wanted to run by his side, but their order had been set by Emanuel.

She would be with Jeremy while the vampires hid from the daylight. They would fight side by side when the time came.

I'll be with him when blood starts to fall.

Nola tried to shake the images of blood-slicked floors from her mind. She studied the ridges and trees they passed, listening for the calls of the night birds.

Julian led them down a different path than the one they'd followed before. He held the rolled up map in his hand but didn't stop to check their route as they cut down the side of the mountain onto a path surrounded by trees tainted by black moss.

He doesn't have time to be uncertain. We're racing against death. Running toward blood and pain.

I've never run toward violence before.

Nola's hands shook, but she kept running.

It's too late for second guessing.

The pounding of the vampires' footsteps chased her north. Somewhere in the long line, Kieran ran behind her. And Emanuel, and Raina. The twins, and Stell. Jude and the blond girl who hated being trapped in Nightland.

I don't know her name. I should know her name.

There wouldn't be as many people running with her on the return trip to Nightland.

If I make the run back.

Nola tipped her chin down, grateful no one could see her face. No moon had risen to replace the burning sun, but the darkness wouldn't have kept the others from seeing the tears in her eyes.

We'll be able to see better than the Domers when we attack. Did Rebecca pick tomorrow night for the darkness?

But Rebecca's people wouldn't be able to see in the dark as Nola could.

They've chosen their sacrifice. They aren't planning on bringing anyone home. They don't know our plan.

The need to hear Jeremy's voice, for him to say something reassuring, pressed against Nola's chest.

She kept her gaze locked on his back as they passed the barren earth left behind by the Nallot.

A faint whisper of murmurs fluttered through the line.

Did Rebecca lead us past this place on purpose? To make sure Emanuel would see what Salinger had done?

Breathe, Nola. Just breathe.

Julian's pace didn't change as they ran parallel with the river and the ruined road, traveling farther north than Nola had ever been.

Movement shifted in the shadows far ahead.

Let it be Rebecca.

Julian didn't slow until he was within a hundred yards of the figures. He moved his hand to the hilt of his sword as the group of shadows turned toward him.

The people wore the brown of the Woodlands. Each had a bow and quiver full of arrows strapped to their backs.

Rebecca stepped to the front. A heavy Outer Guard rifle had joined the bow across her back. "I was hoping you'd make better time."

"It was quite a long journey." Julian bowed.

"I'll cross first and then the nightwalkers follow." Rebecca waved the Northerners out of her path. "Took us damned near a day to get the thing right, but it should hold for all of us."

"What should?" Nola asked. The feeling of speaking felt foreign to her mouth after the long hours of running in silence.

"Our bridge." Rebecca pointed to a pair of ropes hanging over the water.

The two ropes, one six feet above the other, reached from the trunk of a tree on the near bank to another on the far side of the river.

"I'm impressed," Julian said.

"How did you manage it?" Jeremy asked.

"Some damn fine shooting and a raft big enough for one," Rebecca said. "It's not our first time crossing. We're just smart enough not to leave a trail behind."

Jeremy took Nola's hand, lacing his fingers through hers.

Rebecca turned to the vampires. "If anyone falls in, we won't be swimming out after you. One at a time to keep the weight down." She headed to the tree where the ropes had been anchored, patting the trunk before gripping the higher rope and stepping up onto the lower.

Nola clutched Jeremy's hand tighter as Rebecca side-stepped out over the water, moving only a foot at a time as she crossed the raging current.

Emanuel stepped up to the end of the rope.

"Let me go first," Raina said.

"Rebecca and I have much to discuss and no time to spare." Emanuel gripped the top rope.

"Emanuel—"

"If this were a ploy to kill me, there would be much simpler ways than luring me out over the river." Emanuel watched as Rebecca climbed down on the other side, then stepped up and began his own journey.

"This is going to take too long," Gentry said.

"Well, if they had been able to build a nice, big bridge like the one the domes so foolishly blew up, I'm sure they would have." Raina kept her gaze fixed on Emanuel's back until he reached the far bank.

"I'll go next." Stokes stepped up to the rope.

"No chance in hell," Raina said.

"You think I should leave Rebecca alone with a pack of vampires?" Stokes said.

"You think you could do a damn thing against us?" Raina pulled herself up and started over the water, leaving a red-faced Stokes behind.

"We should let the vampires go first," Nola said. "Give them more time to get to ground."

"You're coming, are you?" Stokes eyed Nola. "Where's Jude?"

"I'm here, Captain." Jude stepped up beside Julian, his eyes cast toward the ground.

"Good to see you alive," Stokes said.

"Thanks, Captain."

"Jude." Al appeared at Stokes' side. "I'm glad you made it."

"You too, Al," Jude said.

"Get across the river, Jude," Stokes said. "I didn't send you to get saved just for you to die in the sun. I meant what I said. We need you fighting."

One of the twins stepped up to the ropes.

"We're getting the monsters out of our home." Jude turned his dark eyes up, meeting Stokes' gaze.

"Too right we are," Stokes said. "And now I'll have one guard that won't complain about working nights."

Jude smiled. "I'm your permanent volunteer."

"Go." Stokes waved Jude to the ropes.

"You really did leave," Gentry said.

Stokes blinked at her for a moment before cursing under his breath and turning toward the water.

"Nice to see you, too," Gentry said.

They stood watching while the other twin and Jude made it to the far side.

"Are they going to run on without us?" Nola said.

"They should," Jeremy said. "We can catch up after sunrise. Our job begins in the daylight."

Kieran grasped the top rope.

"Kieran." Nola stepped forward, taking his arm.

Kieran turned to her, a sad smile touching his black eyes. "See you on the other side."

"Stay safe." Nola gripped his hand.

Kieran leaned in, kissing her forehead. "You too, Nola." He looked to Jeremy. "Keep her safe."

"Always," Jeremy said.

Kieran nodded and stepped up onto the rope.

Jeremy took Nola's hand, kissing her palm. "He'll be okay."

"I would have punched him and tossed him into the river, but whatever." Gentry glared across the water.

"And have one less person trying to protect Nola?" Jeremy said.

Nola shrugged out of her pack and leaned it against a tree.

"I can carry that across the river," Gentry said.

"You're not used to Graylock yet," Nola said.

"I've been training for Graylock my whole life," Gentry said.

"Graylock didn't exist our whole lives." Jeremy gave a low laugh.

"Doesn't matter," Gentry said, "it's still what Dad was aiming both of us for even if he didn't know it."

Jeremy took off the black pack Raina had prepared for him, carefully leaning it next to Nola's.

One of the big men stepped up onto the rope. A chip of bark cracked off the tree.

"Got any water in that pack?" Gentry asked.

Nola knelt next to her bag, dug past the bundle of green beans, and reached for the water bottle in the bottom. Something around the metal crinkled as she pulled it free. A folded piece of paper had been tied to the bottle with a thin string.

"What's that?" Jeremy asked.

"No idea." Nola untied the string, pulling the paper loose before passing the bottle to Gentry.

Nola

Her name had been written on the outside of the paper in an unfamiliar hand.

"Crazy how little water you need on Graylock," Gentry said.

Nola unfolded the paper.

Dear Nola,

I hope you read this before you break into the domes. I don't know if you'll make it back to Nightland, or if Nightland will even exist much longer. I don't know if I'll survive having my baby, or if my baby will be healthy enough to live. I don't know anything except that I want my baby to grow up someplace safe.

Thank you for finding us a way to get to Nightland. For trying to help me find Charles. No other Domer would have bothered with outsiders, and you saved us from those awful cages.

I need one more thing from you. I need you to come back to Nightland, and I need you to promise to take care of my baby.

If it's a boy, I'm naming him Charles Catlyn. If it's a girl, she'll be Charlotte Catlyn, but call her Charlie when she's good. If something happens to me, you have to remember her name. Paint it across the mountains if you have to, but never let her forget.

Take care of Charlie and Beauford,

T

Tears fell from Nola's cheeks onto the already smeared paper. Jeremy lifted the note from her trembling hands.

"Did you just find out our plan has been sabotaged?" Gentry asked.

"No," Nola said, her voice thick with tears.

"Then stop crying, we're going into a fight," Gentry said.

"The world is ending," Nola said, "the only mandatory thing is survival."

Jeremy knelt next to Nola, wrapping his arms around her and letting her bury her face in his chest.

She didn't fight the tears that streamed down her cheeks. Didn't care how many of the vampires and Northerners saw her cry.

There are too many people to say goodbye to. Too many people I don't want to lose.

"You're next," Stokes said.

Nola looked up, expecting to find Stokes glaring down at her. His dark eyebrows had pinched together, but there was no anger on his face. "You two go and run after the Vampers. Gentry can follow with the Woodlands group."

"Like hell I'll go with you." Gentry stepped onto the rope. "Sorry, Stokes. Both Ridgeways are running with the fast folk tonight."

Stokes watched her until she had reached the halfway point over the river. "I thought you said you didn't have enough Graylock to save Jude."

"We didn't," Jeremy said, "and we don't. Gentry..." Jeremy dug his knuckles into his temples.

"We're going to get enough to finish Gentry's dose from the domes," Nola said. "No matter what it takes."

"I always knew Captain Ridgeway's kids were going to turn out crazy as hell," Stokes said. "I'm glad they're fighting on my side."

Jeremy gave an almost real smile. "Glad I'm fighting with the evil old bastard Stokes."

Gentry jumped off the rope on the far bank.

"You next," Jeremy said.

"Right." Nola pulled on her pack. "Right."

"Your arms are more than strong enough to hold you," Jeremy said. "Just keep a tight grip and you'll be okay."

"Better than a tiny tunnel." Nola's words came out steadier than she'd dared hope. She gripped the top rope with both hands. The coarse texture of the fibers bit into her palms.

"Keep breathing," Jeremy said.

Nola nodded and stepped up onto the bottom rope. The line bowed beneath her, swaying as she shifted her weight. She leaned farther forward, trying to balance her pack, and the ropes curved backward, away from her body.

"You can do this," Jeremy said. "Nola Kent, I have no doubt in my mind that you can do this."

Centering herself on the rope, Nola slid her right foot sideways. The rope jiggled beneath her but didn't snap and fall away.

No doubt. I will not doubt.

She slid her foot sideways again, stepping out over the river. Though she knew it was impossible, the sound of the racing water seemed infinitely louder once there was no longer solid ground between her and the current.

Ten seconds, Nola.

She took another step sideways.

You get ten seconds to panic.

She stepped again and again.

Then you're done.

She reached the center of the river. The stench of the water pummeled her nose.

That's all you're allowed.

The skin on her palms tore as she slid along the rope, but she didn't ease her grip. Keeping her eyes fixed on the horizon, she repeated the action: move right hand and foot, move left hand and foot.

Her right hand banged into something hard. Nola gasped, preparing to fall into the river. She glanced sideways and found herself nose to nose with the bark of a tree.

"Get down," Rebecca said. "I've still got to get my people through the hills."

Nola stepped down off the rope, taking a moment to convince her hands they really could let go. The pink of her palms was the only sign of the skin the rope had torn away.

She turned east. An empty forest of decaying trees waited for her. The vampires of Nightland had disappeared.

CHAPTER TWENTY-SEVEN

Even as the sun sank over the horizon, its rays burned Nola's neck. She didn't mind. Pain meant life. Life meant a chance at success.

The only sounds of movement around her came from Jeremy, Gentry, Al, and Stokes. The Northerners made no noise as they wound their way through the dead forest in the hills, moving ever closer to the domes.

A pinch of worry prickled the back of Nola's mind even as she focused on the hilltops around her, searching for signs of Salinger's guards.

They're okay. They made it. They all made it.

Rebecca hadn't led the Northerners to the shelter where the vampires had taken refuge, and Julian had left Nola and Jeremy without a map.

A finger pointed toward the woods hadn't been enough for Jeremy to risk striking out to follow Nightland, so they stayed with Rebecca, hoping Nightland had made it. Hoping they wouldn't stand alone at the domes.

Hope is the hardest thing in the world to kill.

Stokes and Al moved at the front of the group, keeping close to Rebecca, as though afraid of getting lost. The Northerners didn't move in one long line as the vampires had, but spread out amongst the trees, winding their way through the forest, as though hoping to leave a maze for whoever might try to follow their path.

Nola walked between Gentry and Jeremy. For the first time since she'd had Graylock, her limbs didn't burn with the need to run. Whether it was the rise in front of them or the one just beyond, soon the domes would take over the horizon.

Then there won't be any choice but to dive in and hope enough of us survive.

Nola studied Jeremy's profile, the slant of his nose, the stubble on his chin.

I love you.

A smile curved Nola's lips.

I love you.

The sounds of movement in front of them stopped. Jeremy's brow furrowed.

Nola tore her gaze from his face to look south. The first glint of the domes' glass peered through the trees ahead of them.

Nola held her breath as she followed Jeremy forward, toward Rebecca.

They'll see us.

They won't look on this side of the river.

Rebecca waited, leaning against the trunk of a tree and peering through its branches. "At least the helicopter's not in the air."

On the east side of the domes, the helicopter waited. A tent had been erected next to the landing pad, though what might be inside, Nola couldn't guess. Two guards stood in front of the tent, facing the helicopter.

"We'll make sure it stays on the ground," Jeremy said. "If Salinger can send Nallot into the air, we're dead before we start."

"What about the guards?" Gentry said.

"We're fast," Nola said. "We can make it."

"Without being caught?" Rebecca asked.

"I'll go," Jeremy said.

"We're going together," Nola said.

"Can you do it?" Gentry eyed Rebecca.

"I'm used to the way the woods work," Rebecca said. "That doesn't make me invisible."

Gentry turned her gaze back to the guards. "If we get caught and the guards send up an alarm, they'll get us with Nallot before we can get back over the river."

"If we don't get to work soon," Jeremy said, "we won't be ready in time."

Nola glanced west. The sun had already begun to sink out of sight.

"If you have to go, then try making a run for it," Rebecca said. "But, if you want my advice, wait for a nice opening before you go sprinting at the armed men."

"What kind of opening?" Nola said.

"I'm not sure," Rebecca said. "But I like you well enough, I'll try and come up with something."

"Thanks," Nola said.

"We'll be listening for you." Rebecca gave a nod and turned north, heading farther into the trees.

"I wish the ground weren't so open." Jeremy bit his lips together, glaring at the domes. "A hundred and fifty yards of open space? No matter how fast we run, it's too far to hope we won't be spotted."

"Leaving cover right next to the domes would make them harder to defend," Gentry said.

"I didn't say it would have been smart, just convenient."

"Touché," Gentry said.

Jeremy took Nola's hand as he headed east, keeping within the tree line.

Nola willed her shoulders to stay relaxed and her breathing to stay even. "Last time I was in these woods, the Outer Guard were shooting at me."

"I'm sure they'll be shooting at us again soon," Gentry said.

"Gentry," Jeremy warned.

"If she's not ready for it, she can wait in the woods," Gentry said.

"I'm not letting Jeremy go in there without me," Nola said. "Besides, neither of you would know what to save."

"Fine," Gentry said. "Just do me a favor and try to look brave."

They stopped level with the helicopter. Nola peeked around the side of a tree, studying the tent and the guards.

Both guards wore helmets and full gear. Both held rifles in their hands.

"I'll take right, you take left?" Gentry said. "You two should grab their helmets and vests."

"If we can figure out how to get there," Jeremy said.

"Jeremy, let me take your pack." Nola slid off her pack of food. "If you two are fighting, then I can set the box."

"Nola—"

"Give her the pack," Gentry cut across Jeremy.

"Promise me you'll get clear," Jeremy said. "No matter what happens, even if you have to pitch the bag and run, you have to get clear."

"I've got it," Nola said. "I promise."

Jeremy took off his black pack, passing the weight to Nola.

"We're going to have to make a break for it." Gentry looked up to the cement tower at the center of the domes, toward the maintenance ladder too small for even Graylock-changed eyes to see. "I'm running out of time."

"How will we know when Rebecca creates a window for us?" Nola leaned forward against the tree, trying not to think of what she wore on her back.

"Do you trust her to come through?" Gentry asked.

"I trust her to do whatever it takes to win," Jeremy said.

Gentry pulled her weapon from its holster, checking the loaded darts.

Nola gripped the hilt of the blade on one hip and the gun on the other.

Hurt to protect. Fight to defend.

A *crack* sounded in the trees to the west.

All three spun toward the noise. Six brown blurs darted out toward the domes. With a faint *buzz* and *thwack*, an arrow hit a tree near the slowest of the brown things, steering the creatures farther east toward Nola.

"Are those deer?" Nola took a step toward the animals.

"They're our opening." Jeremy took Nola's hand and raced to the very edge of the woods.

The deer charged out of the trees, heading toward the eastern side of the domes.

"Damn she's good," Gentry whispered.

The guards spun, their weapons raised, as the deer raced toward them.

"Wait," Jeremy said. "Wait."

The guards turned, watching the deer run south.

"Run."

Still holding Nola's hand, he sprinted into the open.

Nola looked away from the guards, locking her gaze on the helicopter. Halfway across the clearing, Jeremy let go of her hand.

The horrible feeling of emptiness lasted only an instant. Nola veered away from the others, heading for the far side of the helicopter.

A *thump* and a *grunt* punctuated her footsteps, but she didn't dare look to see who had been hit. She skidded to a stop next to the side door of the helicopter. The doors had been closed, but Nola's aim wasn't inside the body of the craft.

Crack.

Nola yanked off her pack.

Not Jeremy. Jeremy is fine.

Three boxes waited inside the bag. Nola pulled out one of the two smaller boxes. Heavy, gray, and made of soft plastic, the box felt like nothing more than a toy. A red beacon poked out of one side of the box. Nola slipped under the helicopter, ripped a hunk of fabric from the base of the box, and stuck the exposed goo to the underside of the helicopter.

In a moment, it was done. Nola rolled away and sprang to her feet, grabbing the pack as she darted to the tail of the helicopter, peering out toward the tent.

Two guards lay on the ground. Blood pooled around the first, while the other's bare head twisted at an unnatural angle.

Gentry stood over one guard, wiping blood from the side of her neck, while Jeremy stared into the tent.

Nola ran from the shelter of the helicopter toward Jeremy. "We have to keep moving," she called as loudly as she dared.

"Give me the pack," Gentry said.

"Shit," Jeremy said.

"Are you hurt?" Nola removed the second small box from the pack.

"How flammable is Nallot?" Jeremy asked.

Nola passed the pack to Gentry and stepped into the tent.
Nallot.

Large white letters marked the fifteen barrels that waited in the shadows.

"We need to move faster." Nola grabbed Jeremy's hand, dragging him out of the tent.

Gentry had already pulled on the half-empty pack. "See you soon." She ran around the far side of the domes, heading for the back of the cement tower.

Jeremy yanked free the undamaged guard vest while Nola pulled off the other guard's helmet. She didn't let herself look at the guard's face.

Jeremy passed Nola the clean vest and pulled on the second helmet.

Taking a deep breath, Nola settled the helmet on her head. The scent of the dead guard's sweat filled her nose. Sour rolled into her mouth as she slung on the vest.

They'll keep me safe. Protect the heart and the neck, that's all I have to do.

"Ready?" Jeremy tightened his blood-covered vest and lifted the box from Nola's hands.

She couldn't see his face beneath the helmet.

He's not one of them. He's Jeremy. My Jeremy.

"Let's go." Nola took the lead, following the same path Gentry had run moments before.

They ran past the Aquaponics Dome and Leaf Dome.

How many people will see us running?

She waited for the *crackle* of a warning in her ear. For someone to have seen the two fallen guards and sounded the alarm.

They rounded the corner and neared the edge of Green Dome. The lights hadn't been turned on for the evening, but still a figure moved on the other side of the glass.

Jeremy sprinted in front of Nola, tearing the fabric from the box before he reached the dome. He planted the box on the glass wall and kept running.

Nola glanced up to the cement tower. A black figure climbed toward the Com Room.

The last of the sunlight faded from the sky.

Move faster, Gentry.

They reached the far side of Green Dome where an open patch of earth separated it from its neighbor.

Jeremy pulled Nola to the ground at the very edge of the glass, planting his body between her and Green Dome.

How long?

Every breath seemed too fast and too slow at the same time.

Raina, it's time.

Her heart raced. Her pulse thundered in her ears.

Bang!

The explosion shook Nola's lungs. Jeremy yanked her to her feet before she could remember how to take a breath.

Boom!

The sound came from beyond Green Dome. A pillar of fire soared into the air. Blue marred the orange of the flames. Nola couldn't tear her gaze from the blaze as Jeremy led her around the side of Green Dome to the newly made break in the glass.

Raina had planned the charge well. A ten-foot hole had been blasted into the side of the dome.

Not so big they can't find a way to fix it.

But how hot will the Nallot burn? Will the fumes kill or be burned away?

Red lights had already begun flashing on the inside of the domes.

Mrs. Pearson stood between the planting trays in the middle of the dome, swaying and staring at the hole in the glass.

"Get to the bunker," Jeremy shouted. "Go. Go!"

Mrs. Pearson started toward the stairs, but Nola and Jeremy were faster. They reached the corridor below before Mrs. Pearson's footsteps clattered on the stairs behind them.

The helmet dulled the blaring of the sirens and shouts of terror, but the tunnel itself shocked fear into Nola's spine.

The whole thing could collapse. What if the tower falls? What if Gentry didn't make it off the tower before the explosion?

The shouts of the panicked Domers grew louder as Nola raced past the corridor that led to the Guard barracks and the bunker near seed storage. Jeremy turned out of the corridor and ran up the stairs to the Aquaponics Dome just as a family with two small children raced by, the toddler sobbing onto his father's shoulder.

The flashing lights seemed out of place in the Aquaponics Dome, where fish swam in slow circles beneath the crops that fed the Domers.

Nola leaned against the wall just out of sight of the staircase.

She found Jeremy's hand without tearing her gaze from the fire that still burned by the helicopter.

"We said we'd keep it out of the air," Jeremy said.

Nola nodded, sending her oversized helmet bobbling. Peeling herself away from the wall, she crept farther into the dome, going down the steps that led to the base of the tanks. High above the domes, a faint glow came from the top of the Com Tower.

"She did it," Jeremy said. "All the communications systems will be out. The guards' coms won't work. They won't be able to contact the Incorporation. All of it's gone."

"You'll have to congratulate her when we get back to Nightland." Nola was grateful the helmet hid the fear on her face.

The screaming in the corridors faded. The pounding of the guards' boots racing toward the threat destroying their home never even passed by the entrance to the Aquaponics Dome.

"Is it time?" Nola asked.

"I don't think we can afford to wait," Jeremy said. "Raina and Kieran will be here soon."

Letting go of Nola's hand, Jeremy led the way back to the steps, pulling his gun from his belt.

Only the flickering red lights moved in the hall.

The dome names painted on the walls were the same as when Nola had called the domes her home, but she felt no welcome at reading them as they ran down the corridor.

Jeremy slowed as they rounded the corner, holding his arm out to keep Nola from passing him. The stairs leading farther down were empty.

Nola pulled her Guard gun from her hip as they ran down the steps at a human speed. Her throat tightened as they rounded the corner and went down another flight of stairs, then another, winding deeper into the earth.

An empty corridor lined with frosted-glass doors waited for them. Her gun slipped in her grip as sweat slicked her palms.

Jeremy stopped next to a glass door, checking to see that Nola was at his side before shoving the door open and stepping into the seed storage room.

The familiar cold tingled Nola's skin. She should have felt safe surrounded by the rows of shelves where seeds waited for the day the world would be ready for the Domers to leave their glass castle, but the sight of the useless bounty sent a surge of anger racing through her limbs.

"What a waste." She turned toward the computer panel in the wall.

"What the hell are you doing down here?" The familiar voice froze Nola's finger an inch above the screen. "I have made it abundantly clear—I will not abandon my seeds, no matter what Captain Ridgeway says."

Nola turned to find her mother glaring at her.

CHAPTER TWENTY-EIGHT

More lines creased Lenora Kent's face than Nola remembered.

Lenora pointed toward the door. "Out of my seed storage, now. Whatever this fresh round of hell might be, I'm sure you'll be much more useful somewhere else."

Nola's hand shook as she tucked her gun back into its holster and removed her helmet. "Mom."

"Magnolia." Lenora shook her head, sending her graying hair fluttering around her shoulders.

"Mom, I need you to go to the back of the room."

"What are you doing here?" Lenora said. "You left. You broke those outsiders out of the cells, and you left."

"Yes, I did." Nola took a step toward her mother. "I left because it was the right thing to do. Now I'm here because it's the right thing to do."

"You betrayed your home," Lenora said.

"No, Mom."

"Don't *Mom* me," Lenora spat. "My daughter died the day the Vampers kidnapped her."

Nola flinched, trying to hide the stab of betrayal in her gut.

"No. I'm alive, and I'm doing more to save the human race now than I ever would have accomplished locked in here."

"Get out," Lenora said.

"Mom—"

"My daughter is dead."

Jeremy took of his helmet. "Get to the back of the room, sit on the floor, and don't move."

"Filthy traitors, both of you." Lenora stepped forward.

"Don't." Jeremy raised his gun.

"I will not let you harm my seeds," Lenora said. "They are worth more than my life."

"And more than your daughter," Nola said.

"Yes." Lenora met Nola's eyes.

"Make sure she can't stop me." Nola turned back to the screen.

She punched in her mother's passcode without having to think. The whole system pulled up. Inventory, files, climate control. Nola tapped on the climate heading. In three quick strokes, she quadrupled the temperature in the room.

"It'll ruin everything," Nola said. The vents turned on, blasting hot air into seed storage. "These seeds were meant to provide for generations."

Jeremy laid a hand on her shoulder. "So is Nightland, and the spring in the Woodlands."

Nola turned away from the panel. Lenora lay unconscious on the floor. The hateful twist of her face had faded, leaving Lenora looking almost like the mother Nola remembered.

"She's still alive?" Nola asked.

"Yeah."

"Move her to the hall." Nola didn't watch as Jeremy carried Lenora out of the room. Instead, she raced down the rows, pulling slim packets of seeds from the different bins.

The door to the hall closed.

"Jeremy?" Nola called.

"It's just me." The sound of Jeremy's boots pounded toward the far side of the room.

Nola stopped at each of the most precious seed bins, loading her pockets with treasures from root vegetables to healing herbs.

A *whine* sounded from the wall as Jeremy pulled the vent free.

Nola stopped in front of the bin labeled *Ficus Carica* and pulled out a packet.

"Nola," Jeremy whispered.

"Coming." Nola shoved the packet into her pocket with more than two-dozen others and ran for the vent on the far side of the room.

There will be no treasure left in the domes.

Jeremy had already pulled the vent free and kicked open the path to the other side. Still, Nola held her breath as she crawled through the few feet of metal vent and pulled herself out into the medical storage room.

Unlike seed storage, closed cabinets lined the walls of medical storage.

"I have no idea where it could be," Nola said.

"Start looking." Jeremy ducked back into the vent, pulling the grate to seed storage closed behind them.

Nodding to herself, Nola ran to the nearest case and wrenched it open. Vials filled with bright blue took up all of the shelves. Snapping the doors shut, Nola moved on to the next. Bottles of pills waited for her. She grabbed four vials of clear fluid and a handful of I-Vents from the third cabinet, shoving them all into the pockets of the dead guard's vest.

A *click* sounded from behind her as Jeremy began searching his half of the room.

Please, even if it's only one dose. Let me find one full dose.

The next case held closed tubs. The next, dishes of golden goo.

We can't have found Gentry just to lose her. Not after everything we've been through.

Cabinet by cabinet, she made her way around the room, dashing on to the next as soon as she was sure she hadn't found any of the deep black Graylock.

"Oof." Nola ran into something hard and glanced over to find Jeremy staring at her.

"Nothing?" Dread filled Jeremy's eyes.

"I'm sorry," Nola said.

"My dad's office," Jeremy said. "You said you saw some Graylock in his office."

"In the cabinet behind his desk," Nola said.

Jeremy raced to the vent, cramming his helmet back onto his head.

Only a floor up.

Nola had made the climb before she'd been given the strength of Graylock. Getting to the next floor would be easy now.

Jeremy tore the vent free with his fingers and began climbing before Nola reached the grate.

She ducked into the shaft, watching as Jeremy pulled himself onto the thin ledge near the Outer Guard barracks and kicked the grate to his father's office free. In one swift movement, he shifted his weight across the shaft and pulled himself through to the other side.

Nola pulled the grate to medical storage closed and put on her helmet. She took shaking breaths, trying to convince her lungs there was still air in the world.

Hot air aiming toward seed storage rushed down on her.

It'll contaminate medical storage, too.

Better than dumping Nallot onto a living person.

"Come on." Jeremy reached down into the shaft.

Nola jumped, grabbing hold of his hands. She closed her eyes as he lifted her up the shaft and dragged her onto the floor of Captain Ridgeway's office.

Everything was as it had been before. Captain Ridgeway's desk with the one chair behind it, a photo of Jeremy and Gentry from years ago when Jeremy was still shorter than his sister. A humming cabinet against the back wall.

Nola sprang to her feet while Jeremy moved to the cabinet and wrenched the drawer open.

"Shit!" He punched the side of the cabinet.

Nola leaned over the drawer. Cool air filtered up from the empty space.

"Where would Salinger's office be?" Nola asked.

"It could be anywhere." Jeremy dug the heels of his hands into his eyes. "It could be a house in one of the domestic domes. He could have taken over the damn Com Room for all we know. The formula could be in the computer encrypted under any of the doctors' files, and we wouldn't have a damned way to open the files even if we could get them."

"We can figure this out." Nola lifted Jeremy's hands away from his face. "You and me together, we can figure this out."

"Gentry's going to run out of time. There's nothing we can do."

"If I needed Graylock, would you give up?"

"Never." Jeremy gripped her hands.

"Then we have to keep looking. We'll go to the medical wing. There's got to be a triage kit somewhere."

The walls rumbled, shaking with the chaos of a far away explosion.

"Raina," Nola said.

"We have to get to the Atrium." Jeremy shoved on his helmet.

"But the medical—"

"If Salinger is hoarding the Graylock, he won't be keeping it in the medical wing. We're supposed to be in the Atrium. If we don't get there, Gentry won't need Graylock." Jeremy stepped toward the door to the corridor. He waited a moment before pulling the door open a crack.

The red lights flashed, but there was no sign of any Outer Guard.

Again, they both drew their weapons as they ran into the hall.

Jeremy looked every bit the Outer Guard, from his boots to his helmet. If his clothes hadn't been torn, the illusion would have been perfect.

Nola ran by his side in shoes that had once belonged to someone else, and Bishop's pants and shirt, both of which were far too large for her.

I'm playing dress up in the middle of a battle.

Signs of chaos didn't litter the domes as they raced through the tunnels. No wounded being carried to help. No guards charging toward the new break in the glass.

Where are the guards?

They found the first signs of true fighting as they reached the corridor below the Atrium. A smear of blood marred the otherwise perfect cleanliness of the tunnel floor.

Around the next corner, a guard lay on the ground, a pool of blood surrounding him.

Nola skirted the red and kept right by Jeremy's side, not allowing herself time to wonder if the man was already dead or only waiting for Graylock to revive him.

Shouts and the *pops* of Guard guns being fired carried from up the steps.

It should be louder. There should be more people fighting.

Unless something went wrong and the vampires were beaten before they started.

Jeremy slowed as they reached the top of the stairs to the Atrium.

The scent of smoke cut through the stench of sweat inside Nola's helmet.

The domes had been working on replanting the trees and grass damaged by Nightland's first attack. The new growth that had replaced the barren patches was now scarred by footprints and blood. A line of twenty Dome Guard stood around the base of the Com Tower, surrounded by shattered glass and chunks of concrete that had fallen through the dome from the blast on top of the tower. A dozen Outer Guard fought the vampires on the far side of the Atrium where all the vehicles were parked.

"Where's Gentry?" Nola asked.

"Stay behind me." Jeremy ran up the last of the stairs and charged straight for the Guard trucks.

Raina fought two guards at once, her knives flashing in her hands as she sliced the gun from one of the guard's grips. The twins fought side-by-side, tackling a guard and ripping his weapon from his hands. By the shattered glass, vampires lay still on the ground near guards with arrows protruding from their bodies.

Nola scanned the unmoving fighters, searching for Kieran and Gentry.

Jeremy charged into the fight, knocking over a guard who had his weapon aimed at Julian.

Nola raised her gun, firing a dart into the shoulder of an Outer Guard who barreled toward Jeremy.

Raina sprinted through the opening toward the trucks, her pack disappearing from view as the guard she had been fighting rounded on Nola.

He struck down, pummeling her wrist to knock her gun from her grip. Nola pulled her knife from its sheath with her other hand, sinking the blade into the man's thigh.

The helmet dampened the man's scream as she wrenched her knife free.

Before she could swing her blade again, Jeremy stabbed the man under the bottom of his vest. The guard gagged as Jeremy tossed him aside.

"Are you—" A *pop* cut across Jeremy's question. A thin silver dart glanced off the bottom of his helmet. Nola spun toward the shooter.

The Dome Guard had turned their weapons toward the fight by the trucks. Whether they no longer cared about hitting their own men, or had decided enough Domers had fallen to make shooting worth it, didn't matter as darts pummeled the fighters.

Jeremy yanked Nola sideways as another round of *pops* sounded from the Dome Guard's guns.

A shrill whistle blasted from behind the trucks. As one, the vampires ran, not toward the opening in the glass or for the shelter of the trucks, but for the far side of the Atrium and the stairs that led farther into the domes.

"Stop them!"

You're too late.

Jeremy grabbed Nola's shoulders, knocking her to the ground the moment before a *boom* shook the Atrium. Heat lapped Nola's skin. The glass above them shattered, raining fragments down on them as a series of *pops* and *bangs* carried over the roar of the fire and the shouts of the guards.

"Are you okay?" Jeremy grabbed Nola under the arms, hauling her to her feet.

"I'm fine." Nola scanned the faces around them.

Raina blew her hair out of her eyes and wiped the blood off her hands. Kieran stood behind her, his hair singed, but looking otherwise undamaged as he stared at the inferno that had been the domes' vehicles.

"Did you get all the ammunition?" Julian looked to Kieran.

"I set the blast on the weapons locker door," Kieran said. "It was the best I could do."

The flames had swallowed the guards they had been fighting before. But the Dome Guard near the Com Tower were getting back to their feet. Wounded and bloody as they were, they turned toward the stairs where the people of Nightland had fled the blast radius.

"We need to leave." Julian raised his sword.

"Salinger," Nola said. "Has anyone seen Salinger?"

"We've only seen the guards in here," Julian said. "The rest must be on Emanuel's side of the fight."

The Dome Guard raised their weapons.

"Go!" Jeremy shoved Nola toward the wide opening in the glass.

We can't leave. We have to stop Salinger. We have to save Gentry.

She didn't have time to speak as a string of *pops* punctuated the air.

Most of the Atrium wall had fallen, leaving a wide gap for them to escape. Open air waited just in front of them.

An arrow flew in from the night, landing right in front of Julian.

"Shit." Raina raised both her knives, her gaze fixed on the darkness beyond the shattered glass.

Captain Ridgeway ran toward them, a pack of Outer Guard by his side.

CHAPTER TWENTY-NINE

A rrows chased the Outer Guard as they ran into the ruined Atrium, their weapons leveled at the vampires.

An arrow struck one Guard in the back and another in the leg, but still the pack moved closer.

"Guards hold your fire!" a voice shouted from beyond the glass. "All of you, hold your damned fire."

Stokes limped in from the darkness. He held his arm to his chest, and his bad leg dragged through the shattered glass. But as he glared at the Outer Guard, he seemed as terrifying as Raina.

"What are you doing here?" Captain Ridgeway turned his gun on Stokes even as his men kept their weapons aimed at the vampires.

"Trying to keep the rest of my Guard from dying." Stokes pointed to the Dome Guard by the Com Tower. "There's enough blood on the ground. Back away and let these people go."

"I'm not taking orders from a traitor." Captain Ridgeway pointed his gun at Stokes' unprotected chest. "I'm not letting these murderers walk out of my home again."

"Dome Guard." Stokes spoke over Ridgeway. "I trained you to protect the people of the domes. Salinger and Ridgeway have turned you into demons. Have made you sit by while they use the women of these domes for breeding. Salinger needs to be stopped."

"You've lost your mind," Ridgeway said.

"He hasn't."

Captain Ridgeway turned at the sound of his son's voice.

"Salinger is a murderer." Jeremy stepped forward, removing his helmet. "He has to be stopped."

Ridgeway stared stone-faced at his son.

Nola joined Jeremy, pulling off her own helmet and taking his hand.

"You've destroyed our home." A guard stepped up next to Ridgeway.

"Think of it as leveling the playing field," Raina said.

"Dad"—Jeremy took another step forward—"where is Salinger? He's the one we came here for. I don't want to fight any of you. None of us can afford more blood on our hands."

"Run," Captain Ridgeway said. "Now."

"We can't," Nola said. "We have to find Salinger. We have to stop him before he kills everyone on the outside. He's trying to wipe us out."

"He is defending the domes," Captain Ridgeway said.

"By dumping Nallot in the woods," Stokes said. "That's bullshit, and even you're smart enough to know it."

"Let us stop him," Julian said. "The demon is damning you as he murders us."

"I cannot let you—"

"We need more Graylock." Nola stepped in front of Jeremy.

"What the hell—"

"We need more Graylock, or your daughter will die!" Nola shouted over Captain Ridgeway.

The *crackle* of the blaze gave the only sound. No boots crunched on the broken glass. The dead had already given their final gasps.

"She took Graylock, but we don't have a third dose," Nola said. "Gentry left because she couldn't be a part of Salinger slaughtering the city. She took Graylock so she could come here to fight. To try and save whatever bit of decency the domes have left. If you don't take us to wherever Salinger has hoarded the Graylock, Gentry will die."

"Where is she?" Ridgeway scanned the faces of the Nightland fighters.

"Captain, she abandoned the domes," an Outer Guard said.

"I did not give you permission to speak," Ridgeway spat.

"She set the blast on top of the Com Tower," Jeremy said. "She's probably fighting Salinger right now."

"If the coms were working, you might have known the prodigal daughter had returned to fight," Raina said. "But I made a little bomb, so whoops."

"Salinger isn't fighting, Captain Stokes." One of the Dome Guard stepped in front of the rest. "None of the Incorporation Guard are."

"We blow a couple holes in the domes and they don't bother showing up?" Raina said. "How disappointing."

"Captain Ridgeway, where is Salinger?" Nola said.

The Captain looked at his son, shaking his head.

"Dad," Jeremy said, "I don't want to lose Gentry. Please."

"Captain—" one of the Outer Guard began.

"Stand down," Captain Ridgeway said. "All of you. I am the Captain of the Outer Guard, the ranking Council Member outside the bunker, and I am ordering you to stand down."

Nola's breath caught in her chest as both Outer Guard and Dome Guard lowered their weapons.

"Salinger and the Incorporation Guard are in the Iron Dome," Captain Ridgeway said. "The order came down from the Incorporation after we lost a guard unit in the northern woods. The people of these domes are disposable. Salinger and the guards he brought in are necessary to the Incorporation and must be protected."

"They're just sitting in there, watching everything burn?" Anger coiled in Nola's stomach.

"I knew this was too easy," Kieran said. "We should have been outnumbered from the start."

"They closed the dome," Captain Ridgeway said. "Lowered the metal."

Jeremy shut his eyes, tipping his face toward the sky. "Where's the Graylock?"

"In his housing unit," Ridgeway said.

"I need you to get us in," Jeremy said. "Open the door, and we'll take care of Salinger and his men."

"Listen to your son," Stokes said.

The pounding of footsteps approached the shattered wall of the Atrium. Emanuel, flanked by Gentry and Rebecca, stood with fifteen fighters at his back. Only three dressed in Northern brown were still standing.

"Dad." Blood covered Gentry's uniform, but she stood straight-backed and proud as her father turned to her. "I've come to take my home back from the monster."

Captain Ridgeway nodded. "We go in, and we don't come out until that bastard is dead. We fight to the last man, and if the Incorporation blows us all to hell, at least our deaths won't come from cowardice. Anyone who doesn't want to fight, get in the Com Tower now."

Two of the Outer Guard moved toward the tower.

"Leave your weapons," Captain Ridgeway ordered.

The guards laid their guns on the floor and walked through the door at the bottom of the tower. Only one Dome Guard joined them.

"Lock them in," Ridgeway said.

Gentry strode forward, grabbing a piece of metal from the

ground. The Dome Guard scattered as she reached the door and rammed the metal between the door and the frame.

"With me." Captain Ridgeway walked past his son and down the steps away from the Atrium.

The guards stared at the vampires and Northerners, unwilling to join their ranks.

Gentry cut through the crowd to Jeremy's side. "You good?"

"Fine." Jeremy smiled. "You?"

"Got a little bloodied up jumping from the damned tower," Gentry said, "but only a handful of Outer Guard showed up on our side to fight. I thought maybe the Nallot fire had scared them away. We waited until we heard the blast."

"And Salinger and his men were hiding the whole time," Jeremy said.

"Cowards," Gentry growled.

"I wonder how hard it would be to blow a hole through the fancy metal dome bits," Raina said.

"I didn't know you were so fond of explosives," Jeremy said.

"Back in the days of my renegade youth, I had a father in construction and a love of chaos." Raina winked. "Took more than shovels to dig the tunnels for our fancy home, lover boy."

Nola held Jeremy's hand tighter as they passed the arrows to Bright Dome.

What will my mother do when she wakes up to find her world shattered?

Captain Ridgeway stopped at the base of the stairs to the Iron Dome. A metal door blocked the entryway.

"You should stay out here, Nola," Jeremy said.

"No." Nola squeezed his hand.

"I always have to try." Jeremy's smile didn't reach his eyes.

"All of you should stay out here," Captain Ridgeway said. "Salinger is our demon, not yours."

"He is a plague on both our houses," Emanuel said. "He's an enemy we both must face."

Captain Ridgeway flipped open a panel on the wall. "Salinger has taken over Stokes' house. Gentry, Jeremy, get in there and get the Graylock."

"We can get it once Salinger is dead," Gentry said.

"I trained you better than to argue with your captain, Guard." The Captain punched in a long code. "Anyone who fires on you is an enemy."

The lock *beeped*. With a grinding sound that cut into Nola's bare ears, the metal door lurched up. Nola took one last deep breath before placing the helmet back on her head.

Before the door had risen halfway, Captain Ridgeway charged up the stairs, Emanuel right behind him. A shout carried from above as Nola raced up the steps by Jeremy's side.

The first *bang* sounded before they reached the inside of the Iron Dome.

Lights burned bright, beaming down from the dome high above. Metal panels surrounded the glass, blocking the night sky from view, trapping them with the line of Incorporation Guard who surrounded the staircase.

A knife whizzed past Nola's ear, hitting a guard in the eye. Another Incorporation Guard took his place, firing his weapon at the stairs. One of the Outer Guard fell. Something hit Nola hard in the stomach, knocking the wind from her, but her body didn't register any pain as she leveled her gun and fired a tiny silver dart into the shoulder of an Incorporation Guard.

Another *bang* shook the air. The person running to Nola's left fell from view, toppling to the ground. Nola tried to see who had fallen, but the helmet blocked her line of sight.

A scream of rage burst from behind her, but Jeremy had reached the line of Incorporation Guard and was fighting hand-to-hand. Gentry leapt high into the air, kicking one of the guards and leveraging herself over his body to land on the other side. Jeremy drove his knife into the neck of the guard he'd been fighting.

"Nola!" he shouted, twisting to look for her as a scream of pain came from Nightland's fighters.

One of the Incorporation Guard turned, aiming his rifle for the bare skin on Jeremy's neck. Nola leapt forward, sinking her blade into the guard's chest.

She felt a scream tear from her throat but didn't pause as she ripped her knife back out of the man's flesh.

"This way." Jeremy sprinted toward the far side of the dome, maneuvering to run behind Nola as a long string of *pops* sounded from near the stairs.

Gentry ran ahead of them, racing toward Salinger's stolen home on her captain's order.

The five guards waiting outside the house turned toward Gentry as she approached.

Nola raised her weapon, firing a string of darts at the guards. One was hit in the arm and crumpled to the ground. The others shifted their attention to Nola.

Gentry lunged forward, punching one of the guards in the side of the head with a sickening *crunch*. Jeremy slashed through another's stomach, taking the doomed man's body and tossing it at his comrade before turning to the final guard.

Nola leapt onto the downed guard, driving her knife into his side before he could struggle to his feet.

Silence fell around the house. Nola's own breaths rattled in her ears over the sounds of fighting by the stairs.

"Nola?" Jeremy kept his gaze toward the house.

"Is Salinger inside?" Nola said.

"One way to find out." Gentry stepped up to the door and kicked, shattering the doorframe.

Weapon raised, Gentry stepped into the house.

Nola's heart thudded in her throat as Jeremy followed his sister. She tightened her grip on her weapon and walked into Captain Stokes' former kitchen.

The tiny room had been taken over by a cabinet, which left barely enough space for Salinger's chair behind the kitchen table.

The spider sat, hands folded in front of him, not even bothering to reach for either of the two guns nestled next to his bowl of dome perfect fruit.

"Who are you?" Salinger said.

"Children born in the glass." Nola stepped up between Jeremy and Gentry. "Children who realized that your kind of survival isn't worth it."

"You know nothing about my kind of survival." Salinger gave a weary smile. "You don't understand the lengths the Incorporation has gone to to ensure the preservation of the human race."

"I don't care," Nola said. "We didn't come here for explanations. We're taking the Graylock."

Salinger looked to the cabinet. "I knew that filth would lead to dark places."

"I don't care what you knew," Jeremy said. "You're done here. We aren't going to let you hurt anyone ever again."

"How?" Salinger said. "Are you going to lock me up in the cells below? The Incorporation will come for me. The women, the children, the damned infants and incompetent guards will be left to rot. But I will not be abandoned by the Incorporation. I, unlike the rest of this failed cesspit, am worthy of rescue."

"Every person is worth saving," Nola said. "The second the Incorporation lost sight of that is the second they failed."

"Well"—Salinger shrugged—"if you aren't going to lock me up, you'll just have to kill me in cold blood."

"What?" Nola said.

"I'm not fighting you," Salinger said. "So you can murder me in cold blood or hold me until the Incorporation comes to collect me."

"Your men are out there dying," Gentry said.

"For the greater good," Salinger said. "For the survival of mankind."

"Defend yourself," Gentry said.

Salinger smiled. "I am saving the human race. I—" Salinger's head tipped back as a silver dart struck his forehead.

Nola spun to find the towering figure of Captain Ridgeway behind her, his weapon raised and aimed at Salinger's corpse.

"Dad," Jeremy said.

"Get the Graylock." Captain Ridgeway kept his gaze and weapon locked on Salinger as a trickle of blood ran down the spider's face.

Jeremy pulled open the cabinet. Dozens of syringes of black filled the chilled drawer.

"The formula," Nola said. "Dr. Wynne needs help with the formula to make more."

"I don't know anything about the formula," Captain Ridgeway said. "Take what you need, as much as you can carry."

Jeremy lifted the precious medicine from the drawer, filling the pouch at his hip before placing extra doses in his pockets.

"The others—" Nola began.

"It's done." Ridgeway turned away from Salinger and led them back out of the house.

Figures moved by the stairs, but the urgency of the battle had faded.

Bodies lay still on the ground.

Nola ran forward, her eyes locked on a head of black hair.

"Nola!" Jeremy called after her.

Kieran knelt next to a bloody corpse.

"Kieran," Nola said.

"I hated him. Even when I lived here, I hated him." Kieran lay Stokes' lifeless hand on his torn chest. Kieran's chest had been torn open, too. His shirt slashed by a blade, but the wound had already healed, leaving blood as the only true mark of the damage that had been done.

They didn't get his heart.

"We hate lots of people until they die for something decent," Raina said.

"And sometimes the good die as well." Emanuel laid Rebecca's body next to Stokes.

Nola tore her gaze from the ruined body of the woman of the Woodlands. Black-clad corpses littered the ground.

Only a few minutes for a hundred people to die.

Torn and twisted, the humans hadn't stood a chance in a fight meant for those who had adapted to survive.

Julian helped Jude limp to Stokes' side.

"Is Salinger dead?" Jude didn't look away from Stokes' bloodied face.

"He is," Jeremy said.

"That's it?" Jude whispered. "After everything we went through, it's over."

"Not yet." Nola looked up to the metal sky.

CHAPTER THIRTY

The bunker door slid open. The wave of whispers that swept up from the Domers swallowed the *swish* of the door's movement.

Nola stepped into the doorway, Jeremy right behind her shoulder, the warmth of his arm against hers washing away her fear.

"Salinger is dead." Nola's voice rang through the bunker. "His guards are dead. Your time under the protection of the Incorporation has ended."

Murmurs sprang up around the room.

Nola waited until silence fell.

"You have no vehicles. No weapons. No seeds. Your communication with the other domes has been severed. Your medical and food supplies are limited. Your population has dwindled. These domes are redundant. The Incorporation isn't coming to save you. We offer you peace. You stay on your side of the river, you try to survive and leave us alone, and we will not attack again. If you threaten Nightland or the people of the Woodlands, we will come back for you. And we will not stop until the threat you impose on the world has been ended for good. We want peace, but we are ready for war." Nola turned away, feeling the gaze of all the people she had known upon her.

"But what are we supposed to do?" a woman asked.

"Survive." Nola turned back to the bunker.

"What about the babies?" A young woman stepped forward, her hand pressed to her stomach. "The Incorporation wanted the babies."

"Not anymore," Nola said. "You've been contaminated by the outside air. You're on your own. What you do from here, that's your choice."

"You've taken everything from us." Dr. Mullins laid a hand on the young woman's shoulder.

"No, we haven't," Nola said.

"We don't know how to survive unprotected," Dr. Mullins said.

"Welcome to the end of the world."

EPILOGUE

The last of the evening's stars glimmered in the sky.

Nola tucked her head onto Jeremy's shoulder, savoring every moment of the night chill before the relentless summer sun would rise. Their view from the mountain's peak let them see as far as the Woodlands and the domes, two tiny places in the world where people still managed to survive.

No smoke marred the horizon. No hint of death or blood ruined the peace of the night.

There was work to be done. The gardens of Nightland had to be protected from the sun. Messages had to be run to the Woodlands and the shattered domes as Emanuel fought to foster their tenuous peace.

Jeremy and Nola would run the messages for the domes together, meeting his sister at the eastern edge of the river to hear news of the new order within the glass.

Before they left, Nola needed to check on sweet little Charlie and make sure T and Beauford had eaten and stolen a few hours' sleep. Kieran would be asking for samples from the mushroom farm. Dr. Wynne would want to tell her about his latest experiments in improving Graylock. The library would be busy with

Emanuel and Julian planning some ambitious project to help those struggling to survive on the highway while Eden ran circles around their feet. Raina would be waiting, knives in hand, to train Nola in the sparring room.

But Jeremy held her tight as the stars shone above them, and for a few perfect moments, saving their tiny piece of humanity could wait.

NOLA'S STORY HAS ENDED. LANNI'S WAR HAS JUST BEGUN.

One will betray her. One will save her. One will destroy her world.

Do the work, steal the goods, keep her sister alive—a simple plan Lanni has been clinging to. With the city burning around her and vampires hiding in the shadows, making it until morning is the best she can hope for.

But order in the city is crumbling, and the thin safety that's kept Lanni alive won't be enough to protect her family. The people who live in the glittering glass domes—lording over the city, safe from the dangers of the outside world—have grown tired of the factory filth marring their perfect apocalypse.

When the new reign of chaos threatens her sister, Lanni faces a horrible choice—accept the fate she was born to, or join the enemy she's sworn to destroy.

Read on for a sneak peek of *Heart of Smoke*.

CHAPTER ONE

The scent of ash blew in through the window, joining the stench of burning oil that always filled the factory. The foreman had been pushing the machines faster for the past week, so a hint of scorched rubber added its stink, too.

I tightened the bandana that covered my face as I waited for the next rack of syringes to rumble down the line.

The outside doors banged open, letting in a fresh plume of smoke.

The foreman greeted the next shift of workers by shouting at them.

I let the hum of the machines drown out his words.

The new rack of syringes slid toward me. I flipped them all into the tray, moving quickly so the heat from the glass wouldn't burn my hands. I patted them all flat as the belt carried the tray past my station, waiting until the last moment to slip one syringe up my sleeve.

The packaging machine ate the tray, hiding the gap I'd created. I reached up to tighten my bandana again, letting the syringe fall farther up my arm. I gritted my teeth as the heat stung my elbow.

With a rumble, the next batch headed down the line.

Three solid taps on the shoulder and I stepped out of my place, gladly giving my station to the worker for the next shift.

I stretched my arms toward the ceiling, letting my back crack as the hot syringe slid down to the base of my spine, landing where my shirt tucked into my pants.

I'd only managed to snag six during my shift. Not a great day's work by any means.

Better than any of the others could manage.

"Check out," the foreman shouted, like he thought we didn't know what we were supposed to do at the end of our shift. Or worse, he was foolish enough to think we wanted to stay.

All of us rushed toward the booth by the door. I didn't run. I couldn't risk a sharp ear catching the faint clinking of my hard-won treasure. By the time I joined the line, there were already six others waiting to be checked out by the foreman's wife.

Mrs. Foreman sat in the booth, scanner in hand, frowning at each person who dared ask for their belongings back and to be paid for their time.

Or maybe it wasn't our wanting to be paid for our labor that she found so offensive. Maybe it was our dirty faces and rounded shoulders. Or the stink of sweat and rubber that had gotten permanently stuck in all our clothes. Maybe she didn't like the reminder that her husband's factory really produced two prod-ucts—syringes and broken people.

I leaned out of line, peeking through the door to the courtyard.

The smoke hadn't fully blocked out the sun, but the ash came down thick. The fires were burning close to the city again.

A knot of panic twisted in my stomach as the line shifted forward. My nerves sent tingles from my fingertips to my toes.

Don't panic. You can't afford it.

I pressed my shoulders back and stood tall, making sure not

even Mrs. Foreman's keen eyes could spot the lumps on my back from the pilfered goods.

"Trip Benson." Trip held out his wrist, offering his chip band.

Mrs. Foreman narrowed her eyes at him, like she wasn't sure if he was the same Trip Benson she'd been checking out after his shift six days a week for a dozen years.

"Trip Benson." He held his wrist right in front of her face, like he wanted her to lick the tarnished metal bracelet instead of scan the chip it held.

Mrs. Foreman turned in her chair, taking her time gathering Trip's bag and jug, before handing them over and finally scanning his chip.

"Thank you." Trip snatched his things and strode out the door.

I took a deep breath, filling my lungs till they ached, pulled off my bandana, and stepped up to the counter, holding out my wrist.

"Name?" Mrs. Foreman pursed her lips at me.

I leaned over the counter, holding my chip band right under her scanner.

"Name?"

I held her glare even as my lungs started to tense.

Mrs. Foreman made a sound between a growl and a sneeze before turning to grab my bag and three jugs. She lingered, enjoying tormenting me, lining the jugs up perfectly on the counter and trying to balance my bag so it wouldn't tip over. When my lungs had started to burn and my brain had started to scream that I needed air, she finally scanned my chip, transferring over my credits and ration for the day's work.

I grabbed my things, making myself walk calmly to the bare patch of wall where I could set everything down. My fingers fumbled as I tied my bandana back around my face. I took a deep breath, and the familiar stink of the thick fabric pummeled my nose. My head spun as oxygen raced through my veins, leaving bright spots dancing in my eyes. Snatching my things back up, I headed out into the square.

My shoulders relaxed as soon as I stepped outside, though walking through the square between the four factory buildings was hardly more cheerful than working the belts.

Litter and ash stirred with the chill wind that swept between the brick buildings. A crumpled, blue pamphlet rolled across my foot.

I grabbed the paper and tucked it into my pocket as a wave of laughter came from the men smoking in the back corner of the square.

They were right to laugh. There was no use in reading the kep-made pamphlet. Even if I was foolish enough to trust anything the glass guards said, weak words of comfort wouldn't offer me any protection.

I glanced up at the sky. To the east, evening light peered down, but to the west, thick, gray smoke blocked out the sun.

"Dammit." I bolted across the square toward the most rundown of the four brick buildings.

The ash must have been falling the whole day. The thick layer of it muffled my footsteps and puffed up around my boots.

"Where's your coat, honey?" one of the men in the corner called.

I tossed up my favored finger rather than waste air shouting back.

The men laughed again.

I flinched as one of the men's laughs dissolved into wracking coughs that made me wonder how much longer I'd have to deal with his daily taunts.

The sound of his hacking followed me into the kids' factory.

There were no machines to offer a blissful, mind-numbing hum on the kids' work floor, where they scrubbed and sorted bolts and scraps. Everything had to be done quietly so the teacher standing on the scaffold could be heard as she shouted her lessons to her three hundred students.

I stood on my toes, trying to catch a glimpse of Mari's shiny, black hair.

A kid started wailing in the far corner.

The foreman strode toward him, but the teacher didn't pause her lesson on the decimation of the oceans.

I tried not to wonder if the kid was wailing because he'd cut himself or because he couldn't stand the misery of knowing that something as beautiful as a sea turtle had once existed and he'd never get to see one in real life.

One of the minders finally caught sight of me. "Mari Sampson."

I gave the minder a nod of thanks as Mari hopped up from her place at one of the back tables and ran toward me.

"Slower, Mar," I whispered, though I knew my sister couldn't hear me.

"I thought you'd never come." Mari grabbed the jugs from my hands, setting them on the ground while I dug through my bag.

"I come at the same time every day." I pulled out Mari's hat, coat, and gloves.

"But some of the other kids have already been collected." Mari spoke so fast she sucked a bit of her bandana into her mouth and had to spit it out before continuing. "I got stuck on bolt scrubbing today, so you'll have to dig the metal bits out for me."

She held up her hands. Slivers and scratches deep enough to bleed marked her fingers.

I shoved down my sympathy and held out her coat.

Mari sighed before letting me dress her.

I didn't blame her for hating the coat. The ratty outer and inner layers hid the dense material that was worth its weight in credits and would make any decent thief drool. But knowing you were lucky to have a bit of protection from the lethal sunrays and liking to wear the damn thing were two different matters.

I fastened her coat and held out her gloves.

"My fingers already hurt." She tucked her scratched hands behind her back. "I won't get burned. The sun's almost gone, and the sky's filled with smoke. I don't want to wear them."

"Hmm." I tugged Mari's wide-brimmed hat onto her head and tied the rope beneath her chin. "I heard a rumor that someone's been hoarding peaches. I was going to nab them as a treat for you, but if you don't *want* to wear your gloves—"

Mari snatched her gloves away from me and tugged them on.

Biting back a smile, I pulled my own layers from the bag and dressed myself in a quarter of the time it had taken me to dress Mari. I slung my bag on and passed her one of the jugs, keeping two for myself.

"We're going to jog today," I said.

"Why?" Mari tipped her chin up so I could see her eyes below the brim of her hat.

"Smoke's coming in from the western side of the city."

"Oh, reef bleachers!" Mari cursed, grabbing my hand and running out the door.

I let her set our pace as we cut through the litter-strewn square and out onto the street beyond the factories.

The streets themselves had been kept clean of trash—the kep laws made sure of it—but not even the sweepers could keep up with the ash coming down from the sky.

Most of the people we passed had covered their heads, trying to keep the falling grit from settling into their hair. Some held cloths over their mouths or had tied rags around their faces. All of them wore the same painful air of resignation.

We all knew the city could drown in ash, and there wasn't a damn thing any of us could do about it. But watching hopelessness smother us when the ash was only a few inches thick...it almost seemed worse than letting the whole city burn at once.

I glanced up. The smoke had drifted farther in, close enough to coat the western edge of the city. I ran a little faster as we reached Generation Way, trying not to grip Mari's hand tight enough to make the scratches and slivers any worse.

The thumping of a club's music pounded through the air as we rounded the corner onto Endeavor Avenue. The handful of daytime bars that had been allowed to stay open had all been packed into the same few blocks with the shops that still sold non-essential goods. Cheers came from the nearest bar as a singer started a new song.

Mari took the lead, weaving a path through the customers eager to spend their credits.

Before we managed to break through the shoppers, I caught sight of the end of the line. It already stretched a block back from the tanks.

We dodged around a few of the slower people carrying jugs and claimed a place in line behind a man who stank with a tang exclusive to chem plant workers.

"The line's too long." Mari gripped my hand.

"We'll be fine," I said.

"What if the fires get too close and they call the kep away? What if the smoke stays in tomorrow?" She stood on her toes, trying to see between the adults in front of her. "What if they can't push the fires back?"

"Everything is going to be fine. We got here in time. We'll make it to the front." My guilt at lying to my little sister crashed into the hunger rumbling in my stomach.

"Two tanks," a woman a few people ahead of us shouted. "Smoke's coming in, and they're only running two tanks!"

I caught a glimpse of the start of the line as we all shuffled forward.

The woman was right. They were only distributing from two of the three tanks. The kep had only bothered to send twelve glass guards in fancy black uniforms to deal with the thirsty masses.

"Keep to a single line," a kep guard shouted. "If you all keep to a single line, we can get you through faster."

We won't all make it.

I turned my gaze up to the edge of the overhang that protected the tanks, choosing loathing over worry. Years of smoke and soot hadn't managed to destroy the image some idiot had painted to loom over the city scum.

Pictures of a happy family and a blooming tree flanked the words *For the Future of Our Children.* Like the kep cared about Mari's future or mine.

I kept my gaze fixed on the painted family until Mari started bouncing.

There were only five in line ahead of us.

"Come on," Mari muttered. "Come on." She pressed her cheek to my waist, tilting her hat.

I unfastened my coat and draped the side over her, covering the bit of her neck the hat had left exposed.

I glanced west.

The smoke had shifted again. The entire western side of the city would be covered.

One jug. If we can fill just one, we'll be fine.

A grating beep came from the front of the line, near one of the two working green tanks.

"I'm sorry, ma'am. Your chip shows no ration." The guard with the scanner turned away from the rationless woman.

"That's not possible." The woman stepped in front of the guard, holding out her wrist. "I did my day in the factory. They added my ration to my band, I know they did."

"Next."

The chem worker walked past the woman to the other running tank.

"Check it again." The woman shook her wrist at the guard. "I have a ration."

"The factory may have placed the ration on your chip," the

guard said, "but fresh fires sparked to the west. Water was diverted from this station for the protection of the city. We have to make sure everyone is provided for."

"I'm part of everyone." The woman edged closer to the tank. "I need my ration."

"We've had to prioritize, ma'am." The guard held up his hand, blocking her path. "You are not in the approved group."

"I will die." The woman clutched her jug. "You are throwing my life away."

"Difficult decisions had to be made," the guard said. "We thank you for your sacrifice."

The woman threw her jug at the tank and leapt toward the guard, reaching for his neck like she thought she could choke him.

Another guard lunged forward, cracking the woman over the head with his club before her fingers had even grazed his fellow's neck.

The woman crumpled to the ground and lay still. She wasn't even breathing.

Mari started to shake as the woman's blood stained the ash on the street.

"Next," the guard called.

I held Mari close, guiding her around the growing patch of red sludge. We stopped in front of the tank. I raised my wrist for the guard to scan my chip band. My heart froze as I waited for the beep.

"Cleared for three jugs," the guard with the scanner said.

The other kep took Mari's jug.

My heart didn't start beating again until he turned on the tap and water began filling the container.

I let go of Mari to open the other jugs.

The guard passed the first back to Mari and had started filling the second before all the kep tipped their heads to the side at once, as though listening to a voice only they could hear.

I reached forward, bracing the still-filling jug the moment

before the guard let go of it and bolted for the side of the overhang.

Mari squeaked as I caught the jug, managing to keep it upright so it wouldn't spill. I twisted the top back on, taking the second to protect the slim bit of our ration we'd claimed before grabbing Mari's hand.

"Run." I didn't have to say it.

Mari darted for the corner of the overhang as the high whine of the closing gates began. We slipped into the narrow alley beside the tanks before the crowd still waiting in line started to shout.

The water station would be closed while the glass guards hid, or fought the fire raging to the west, or whatever it was the kep in black guard uniforms did when they abandoned their petty attempts at helping the city scum.

Everyone left in line would have to go without.

Thank you for your sacrifice.

Order your copy of Heart of Smoke *to continue the story.*

ESCAPE INTO ADVENTURE

Thank you for reading *Son of Sun*. If you enjoyed the book, please consider leaving a review to help other readers find Nola's story.

As always, thanks for reading,

Megan O'Russell

Never miss a moment of the danger or romance.

Join the Megan O'Russell mailing list to stay up to date on all the action by visiting https://www.meganorussell.com/book-signup.

ABOUT THE AUTHOR

Megan O'Russell is the author of several Young Adult series that invite readers to escape into worlds of adventure. From *Girl of Glass*, which blends dystopian darkness with the heart-pounding danger of vampires, to *Ena of Ilbrea*, which draws readers into an epic world of magic and assassins.

With the *Girl of Glass* series, *The Tethering* series, *The Chronicles of Maggie Trent*, *The Tale of Bryant Adams,* the *Ena of Ilbrea* series, and several more projects planned, there are always exciting new books on the horizon. To be the first to hear about new releases, free short stories, and giveaways, sign up for Megan's newsletter by visiting the following:

https://www.meganorussell.com/book-signup.

Originally from Upstate New York, Megan is a professional musical theatre performer whose work has taken her across North America. Her chronic wanderlust has led her from Alaska to Thailand and many places in between. Wanting to travel has fostered Megan's love of books that allow her to visit countless new worlds from her favorite reading nook. Megan is also a lyricist and playwright. Information on her theatrical works can be found at RussellCompositions.com.

She would be thrilled to chat with you on Facebook or Twitter

@MeganORussell, elated if you'd visit her website MeganORussel-l.com, and over the moon if you'd like the pictures of her adventures on Instagram @ORussellMegan.

ALSO BY MEGAN O'RUSSELL

<u>The Girl of Glass Series</u>

Girl of Glass

Boy of Blood

Night of Never

Son of Sun

<u>The Tale of Bryant Adams</u>

How I Magically Messed Up My Life in Four Freakin' Days

Seven Things Not to Do When Everyone's Trying to Kill You

Three Simple Steps to Wizarding Domination

Five Spellbinding Laws of International Larceny

<u>The Tethering Series</u>

The Tethering

The Siren's Realm

The Dragon Unbound

The Blood Heir

<u>The Chronicles of Maggie Trent</u>

The Girl Without Magic

The Girl Locked With Gold

The Girl Cloaked in Shadow

<u>Ena of Ilbrea</u>

Wrath and Wing

Ember and Stone

Mountain and Ash

Ice and Sky

Feather and Flame

<u>Guilds of Ilbrea</u>

Inker and Crown

Myth and Storm

<u>The Heart of Smoke Series</u>

Heart of Smoke

Soul of Glass

Eye of Stone

Ash of Ages

www.ingramcontent.com/pod-product-compliance
Lightning Source LLC
Chambersburg PA
CBHW050233110726

47898CB00007B/2134